THE LOVE LETTER

TWO SISTERS. ONE LETTER. A HIGHLAND ROAD TRIP OF SECRETS

CLAIRE GILLIES

GREEN ISLE PUBLISHING

Published by Green Isle Publishing

www.clairegillies.com

Paperback ISBN: 978-1-7392452-6-9

Ebook ISBN: 978-1-7392452-7-6

The wee birdies sing and the wildflowers spring,
And in sunshine the waters are sleeping.
But the broken heart it kens nae second spring again,
Though the waeful may cease frae their grieving.

— UNKNOWN

1

MEG

Meg MacDonald lived at 1 Sycamore Avenue, and she loved how that sounded. Nestled in the leafy inner Melbourne suburbs, the streets whispered tales of bygone eras, where famous writers once roamed amidst Victorian splendour. Tourists thronged to admire the architectural marvels, while film crews, like clockwork, transformed the perfect terraces into cinematic backdrops every other weekend. Each house stood as a testament to craftsmanship, with intricate iron gates, stained-glass windows, and meticulously maintained gardens.

Among these treasures, Meg's own home shone brightly. Years of dedication and renovation had transformed her once crumbling 1850s terraced house into a sanctuary. The fresh black paint above her door marked not just an address but a sense of belonging.

1 Sycamore Avenue was more than a location. It was a part of her identity.

In Meg's world, order wasn't merely a preference – it was her lifeline. Like that first invigorating sip of morning coffee, she craved it with a desperation that bordered on obsession.

So when she finally achieved it, cocooned in the tranquil embrace of her routines, it felt like an undeniable victory.

Like any other day, this one began with the comforting familiarity of her rituals. Perched on her sofa, bathed in the soft morning light filtering through billowing white curtains, Meg cradled her favourite oatmeal-coloured mug in one hand and a pen in the other. With each sip, a triumphant smile graced her lips as she conquered her to-do list before the day had truly begun.

It was all so familiar. Reassuring.

The symphony of everyday sounds enveloped her – the postman's shuffle, the neighbouring children's playful banter – creating the backdrop of an ordinary morning. Yet, beneath the veneer of familiarity, a subtle unease lingered.

As she smoothed the pages of her diary, her eyes fell upon the day's quote:

Look back, and smile on perils past. - Walter Scott.

The words failed to uplift or motivate; instead, a frown line appeared on her usually smooth brow.

As she methodically crossed off another item on her to-do list, a nagging sensation tugged at the back of her mind. With a sigh, she shrugged off the comforting weight of a knitted throw, her gaze wandering to a recent addition to her decor – an out-of-place rattan chair with mismatched cushions, a relic of an impulsive moment. Hastily stashing the offending cushions away, she resolved not to yield to such whims again, no matter how tempting.

Her attention shifted to the scattered books on the coffee table, each one a tempting distraction. Perhaps she should call her mother before work to understand what might be lurking underneath her thoughts, but as the idea took root, a familiar sensation began to build in the pit of her stomach. Pulling herself away, she wandered barefoot to the kitchen, where a giant calendar dominated the wall. Her fingers traced over the colour-coded appointments, lingering on the glaring blank square – today's ominous reminder.

Of course, she couldn't call her mother.

The feeling gripped her chest, travelling up her throat and threatening to suffocate her.

She knew what day it was. The ticking clock echoed in the silence, but the blank square on the calendar screamed at her – today was anything but routine. Unwilling to confront the reality, she had left it empty, a stark reflection of the void it had left in her life.

As the significance of the date washed over her, her heart sank, and the weight of grief settled heavily on her shoulders, threatening to engulf her. With trembling hands, she reached for her phone, instinctively dialling her sister's number. But the disheartening tone of voicemail greeted her, a painful reminder of her loneliness.

A whole year had passed in the blink of an eye. She remembered how she used to talk to her mother, sharing plans and stories, her voice a comforting presence on the other end of the line. Now, on the anniversary of her mother's passing, she was faced with the daunting task of clearing out their family home, erasing all traces of their shared memories.

A chill ran down her spine as she distracted herself with wiping a dust particle from a framed picture of her mum in the kitchen. Overwhelming sorrow threatened to consume her, but she forced it down, blinking back tears and biting her lip until it hurt. There was no time for tears – everything must be clean, packed, and cleared before her workday. The office would understand if she was a little late.

Only after the remnants of her family life were packed away and order was restored would Meg allow herself to confront the pain gnawing at her chest.

* * *

As she approached her mother's house, she couldn't help but notice the contrast to her own elegant terraced home. The seventies brick bungalow her mother had owned, purchased by her grandparents for their retirement, once posed a challenge to fix up. During Meg's teenage years, they each took a stab at revamping the garden or the kitchen after her mother had been taken advantage of by too many handymen. It had been run-down, everything out of order, patched together with no real rhyme or reason. However, with the economy on the upswing, its location had become highly sought after, with companies sprouting nearby and fashionable cafes enveloping it. To Meg’s astonishment, when auction day came, bidders drove the price sky-high.

She parked her car beside her mother's fruit trees, a spot that had once been a refuge from the relentless summer sun. Particularly the large fig tree that dominated the area, its bare branches now shaking in the cool wind, awaiting the arrival of spring and promising plump, juicy figs. Meg's little sister, Lexi, had a penchant for plucking and devouring its juicy plum figs before fruit bats could steal a taste. That one tree held more memories than Meg could allow herself to acknowledge. Their summer halcyon nights were spent playing under its leaves and carving their initials in its trunk.

She called her sister again. No answer. With a heavy sigh, she tossed her phone into her handbag, resisting the urge to check if their graffiti was still etched into the tree.

A silent hallway greeted her as she entered the house, with only a few boxes sitting side by side for her arrival, an eerie contrast to the once lively home where her mother's hippy friends and the neighbourhood kids freely roamed. With a final check, Meg ensured everything was clean and in order. She rummaged through cupboards and closets, searching for any overlooked items, but everything seemed as clear as she had hoped.

She settled onto the new beige carpet in her mother's bedroom, noticing the different, almost sterile atmosphere. Some changes were welcome, like bidding farewell to the faded red paisley print carpet and the gaudy purple curtains her mother had adored. Her mother's unique style embraced vibrant colours with the motto "the more, the better", earning her the nickname Parrot from a disgruntled neighbour – an incident that always amused her mother. As Meg's eyes roamed around the pristine room, memories flooded back. In her mind's eye, she saw her mother at the dresser, applying make-up and dabbing on homemade perfume. Yet even in the stripped surroundings, the scent of pine and her mother's warmth lingered in the air, even now.

She wanted to hold on to those memories, not the ones that followed.

The image of her mother in her final days haunted her. Raspy breaths filled the room as Meg and Lexi took turns by her side, witnessing the drastic change – sunken eyes, thin arms, a fading presence. Angry tears welled in Meg's eyes, but her frustration shifted towards Lexi. Ignoring messages and calls, especially today, felt like an unforgivable act of selfishness.

In frustration, she kicked out her feet, desperate for support. Before she could let her emotions fully surface, something caught her eye – a vent slightly ajar. She shuffled towards it and gently pried it open, half expecting damage inside. To her surprise, folded papers greeted her – letters and envelopes, all in her mother's handwriting. Some pages were dated, resembling entries from her mother's diary.

January 1, 1995

My heart feels heavy today. I'm starting a new year

without you, my love. The girls are asleep after we spent the night celebrating the new year. I made sure to make a party of it, eating snacks after midnight and dancing in our pyjamas. All the while, I feel like my heart is breaking without you here. Is this the life I'm meant to live? Alone?

I think of last year and how you had your traditions – staying outside until the midnight bells, then bringing in coal, whisky, and bread. I still don't know what those gestures meant, but it pains me even now that the girls will forget. You are slipping away.

So it's the first year without you and I am miserable.

I love you. I will always love you.

Meg squinted at the date again. Her mother had written those words when Meg was just a young girl.

Her phone rang, jolting her back to the present – work calling. Glancing at her watch, she gasped. She was already running late. The keys to the estate agents had to be handed in today.

In a hurry, she gathered the letters, locked up the house, and stepped past the fig tree, leaving behind a home brimming with a lifetime of memories.

* * *

Meg thumped on the imposing door, attempting to peer through the stained-glass window. After a moment, the door creaked open, revealing a girl with a pierced nose and black hair. She glanced up from her phone, barely acknowledging Meg's presence.

"Hey, I'm looking for Lexi. Is she around?" Meg inquired.

The goth girl, with a nonchalant expression, replied, "Lexi? Yeah, she's in there somewhere."

"Great, um, mind if I come in?" she asked, her words trailing off slightly as she shifted uncomfortably.

"Whatever. Just watch out for the cat. She's in a mood." The goth girl shrugged.

Cautiously, Meg stepped inside, scanning the communal area cluttered with mismatched furniture and art supplies. She wasted no more time with small talk and made her way up the narrow staircase, the goth girl returning to her phone, indifferent to the family drama unfolding around her.

Reaching Lexi's door, she knocked. No answer. She waited, knocked again, but still no response. Pulling out her phone, she called her sister, hearing the ringtone from inside the room. Where was she? With growing concern, she placed her ear against the door, and just as she was about to give up and leave, she heard a faint groan from the other side. She pushed the door, but it was locked.

"Lexi, it's me, Meg – let me in!" she shouted, her voice tinged with panic. Rushing downstairs, she found the goth girl in the kitchen, her ear still glued to her phone, hunched over a bowl of cereal. She opened her mouth in a daze at the disruption.

"I need to get into Lexi's room; I think something's wrong. Do you have a spare key?" she asked urgently. Her heartbeat quickened as she frantically tore through the kitchen drawers, searching for anything that could help. A knife caught her eye, and she snatched it up, rushing back upstairs. Her mind raced, hoping her skills in unpicking doors from her teenage years hadn't faded entirely.

The narrow knife slid into the lock, its metal teeth rattling around, but it proved to be the wrong tool. Desperation tightened its grip as she surveyed the hallway. In a moment of sheer urgency, she plucked a clip from her dishevelled hair, strands falling loosely over her shoulders and flopping into her eyes. Sweat poured down her face as she delicately fiddled with the lock.

Relief surged within her as she heard the click.

The door swung wide, revealing her sister lying unconscious on the floor.

2

MEG

"Stop overreacting, Meg," Lexi croaked, her hand over her head, her face drained of its usual pink glow. "I just had a lot to drink and must have passed out on the floor. That's all!"

Meg settled onto the edge of the bed, wrapping her pink dressing robe tightly around herself. Her dark hair, tousled after spending a restless night on the sofa. She had driven Lexi back to her own house, agonising over whether to take her to the hospital or not. Eventually, she decided that the best place for her sister was with her. She wanted to keep a close eye on her without involving the hospital, afraid of what might happen if they started asking questions about her sister's mental health. This was something they needed to do alone, without intervention. Meg herself had never even taken a pill for a headache, let alone antidepressants and wouldn't let her sister fall through the gaps so soon.

Lexi avoided eye contact, her gaze fixed on the floor. A helpless, feeble creature; a far cry from her usual bright and spirited self. The image of Lexi lying face down had haunted Meg all night. She'd thought the worst and was unlikely to recover from the scare so easily.

What confounded her was the extent of her little sister's recklessness. She couldn't help but feel a surge of frustration – if only Lexi listened to her big sister once in a while, she would never find herself in such predicaments. She was convinced it all stemmed from a man – Lexi's penchant for falling in love at the drop of a hat made her seem like a character straight out of a Brontë romance novel, rather than someone navigating real life. Now, as Meg observed the shadows under Lexi's eyes and her dramatic weight loss, she chastised herself for failing to recognise the transformation in her sister sooner. And for that, she placed the blame squarely on her own shoulders.

"Tell me what happened?" Meg leaned over her, offering a glass of water and assisting her with a slow sip.

"I just had a lot to drink. Meg, please, do we have to do this now? I'm tired." Lexi's voice wavered, a frail attempt at nonchalance.

She kept a watchful eye on Lexi until her sister succumbed to sleep. Strands of Lexi's once-blonde hair cascaded long and unkempt on the pillow, revealing dark roots that whispered neglect. Though Meg had grown accustomed to Lexi's ever-changing looks, seeing her stripped of her usual charm was disconcerting. To the casual observer, the sisters seemed an unlikely pair, their personalities and appearances diverging so much that the only shared trait was a scattering of freckles across noses and shoulders, more pronounced in the summer months.

Retreating to the kitchen, Meg cradled a cup of coffee and extracted papers from the box containing her mother's belongings. Uninterrupted, she delved into her mother's words, reading through the letters addressed to Meg's father, spanning many years. She shook her head, considering the dates that coincided with her childhood. Her mother had never uttered a word about this.

The letters didn't portray her mother as the happy and content woman she'd thought her to be. Why would an intelligent and charming woman yearn for a man who was a useless drunk, squandering his time on gambling instead of being there for his kids?

Meg's fists clenched, her fury bubbling. A juvenile reaction, but one she couldn't ignore. Even after the years her father had been absent, she still couldn't forgive him.

Sometimes, as she watched movies or observed a friend interacting with their father, she found herself drawing comparisons. Would she, in that moment, embrace her father tightly, expressing boundless love? Mostly, it brought on resentment – a reminder of something she had never, and would never, have.

Yet, she'd had her mother – an unwavering source of strength, prioritising her children's well-being and even telling their father to leave. She recognised her mother's decision as the best way to shield them from the fallout. However, as she delved into more of her mother's words, a sense of disorientation settled upon her. Did she truly know her mother? It seemed more like a heartbroken woman waiting for a lost love to return.

Beneath the pile of letters, Meg discovered a thick envelope, unlike all the others. Marked by her mother's unique scrawl, it was addressed to Graeme MacDonald in Glenardburn, Scotland. She scrutinised the envelope. It was sealed with last year's stamp.

It should have been sent.

A cold shiver ran up her spine and her stomach lurched. Pushing her coffee away, she moved to the kitchen sink, gulping down a glass of water. Did her mother intend to send this letter all along? Right before she was diagnosed, and the floodgates of her illness opened, immediately pushing her into her deathbed?

The weight of her mother's earlier words pressed upon her. She had loved him – year after year, writing letters filled with pain and heartbreak from losing him. Had she intended to meet him again? To mend and reunite the family? Meg scratched at the letter's seal, hoping it would miraculously open without tearing. But she couldn't. She wouldn't. This letter was not for her, yet had been destined to remain within the walls of their old home.

Meg believed her father to be somewhere in Australia or perhaps New Zealand, not Scotland. Clinging to the kitchen counter, she gazed out of the window, where little brown birds flitted in and out of her rose bushes. Their carefree movements made her envious of their uncomplicated existence.

Grabbing her phone, she typed in "Glenardburn". Images of rolling hills and serene lochs appeared, along with snapshots of houses scattered sparsely along a roadside – a vast peninsula in the Scottish Highlands encompassing numerous villages and towns. Did her mother truly intend to send a letter to their father, or was it another missive meant mainly for herself? She massaged her forehead, sensing a migraine threatening behind her temples.

In the distance, her sister's groans drew her attention. Quickly, she stashed the letters away. Now was not the time. Lexi needed her help. If she hadn't found her sister last night, the situation could be markedly different now. It was her responsibility to care for Lexi, and that began with diverting her mind from her foolish ex.

She peeked into the bedroom. Lexi was sitting up, her voice groggy as she inquired, "Do I smell coffee?"

* * *

Meg settled onto a scratchy tartan blanket spread across lush grass. An earthy scent hit her, mingling with the distant fragrance of blooming purple flowers from a far-off hill. She was next to her mother, staring towards a mysterious dark expanse of water, its surface reflecting hues of purple, blue and green above. She looked up, holding her breath. She had never seen anything so beautiful; the night sky came alive with a mesmerising display – the Northern Lights danced across the horizon, painting the heavens with vibrant streaks of colour. Stars twinkled and the Milky Way stretched across the sky. In the blink of an eye, the scene shifted, revealing clear blue skies.

"Mum, how long do we wait?" Meg whispered but received no response.

She let herself be lulled by the shimmering lights above and the pine of her mother's perfume. And so they waited until a shadow cast itself over them, heralded by a haunting cry that resonated with Meg's soul. She held her breath as a large eagle materialised from lofty heights, a mesmerising and ethereal sight. Descending with grace, majestic wings unfurled, the eagle sliced through the air, its path kissing the water's surface with minimal disturbance – a dance of perfect equilibrium.

As the eagle descended, Meg's gaze sharpened, capturing the astonishing truth. With swift precision, its talons secured a sizeable salmon, and with seamless elegance, the eagle ascended, blending into the rugged landscape of stony hills.

Meg stole a glance at her mother, whose countenance radiated serenity as they watched the majestic creature disappear.

* * *

She spent the next few days immersed in her sister's company, a comforting routine of whipping up nutritious dinners for her and indulging in cosy Netflix marathons. Despite the bittersweet circumstances that brought Lexi under her care, a small part of Meg revelled in the cherished time together.

Yet as they shared these moments, a subtle but palpable shadow lingered over Lexi. Nothing too obvious, just a distant gaze in her eyes that jolted Meg back to the realisation that if she hadn't reached Lexi's door that night, things might have been drastically different.

After days of contemplation, and after gauging Lexi's current state of mind, she had come to a decision regarding her mother's letters. She determined that delving into the past by attempting to reconnect with their father might only send her sister into another tailspin. No, she concluded, her focus should be on helping Lexi regain her footing.

"I was thinking of checking with work for any job openings. Maybe there's something that might catch your interest. What do you think?" Meg asked, stacking another washed dish on the drainer. Lexi remained seated at the table, absorbed in her phone.

It was only when Meg cleared her throat that Lexi jolted, her eyes snapping up. "What? No thanks, absolutely not. I can't think of anything more dull." Her eyes remained glued to the phone screen, leaving Meg to wonder if her sister was scouring the internet for any trace of her worthless ex-boyfriend.

"Hey, there's nothing wrong with being an accountant!" Meg took pride in her career. She found solace in the fact that accountants were essential no matter where you were in the world, even though she hadn't ventured much beyond her current surroundings.

"That might be your thing, Megs, but it's not for me.

What would I do? Run errands for you and your colleagues, mindlessly type emails on a keyboard? No, I'm not cut out for office life – I much prefer the café scene."

Meg's heart ached for her sister to pursue more meaningful endeavours. After Lexi dropped out of art school years ago, she had drifted through various café jobs in Melbourne, seemingly content with the only art in her life being tattoos, which Lexi ploughed all her wages into.

Observing Lexi's friends, Meg noticed they shared similar interests, complete with eccentric haircuts and body piercings. Lexi, however, seemed to lack concern for the importance of planning for the future.

As Meg wiped down the countertop and wrung out the cloth, she couldn't help but ask, "But won't he be at the café? This man that's done this to you!" Her sideways glance caught Lexi's attention, yet her sister remained tight-lipped. "Lex, you're not trying to reconcile with him?" She folded the cloth and leaned against the sink.

"He made a mistake, I'm sure. I might have overreacted. Perhaps I didn't give him a chance to explain," Lexi mumbled.

"He was cheating on you with other women – what's there to explain?"

"But there's more to it, I believe. If I just talk to him … Maybe I wasn't clear with him, perhaps he thought we were more of a casual thing?"

Meg blinked at her sister, momentarily at a loss for words. "But … you can't take him back?"

Lexi shrugged, her gaze drifting back to her phone.

* * *

Go, Meg. Go.

Her mother's words followed her, whispered by the night wind as it swept through the heather-covered hills. In the quiet stillness of the night, Meg jolted awake, sheets tangled around her, and sweat clinging to her skin. Blinking into the dimness, she rose on shaky legs and tiptoed to the kitchen for a glass of water.

The hush of the house amplified the vividness of her recent dream – a scene so clear that she could easily get lost in it again. The image of the Northern Lights, the majestic eagle, and her mother's presence lingered in her mind, haunting her like a persistent echo.

It was the same dream as before, but its meaning eluded her grasp. She couldn't quite piece together the puzzle, or rationalise what she had seen and felt. Yet, an inexplicable compulsion welled up within her, driving her forward with a sense of urgency.

With resolute determination, she understood what needed to be done. Her mother's letters and her father's unanswered past pressed upon her thoughts, weighing heavily on her conscience. She knew she must find him, deliver the letter, and help her mother, wherever she may be now.

A journey beckoned, one Meg never thought she'd take – a journey fraught with uncertainty, but also with the possibility of closure.

3

LEXI

Lexi sat alone in the garden, quietly watching the evening sun fade away. Her mind was consumed by thoughts of Chris, his absence a painful ache that cut through her. Would this torment ever ease? She'd been left shattered and discarded, with no trace of explanation. She brushed away the fresh tears with a weary hand.

"Chris," she whispered his name, like a lament carried on the wind. Memories of their time together played before her eyes. His laughter, his boundless affection, a master of impromptu adventures. Sometimes, he'd show up at her doorstep, declaring his intention to sweep her away for a spontaneous weekend by the beach. In those stolen hours, they'd lose themselves in each other's company, nights melting into mornings beneath the stars, their bodies entwined. Lexi could have stayed like that forever, with the promise of endless possibilities and adventures ahead.

They spoke of wanderlust and far-off lands, painting vivid images of their journey across continents. Lexi's savings had slowly grown, earmarked for travelling – to Bulgaria, with its promise of unfamiliar beauty, and Ireland, with its rugged charm. They'd dreamed of getting a van and exploring all the countries in between, just the two of them and the open road ahead.

Lexi downed her beer and felt the cold settle around her after the sun dipped further. She stayed outside, wrapped up in a blanket and wished Chris was there to hold her. She allowed herself to drift further into the recesses of her memories. Chris's touch like a whisper against her skin. His shaggy blond hair brushing against her shoulder, his lips tracing a delicate path just beneath her earlobe. The rush of his breath, the warmth of his embrace …

She swiped her phone to see if she had missed any messages from him since the last time she'd looked. No messages, no updates. His online presence remained static, and her gaze lingered on a picture she had taken – an image of Chris surfing, the sunlight kissing the waves as he surrendered to the sea's embrace. That moment encapsulated his true spirit. Lexi had stood on the rocks, capturing a fragment of his allure before he disappeared beneath the waves. It was in those waters that he found solace. And she was part of it, if only by witnessing it.

Lexi, on the other hand, had a fear of sharks. No matter how often she went into the water, she would half expect a great white to emerge from the waves and swallow her whole.

With a heavy sigh, she wiped her nose and grabbed another bottle of beer she had stashed under the bench earlier without Meg seeing. The desire for something stronger gnawed at her, a longing she'd quench once she returned to her own place.

A sudden creak of the door sent a jolt through her, prompting her to swiftly return the beer bottle to its hiding place, obscured by the undergrowth. "This is where you are?" Meg settled beside her, holding two cups of hot chocolate. "I figured you might need this. It's chilly out here, and you've been out forever!"

Lexi accepted the cup with a nod, though her heart ached for solitude and her secret stash of beer. All she craved was a moment to herself, a chance to reminisce about the good times she'd shared with Chris. “I like the cold.”

As her sister sipped her hot chocolate and settled beside her, a silent agreement hung between them. Lexi lit a cigarette, inhaling deeply before exhaling into the crisp night air. She relished the familiar swirl of smoke, while Meg shifted slightly beside her.

Meg tutted. “You still smoke? I thought you quit.”

Lexi's smile carried a hint of defiance. “Nope, not yet.”

Meg twirled a strand of her dark hair between her fingers. “I’ve been doing a lot of thinking recently. Maybe it's because it's a year since Mum passed, but I've been feeling drawn to do something in her memory.”

Lexi remained quiet, her eyes fixed on the small patch of grass before them.

“Remember Mum travelled before she had us?” she continued. “She would often talk about her time abroad.”

“Yeah, she went on and on, like a broken record sometimes.” Lexi fidgeted with the zip on her sweatshirt, looking down. “I wondered why she ever came back here to settle down?”

Meg shrugged. “It was just what people did. I think she had hoped we would do the same thing – live in another country for a bit … but we haven't, have we?”

“I just never had the money.” Lexi inhaled another drag from her cigarette.

Meg nodded, watching her exhale smoke. “She talked about Scotland.”

“Yup.” Lexi's attention fell onto her zipper again.

“Mum loved that trip. I’ve been thinking of how she would tell us stories of the castles she visited. Remember the fairy tales?”

"They were romantic, I guess. I liked the one about the laird's daughter and the stableboy."

"I know you did, you'd always ask to hear it." Meg's features softened. "Although most of the stories were the same – basically, in every story there would be a damsel in distress and a hero to save her." She rolled her eyes.

"She did meet Dad there, maybe that's why it held such strong memories for her."

With a frown, Meg stopped twirling the strand of hair, turning to Lexi directly. "This may sound mad … but since I moved the last of her things, I've had this nagging feeling. Like she wants us to go."

Lexi's mouth opened in alarm. "What? To Scotland?"

"Yes. I know, it may seem a bit impulsive."

"I'll say! Especially for you!"

Meg raised an eyebrow. "But I feel this is what she wants. She often talked about going back. It was like her bucket list … before she realised she was ill."

Lexi placed her cup down, memories of the last few days before her mother's passing flashed before her, and more tears fell down her cheeks.

"Oh hun, I'm sorry, I didn't mean to upset you." Meg put her arm protectively around Lexi's back. "It's maybe not the best time now. We can talk about this another time," she said gently.

"No, I'm fine." Lexi sniffed and wiped her red eyes, stubbing her cigarette on the bench. Meg shuffled next to her. "Carry on, what did you want to say?"

"I think we should go to Scotland together," Meg said. "Scatter the rest of Mum's ashes and do the trip she wanted to do."

Lexi looked at Meg, who was still gently stroking her back. "What?"

"I can take time off work, and my share of Mum's inheritance came through. I would pay for the whole trip. I think we need to get away."

Lexi shook her head. "I have a lot of things to sort out here …"

Meg pulled her hand away. "I think you need to get away, get out from under this cloud and clear your head."

She reached for another cigarette and lit it. "But, I need to see Chris."

Meg sighed and drank her hot chocolate. She crossed her legs, her body turned from Lexi.

"It's a nice idea, but there's no rush, right?" Lexi continued. "Perhaps next year, when—"

"I just thought it might be a nice thing for us to do. Together. You never talk to me anymore Lex. You never call. I feel like I'm forever forcing you to do things with me. I mean, you didn't even help me with Mum's things."

"I said I was sorry … I … I told you." Her voice cracked, and she turned to her sister.

"Yes, yes." Meg muttered under her breath and stood up. "Well, it's cold. I'm going to have an early night and turn in." She walked back inside the house, leaving her sister in darkness.

* * *

Lexi stared at her phone, her heart lurching as a wave of nausea washed over her. She couldn't tear her eyes away from the photo Chris had just posted – his arms wrapped around a beautiful blue-eyed brunette by the beach.

Having the best weekend with this one, read Chris's caption underneath.

Frustration surged within her, and she flung the phone into the grass. Suppressing the urge to scream, she clenched her fists with sheer willpower and paced back and forth around the small garden space. For a moment, she hesitated, her mind racing with conflicting thoughts. Then, fuelled by a surge of emotions, she snatched up an empty beer bottle and smashed it against the garden wall.

"Well, he can piss off and go to hell!" she muttered, still pacing. She felt the heat rising in her chest, the anger consuming her. At this angle, she could still see the faint blue light of his declaration shining through the grass.

Despite the shattered glass strewn across the ground, a brief moment of realisation washed over her. What had she gained by succumbing to her anger? With a weary sigh, she bent down to pick up the shattered pieces, foolishly cutting her finger in the process.

She sucked her finger, stomping her Doc Marten boot, and backed away. Each step back toward the house, her temper ebbed slightly, replaced by a weary resignation.

Brushing her tears away, she craved the warmth of Meg's house, no longer willing to dwell in the darkness of her heartache. As she reached the door, she paused, taking a moment to compose herself. With a steadying breath, she gently pushed it open, the soft glow of the hallway light spilling into the dimness of Meg's room.

Inside, Meg, with tousled hair, propped herself up on her elbow. "Is everything OK?" she whispered.

Leaning against the door, Lexi made up her mind. "Yeah, I think I need a holiday after all. When shall we leave?" she asked with determination.

4

MEG

Surprising even herself, Meg dived into trip planning, drawing inspiration from her mother's tales. Crafting an itinerary, she turned the distraction into a welcome escape. As Melbourne's winter sun shifted to the hues of spring, she immersed herself in the process. Acknowledging Scotland's shift from summer to autumn, she relished the thought of cooler months, a contrast to stifling Melbourne summers. Meanwhile, Lexi, unaware, enthusiastically packed for a beach holiday until Meg broke the news about Scotland's weather.

"What?" Lexi exclaimed, her eyes pleading. "But it's summer there!"

"The tail end of summer, Lex," Meg clarified, swiping through photos on her phone to reveal bundled-up holiday-makers braving the Scottish summer.

Lexi dramatically flopped onto the bed, feigning disappointment. "And there goes my chance at a beach holiday!"

"We're not headed to the Bahamas," Meg deadpanned, holding up a sarong from Lexi's suitcase. "It's all about hills, rain, and castles."

Lexi shot back with a grin. “Can we at least trade castles for the Bahamas?”

Meg couldn't suppress a laugh, though she maintained her resolve. “Nope, no Bahamas. You need to pack some practical stuff, Lex.”

With a theatrical sigh, Lexi slumped back on the bed, pretending to pout. Meg raised an eyebrow and left her sister wriggling with mock protest as she continued organising their Scottish adventure.

* * *

After enduring twenty-four hours of turbulent plane travel, the two girls stumbled off the plane in Edinburgh, bleary-eyed and nerves frazzled. As they disembarked, both girls nearly kissed the solid ground beneath them. Their flight had been a nightmare, plagued by the wails of not one, but three crying children, leaving them with minimal rest. There had also been relentless turbulence.

Blinking against the glaring signs, they stuck close together, seeking solace in each other's presence. Amid the crowd, a red-kilted figure emerged, hoisting a sign with their names. Meg wondered if he had just survived a long-haul fight too; his scraggly beard nearly obscured his face, and his grey jumper was covered in lint.

“Welcome to Edinburgh,” he croaked.

Meg could barely muster a meagre “Thanks” as the furry man assisted them with their suitcases. The trio navigated their way through the airport at a snail's pace.

“Good flight?” he attempted, his voice strained, and Meg struggled to respond. She longed for nothing more than a warm bath and a soft bed.

As they stepped outside, an icy gust threatened to knock them off their feet. The sky overhead was a blanket of grey, and Meg mentally cursed her decision not to wear her thick winter coat, which was buried somewhere deep within her suitcase.

"Bahamas … if only," muttered Lexi beside her.

"Just up here," the tall man called, his kilt swaying as he led the way.

Once inside a compact people carrier van, the sisters huddled together, their eyes heavy with exhaustion. Time seemed to blur, and before Meg knew it, she was being gently shaken awake by the stranger, his voice a loud intrusion.

"You're here," he announced, and she winced at the sudden noise. The fatigue in her body made every movement feel like trudging through mud.

Guiding them to their hotel rooms, he gave a salute to the hotel staff and then effortlessly lugged their suitcases up a spiral staircase. When they reached their rooms, he clapped his hands together and boomed, "So I thought I'd show you a nice lunch spot and then we could visit Edinburgh Castle."

The girls exchanged alarmed glances. "No, thank you," Meg quickly replied, her head spinning slightly with the motion.

"I understand, I understand," the man placated, raising his hands. "But you've only got one night here in Edinburgh before we head to Glasgow tomorrow. Trust me, it's best to push through the exhaustion and stay awake a bit longer. That way, you'll adjust to the time difference without feeling too jet-lagged."

"Great advice," Meg murmured. Lexi had already succumbed to exhaustion, collapsing onto one of the beds. "But honestly, we're just too tired to think right now. We'll catch up with you in the morning."

She ushered him out and closed the door on the slightly miffed, bearded man. Collapsing onto the bed herself, she had every intention of taking a brief rest before showering.

However, as soon as her eyelids fluttered shut, she joined her sister in slumber, both of them sleeping away the rest of the day.

* * *

"Morning," Meg greeted the kilted tour guide at breakfast.

"Oh, aye," he grunted. "How are you?"

"Feeling good." Meg nodded. "I needed that rest. I've been up for a while planning a few things to do on our trip. I thought when we go to Inverness, we could spend two days there instead of one, and we could visit—"

"I've already made up the itinerary. We can't be changing too much now." His serious dark eyes bored into her.

"We can talk about it again." She waved her hand, eager to move on to breakfast. The hotel exuded an old-world grandeur, with a dark tartan carpet and waiters donning green waistcoats and white aprons darting between tables. Beside her, Lexi was busy polishing off a plate piled high with a hearty fried breakfast, savouring every last bite of egg with buttered toast. Lexi leaned back in her seat, emitting a blissful sigh.

"I could eat that all over again!" she dreamily shared with her captive audience. Meg settled for a cup of coffee and a piece of toast, still feeling a touch out of sorts. She dared not push her appetite too far.

"Alright, so as we didn't chat yesterday." The tour guide put down his cup of tea and began reading from a sheet of paper. "My name is Angus, I work for Highlander Tours, and I want to welcome you to Scotland," he delivered in a monotone voice, scratching his cheek as he continued reading.

"Can I just stop you there?" Meg raised her hand. "Maybe we could just have a conversation? I came across your tour company because you specialise in the north-west Highlands, isn't that right?" She took a bite of cold, chewy toast and felt her appetite wane.

He blinked. "Yes, we're based in Abergow within the Glenardburn peninsula."

Glenardburn – Meg's heart skipped a beat.

"So … if I could circle back to the introduction?" Angus didn't wait for her response, promptly diving back into the scripted words, and Meg internally groaned. As she sipped her now cold coffee, she glanced at Lexi, who was quietly swiping her cell phone. Breakfast with Angus promised to be an educational affair, though not in the way Meg had initially anticipated.

* * *

"So are we ready?" Angus stood outside the girls' hotel room. "I can take your bags downstairs?" His expression fell as he took in the unpacked suitcases and Lexi's bed strewn with clothes. "We need to check out! In five minutes!"

"Couldn't we stay another night?" Lexi asked with a sugary sweetness. "We just got here!"

"But we're on a tight schedule. You said you wanted to get to the Glenardburn region, then we need to go—"

"Alright," Meg intervened, hoping Lexi wouldn't find any significance in that specific destination. "Let's skip Glasgow and stay another night here."

"I've already booked the next hotel!" Angus's face flushed pink. "I sent you all this information when you booked with us." His gaze locked onto Meg's, a touch too intense for her liking. It was like he was trying to hypnotise her into compliance. She couldn't help but wonder if he practised his stare in the mirror every morning. She briefly entertained the idea of calling the whole alliance quits and asking for a refund. After all, dealing with a tour guide who could stare down a grizzly bear wasn't exactly what she signed up for.

"I want to see Edinburgh Castle!" Lexi chimed in, her voice nearly reaching a petulant pitch.

"Look, Mr …?" Meg began in her professional accountant's tone, not allowing the towering presence before her to intimidate her. After all, they were the customers here, paying good money for assistance with their travel. If they wanted to stay, shouldn't the company make every effort to ensure a smooth experience? The customer is always right, or so the saying goes. Yet, she knew she needed to tread lightly. After all, she did need his help in finding her father. Selecting this tour company was no random choice; they offered the best chance of uncovering her father's whereabouts or connecting with people who could in Glenardburn.

He crossed his arms. "It's Angus."

"Mr Angus, my apologies if we got off on the wrong foot. We were jet-lagged yesterday, and if we could just extend our stay in Edinburgh by one more night, we would greatly appreciate it."

"You'll still be jet-lagged today," he muttered.

"Look – we are paying customers. So kindly head downstairs, secure us another night, and we'll go see the castle, have lunch … do all those things you suggested yesterday."

"It's not that simple," he huffed, throwing his head back, glaring at the ceiling. "We're in the busiest month of the year. Haven't you noticed? It's the Fringe Festival, Edinburgh's largest event." His eyes widened. "Everything will be fully booked!"

"Well, it's best to try before giving up, isn't it?" she responded tersely, her voice firm as she waited for Angus to leave.

Lexi popped her head out of the window. "Hmm … it does seem pretty crowded out there!"

“Don't mind him,” Meg retorted. “He's just being difficult – probably used to having his way. How has he not faced customer complaints before if he treats clients like this? Well, I'll show him who's boss!” She rolled up her sleeves and tidied the scattered mess Lexi had created on her bed, taking note but not bothering to ask why she still had packed so many different bikinis.

The sisters readied themselves shortly after and descended the winding staircase, met by Angus's stern expression.

“Well?” Meg inquired.

“It'll cost more,” Angus said.

“Fine.” She bit her lip, suppressing a smirk as Angus walked away. Clearly, he wasn't used to assertive women; she stifled a laugh, confident she'd won.

5

MEG

They walked the busy cobbled street of the Royal Mile, passing actors, comedians, magicians and singers who performed their arts along the way, luring potential audience members to their shows. Meg had never seen anything like it. The buzz was electric, and she drank in the different cultures, feeling like everyone in the world was crammed into this one city, walking past her. Aromas of roasted meats wafted by, and craft stalls displayed intricate silver Celtic jewellery that caught Lexi's eye. Meg and Angus stood nearby, both in an awkward stance.

Meg couldn't shake the tension from their earlier spat. She crossed her arms, determined not to break the silence first. Angus cleared his throat and gestured towards an imposing dark building. "Would you like to explore the inside of the church?"

Her gaze lifted to the structure she had missed, lost in the crowd. They left Lexi admiring craft stalls and moved across the road. "It dates back to the thirteenth century," Angus shared as he surged ahead, his distinctive red kilt drawing curious glances.

"Magnificent," Meg remarked, stopping to admire the view, only to be abruptly scolded.

"Don't step there!" Angus ordered, and she froze, bewildered. She glanced down at a heart-shaped cluster of cobbled stones. "Oh, how beautiful!"

"Get off them!" Angus insisted.

"What?" she hesitated, alarmed at being shouted at in public.

"It's bad luck!"

She sidestepped, face flushing.

Angus breathed out. "I apologise – I didn't mean to startle you." His mouth twisted. "You see, this spot has a history. A tollbooth once stood here – a prison. Unspeakable acts occurred: hangings, torture, the darkest of deeds. People paid their taxes, and others were punished here."

Meg shuddered involuntarily, just as an older man walked by, his face hidden behind a green and white scarf. He hawked up saliva and spat on the heart-shaped ground, barely missing Meg's shoe.

"Urgh that's disgusting!" Meg's mouth opened, repulsed at the retreating figure.

"Yes, that's another tradition," Angus affirmed. "An acknowledgement of the site's grim history, and also a gesture for good luck. That, or maybe they just dislike Hearts Football Club!" He chuckled at Meg's bewildered expression.

"Hey!" Lexi appeared behind them, proudly holding a pair of long, emerald-green drop earrings and a matching ring.

"Lex, get off the heart!" Meg called out, shooing her sister off the stonework. "It's bad luck!" she whispered, more concerned that someone would spit on her.

Beside her, Angus's shoulders shook with suppressed laughter as he walked off ahead of them. "Watch out for those Hearts fans," he teased, making Meg bristle.

* * *

After hours of sightseeing, Meg felt exhausted. Her eyes drooped as they ate lunch in a café overlooking another old street. She knew she needed to rest soon.

“Let's go up Carlton Hill after this, and I'll show you the city views,” Angus suggested between bites of his meat pie and chips. Meg winced, disliking people talking with their mouths full. She waited for him to finish chewing before responding.

“Sounds good!” Lexi chimed in cheerfully, stirring her coffee and gazing dreamily at the passers-by.

“I’m not sure … I'm really tired. I think I need a lie-down,” Meg admitted. She couldn't imagine walking any further. They had already visited the castle, and after the long flight the day before, exhaustion weighed heavily on her.

“It's the jet lag catching up with you. If you go to sleep now, you'll be up in the middle of the night, and you'll never get into a good routine for the rest of the trip,” Angus explained.

“OK, Dad!” Lexi teased, taking a sip of her frothy coffee.

“If you had listened to me yesterday, you would feel a lot different today,” Angus added.

“I’m not looking for a lecture, Mr Angus,” Meg sighed.

“No, sorry,” he backtracked, his tone changing. “We can take it slow, enjoy your lunch, maybe have something sugary or another coffee, and then we'll stroll up the mound. That way, if we keep you both awake as long as possible today, you can still see Edinburgh and feel better tomorrow.”

“OK,” Meg agreed, reluctantly ordering an iced coffee with extra cream. If she was going to continue walking, she needed all the energy she could get.

Angus guided the girls up a hill that offered panoramic city views. He had taken them to various spots that he considered “historical”, but the girls' interest began to fade, and they soon agreed that a rest at the hotel was in order.

Meg yearned for sleep, even if just for a brief respite. Her eyes gently closed, and she drifted off until Lexi prodded her.

“What's going on?” She jolted awake, alarmed.

“We can't sleep, Megs. We'll never sleep tonight.” Lexi's dark outline loomed over her. “Remember what Angus said?”

“But it's so comfy and warm.” Meg turned onto her side, nuzzling into her pillow. “Plus, you had four coffees – you’re running on pure caffeine.”

“Come on, it's still sunny out there. I fancy fish and chips.”

Meg's stomach gave an involuntary gurgle, and she had to admit that she was hungry again too. Earlier that day she had noticed a fish and chips takeaway with a long line of eager customers queuing outside.

“Should we tell Angus? We could grab some for him as well,” Lexi suggested, donning a light denim jacket and slinging an orange crossbody bag over her shoulder. Her recently dyed blonde hair shone brightly, the roots still fresh.

Meg wasn't particularly keen on engaging with Angus again for the evening if she could avoid it. There was an air of bossiness and unfriendliness about him, and the way he treated her like a mischievous schoolgirl – rather than the professional woman she was – truly irked her. “Let's skip that. How about we explore on our own?” she proposed.

“Maybe we could check out that cool graveyard he mentioned earlier?” Lexi chimed in, brimming with energy compared to her sister.

They glided through the ancient streets of Edinburgh, the setting sun casting long shadows. The crowd had thinned since earlier in the day, making it easier for them to order fish and chips without a wait. As they approached the graveyard, a couple of bashful-looking youths stumbled past, one of them sporting a baseball cap and clutching a clinking plastic bag. Lexi took the lead and settled on a bench at the far end of the gated graveyard. She tore open the newspaper-wrapped package and dived into her meal with gusto, filling the air with the scent of salt and vinegar.

"Slow down, you might give yourself indigestion," Meg advised.

"I don't know what it is, but ever since we got here, I've been starving," Lexi admitted, shoving another fat chip into her mouth and brushing off her sister's concern.

"I'm the opposite … I think it might be the jet lag."

Lexi continued eating with relish until all was devoured and scrunched up the newspaper, smacking her lips together. She draped herself on the bench and sighed. "It's beautiful, the evening sun spilling over the stones like that. It's really a tranquil spot, don't you think?"

Meg, still munching on her chips, nodded. Lexi had always been a speed eater, a trait that had persisted since their childhood. Back then, Lexi would have polished off her dinner and dessert and settled in for cartoons, while Meg would be labouring through the main course.

"There's a folklore tale about this place," Lexi began, crossing her arms and reclining on the bench, stifling a yawn. "It's about a man who worked as a nightwatchman in the police. He used to bring his little terrier dog along on his nightly rounds. They were inseparable. But when the man passed away, he left his dog all alone. Strangely enough, the dog came to this graveyard every single day and night, standing watch over his master's grave. Isn't that just heart-wrenching?"

"Did Angus tell you that?" Meg asked.

"Yup, and it was also on the plaque near the entrance," Lexi confirmed with a nod.

"I must have overlooked it." Meg set aside her chips as

her appetite waned. “There's something special about loyalty. Don’t you think? It's a quality we don't always see in real life, so when we come across it, even in a tale about a dog, we can't help but romanticise it. Loyalty is definitely one of the finer traits of humanity.” As she spoke, her thoughts drifted to her father. She closed her eyes, a mix of emotions swirling within her, hoping that the gentle breeze would carry them away.

* * *

“Oh my god!” Meg nudged Lexi.

“Eh?” Lexi wiped her mouth, a sheet of newspaper sticking to her cheek. “We actually dozed off!” Meg stood up abruptly. “In a graveyard!”

“It's OK, it's still early evening,” Lexi said calmly.

“No, it's not! It's eleven p.m.!” Meg glanced at her phone. She had several missed calls.

“It can't be – it's still fairly light!” Lexi chuckled.

“Lexi, it's late … let's get out of here!”

The girls quickly marched toward the gate, only to find it locked.

“But – but, nobody came to check if anyone was here before they locked up?” Meg stuttered.

“How do you know? We were both asleep!”

“Someone would have seen us, surely!” She rattled the gate and was instantly relieved to see people passing on the other side. “Oh, hello! Can you help us? We've been locked in. Is there a security guard somewhere?” Meg pleaded with the couple, who looked at her in confusion and carried on walking.

“Wait!” Lexi called after them.

“They probably don't speak English. No, no no!” Meg racked her brains. She couldn't call the emergency hotline – it wasn't that kind of emergency. But the more time they spent locked on the wrong side of a graveyard gate, the more she was tempted.

"Call Angus!" Lexi ordered. "I don't have his phone number. Do you?"

Meg really didn't want to call Angus – he'd make all this out to be their fault, and chastise her again. Plus, she felt bad about leaving the hotel without letting him know where they were. But they were grown women! She fumed to herself quietly. They had every right to explore the city by themselves, without having him chaperone them with a permanent sour expression plastered on his face.

With a groan, she eventually pulled out her phone and accepted the inevitable expense it would be to call him on her Australian SIM card.

"Where are you? A graveyard?" Angus's voice sounded surprised.

Meg put on a breezy voice. "Yes, the one you were talking about earlier. Someone has locked us in, and no matter who walks past, no one knows where to find security."

"Maybe we could climb out another way?" Lexi suggested. "We could check around the back, maybe there's a hole in the wall?"

She looked at her flatly and listened to Angus, who left instructions for them to stay put, promising to arrive soon. "He's coming," she said, shifting uncomfortably. It was now almost dark, and they had given up asking people for help. Huddled together, the girls waited, jumping at every noise behind them. Meg finally stood up abruptly after hearing one too many sounds. "You're right, let's see if there's another way out. It's cold, and I'm not waiting around for a man to rescue us."

She trudged into the graveyard, Lexi following closely. She walked along the walls, feeling her way in the darkness, hoping to find an opening. Suddenly, something crashed into her side and she spun around. "Lex, watch it!" she yelled. "What's wrong with you—?"

Lexi stood huddled, rubbing her arms against the cold wind. "Eh?" Her voice sounded confused. "Have you found anything yet?" she asked impatiently.

Meg's blood ran cold. "You didn't just push into me right now?"

"How could I? I'm all the way over here. Plus, I want to get out of here as much as you!"

"But I could have sworn I felt a push …" A shiver ran down her spine just as a rattling of chains echoed. Frozen, she looked at her sister and then to the dark figure standing tall on the pathway behind them.

"So, this is where you are?" the deep, familiar voice cut through, and Meg had to stop herself from running up to him and jumping into his arms.

* * *

In the hotel bar, Angus handed Lexi and Meg a glass each with a knowing nod. "Here you go, ladies, the ultimate remedy for all life's little mishaps," he declared, raising his glass in a mock-toast. "A wee dram of this magical elixir, and you'll find yourself immune to everything – from locked graveyards to pesky jet lag."

"You're enjoying this a little too much," Meg remarked dryly.

"Well, it's a first for me, rescuing two lasses from a graveyard," he replied with a grin.

"I wouldn't say *rescued* – we were finding our own way out." Meg cast a sceptical glance at the whisky and noted Angus's altered demeanour. He was poking fun at them, and it irked her. "And I doubt whisky is necessary for every occasion."

Angus chuckled, taking a sip from his own glass. "It's a universal truth that a good Scotch can solve just about anything. Bad day at work? Whisky. Locked in a graveyard? Double whisky."

"Sounds to me like you're encouraging alcoholism!" Meg quipped, frowning at Lexi's already empty glass.

Her sister's gaze lingered on Angus, who leaned on an elbow with his eyes half closed. "And what about heartbreak, Angus?" she asked, surprising Meg. "Does it heal that too?"

A moment of quiet settled over them, and Angus glanced at Meg before responding. His expression was unreadable. "Well, heartbreak … that's a bit different," he said soberly, tapping his hand against the small wooden round table. "People think it will help, but often times you get to the bottom of the bottle and feel worse than when you started." He grimaced, folding his arms, while Lexi watched him in wonder, hanging on his every word as if they were drops of wisdom from an oracle. He shrugged. "But for now, it should help with your shivering, Lexi."

"I think a bath will do more to stop my shivering," Lexi said slowly, her teeth audibly chattering.

"Even so, whisky will settle your nerves," Angus insisted.

Meg looked out the window, her jet-lagged mind trying to process the day's events. She felt a bone-deep coldness as fatigue overtook her.

"Are you OK, Meg?" Angus gently nudged her shoulder.

"Yes," she replied blankly.

"That's good. There's a lot of history about that graveyard. Honestly, I'm surprised it was locked while you both were in it. Really strange they didn't notice you. The security guard said he did his usual checks and hadn't seen a soul. Anyway, it's good you both are well and didn't see anything?"

“What do you mean?” Meg's mouth opened slowly.

“Oh well, it depends what way you're inclined. Judging by what I know so far, I’d think you wouldn’t believe in anything other than what's right in front of you.” He shrugged, not noticing Meg’s inner outrage. “You see, that place used to be an open prison, and rumour has it, it's still home to a few poltergeists. They say the spirits like to keep an eye on things, especially when unsuspecting tourists take an unexpected nap.”

She raised an eyebrow, her expression a mix of scepticism and amusement. “Poltergeists, Angus? Really?”

He nodded, maintaining a straight face. “Oh, aye! Edinburgh is a city steeped in history and mystery. You walk with ghosts here.”

Lexi shook her head and chuckled lightly, the whisky going to her head. “Of course it's haunted – everywhere here is!”

Meg remained motionless as her jet lag conjured vivid imaginations. The push in the graveyard had felt unsettlingly real, yet her rational mind rebuffed the notion. Downing the whisky, she aimed to quiet her racing thoughts. She refused to succumb to fairy tales.

6

ANGUS

Angus unclasped the belt of his kilt, the fabric finally releasing its hold on him. A deep breath escaped him as he pulled on a pair of jeans, the tension of the day melting away. The charade for the day was over, and he could return to his usual self. Leaning against the window overlooking a softly lit courtyard, he pondered whether now was the right time to make a call he'd been putting off. He peered down. A sleek black cat ambled along the moss-covered stone wall, its graceful movements silent against the distant hum of nightlife. The small green patch below, surrounded by ivy-laden walls, served as a haven within the city's heartbeat.

Despite the late hour, the quiet evening seemed perfect for an uninterrupted conversation, free from the distractions of guiding tours or saving locked-up lasses. With a determined nod, he dialled the number, mustering his resolve.

"Angus, how're ya?" a chirpy voice greeted him from the other end.

"Jake, I'm doing alright. How's the Expo in London?" He leaned against the window with the city's ambient glow casting a warm hue on his face.

"Great! I'm already booking new clients for next year. Can you believe how busy things have gotten? Suddenly, everyone wants a guided tour around Scotland!"

"Good on you, Jake," he said, glancing at the courtyard below. "So when are you coming back?"

"How? What's happened?" Jake's voice shifted from playful to concerned. "Did you pick up those girls? Is everything OK?"

He settled onto the hotel bed, propping himself up against the wall by the window. The room was small, with just a bed and a small side table – one of the staff quarters Jake had arranged during his Edinburgh tours. Angus rubbed his forehead, his legs dangling off the edge of the bed. "Yeah, I did. Everything's fine. Though, they're making changes to the itinerary, which is … irritating."

"Oh, I see." Jake's tone lightened. "Look, they've paid us extra, so if they want to tweak a few things, I would go along with it. Sorry I couldn't be there, but you've been a huge help. I think I need more staff, don't I?" Jake chuckled.

"Yeah, I'd say so." Angus's fingers drummed restlessly on the bedspread as he stared at the ceiling, frustration mounting. This was turning into more work than he had anticipated. Despite hoping someone else could handle the two Australian sisters' trip up north, it seemed unlikely. Jake needed his help after all; Angus just needed to endure a little longer.

Jake's gratitude echoed through the phone. "Thanks for doing it, Angus. Every penny matters – especially now with all the outgoings we're having. You're a great pal!"

He ran his fingers through his hair, steering the conversation in a new direction. "Are you enjoying London? Have you visited any interesting places – aside from the Travel Expo?"

"Yeah, managed to hit up a couple of museums … and pubs!"

"Of course, pubs." Angus chuckled.

“It's been fantastic. I can't believe it took me this long to explore the city. Even when you were here, I never came to visit! What a missed opportunity. I could've been drumming up business down here for years. Or better yet, I could've convinced you to join me long ago!”

Angus quirked an eyebrow. “You forget, I was working at least sixty hours a week.”

“I know, but aren't you glad you left that job behind?”

“I’m still getting used to the pay cut.”

Jake laughed. “Don't worry, you'll adjust. Maybe give it a few more years!”

“I’m only helping you out because you begged me, remember? Don't get any ideas that I'm here to stay!”

“We'll see …”

Angus chuckled. “We will see. Just so you know, dealing with customers isn't exactly my strong suit. You know the customer isn't always right.”

“You're getting along with them, though, right? They're paying us well, after all.”

“Aye, I know. I'll take good care of them. It's just that the elder sister is a bit … challenging.”

“Not used to your rugged charm, I suppose?”

He bristled. “What does that mean?”

“You can be a bit imposing at times. Try to be flexible, mate. Remember – they're paying—”

“Yes, yes, I know. They're paying well. OK, I won't dwell on it anymore. You focus on getting more business for next year, and maybe keep an eye out for potential new staff members!”

The click of the phone echoed in the small room, leaving him staring at the device in his hand. The excitement from the call drained away, leaving him with a heavy sense of duty. His shoulders sloped. Jake needed him, and that meant he had to put up with things and soldier on. He would have to remain professional at all times, putting on his tour-guide persona. This new job wasn't coming to him as naturally as he had hoped, unlike his last work, which had been natural.

He found himself chasing after people who didn't seem to want him around in the first place. It just wasn't him. He groaned to himself, and moved his head onto the mattress, looking up at the ceiling which had paint peeling around the cornices. It was simple in London. Success, money, business magazine features, beautiful women – people listened to him, his opinions mattered. And now? Here he was, lying in a budget hotel room, trying to entertain two wee lassies in his kilt, and for what? Spare change. What had he done? He allowed his thoughts to drift back to his old life, focusing on the rosy days while ignoring the stress and burnout. He flicked on the TV, watching the end of the news and sports, mulling over the day's events. He needed to relax and make this trip as smooth as possible – not just for himself or the girls, but for Jake's sake as well.

* * *

The following morning, he settled down with the itinerary, his mind more open after a night's sleep and the realisation that flexibility was key if they wanted to keep their clients happy. Sitting with the girls, he discussed their plans for the upcoming days. Lexi cast a cursory glance at the itinerary before pushing it over to Meg, who examined it closely.

"Let's skip the cities," Meg proposed, her finger tracing a route on her own map spread out on the table. "We should head north now to allow enough time for us to visit the places our mum went to."

"Are you certain? That means we'll be wasting money – we've already booked these hotels in Stirling, Glasgow, and St Andrews. You agreed to those arrangements." Angus attempted to sound nonchalant and unperturbed, though his efforts didn't convince anyone, especially not himself.

Meg nodded, her expression calm as she casually shrugged. “It's OK. While it would be nice to see those places, now that we're here, the most important thing is to explore where Mum actually travelled.”

“Fine, we'll do it your way.” He inwardly sighed, his mind already bracing for the extra work and stress of rearranging accommodation at this late stage. His jaw clenched as he eyed the itinerary spread across the table. Promises weighed on him like burdens. An unexplained discomfort lingered; he couldn't put his finger on it. It wasn't just the power play unfolding before him with Meg, there was an uneasiness, a subtle tension he couldn’t shake. But, as Jake had requested, this wasn’t about him. He needed to let himself be led. And he had no option but to trust in that.

7

MEG

The compact tour van left the labyrinthine streets of the gothic city behind, venturing through urban sprawls, busy motorways, and endless streams of cars until it finally arrived in the breathtaking countryside with its winding roads. Lexi occupied the front seat, engaged in easy conversation with Angus, while Meg sat in the back, her gaze fixed on the landscape racing past.

Pulling out the map, Meg attempted to pinpoint their location, guessing they were on the outskirts of Loch Lomond. The overcast sky cast a muted reflection on the still water. Through the trees, glimpses of hills broke the horizon, evoking images of the eagle in her dreams descending from the dark mountains in search of food. The notion that her mother was guiding her toward her father lingered, a persistent thought she couldn't shake. But it seemed absurd, even foolish to acknowledge it.

She kicked her feet out and leaned back, tuning in to Lexi's conversation with Angus. Suddenly, she felt a pull to look up, meeting Angus's intense blue gaze in the rear-view mirror. A peculiar sensation rippled through her body, like electric sparks dancing up her spine and tingling down her arms. His stare seemed to hold a depth she hadn't noticed before, triggering an inexplicable curiosity within her. Quickly, Angus averted his gaze, returning to the road, but the moment lingered in her mind, leaving her both unsettled and intrigued. She shook off the feeling, refocusing on the passing views outside the window.

"Alright, here's our first stop," Angus announced as he manoeuvred the vehicle into a car park. "There's a waterfall up the path there. We can grab a drink and take a breather."

"Sounds good." Meg eagerly slid open the van's door and stretched her legs. Swiftly, she changed into her comfortable trainers and threw on a waterproof anorak. Lexi stretched her back before striding ahead.

"Lex, you might want a jacket. Rain's likely." Meg slipped back into her role of older sister, a maternal instinct kicking in. Lexi waved off the concern and followed Angus up a dirt path shaded by trees.

It seemed to Meg that her sister was quickly forgetting about Chris and focusing all her attention on Angus. She hoped this wasn't the case; her sister needed to focus on herself rather than looking around for the next man to come along. Keeping her distance, she inhaled the fresh scent of pine, which grew stronger as she ascended. She tied up her hair, corralling the stray strands that always fell loose, and savoured being outside after what felt like hours in the van.

The air was damp but invigorating, and she strolled at a leisurely pace, drawn by the distant sounds of rushing water. As Lexi and Angus turned a corner up ahead, she followed suit and was greeted by the sight of a powerful waterfall cascading over a cliff and into a pool below. Other tourists passed with nods and smiles. Angus looked back and beckoned Meg to join him. Amid the roar of the water, not much could be heard.

A sudden urge seized her, compelling her to wade into the

cool pool, as if to cleanse herself of what she'd left behind. The scents were intoxicating, like unspoiled wilderness she wished to absorb. Then, rain poured down. Lexi briefly took shelter under a tree, then she said something to Angus – who handed her the keys – and she hurriedly left.

"She's gone back to wait for us in the van," he shouted, pointing at the retreating figure.

"I told her to take a jacket!"

"I'm sure you can't tell Lexi to do anything," he said, closer to her ear.

She pressed her lips together, resisting the urge to list the many ways she and her sister were different from one another.

"Do you want to go in closer?" Angus pointed to the rushing stream ahead.

Meg nodded eagerly, following him as they skirted around the dark pool. They spent some moments watching the powerful stream crash into the depths below. Angus pulled out a water bottle, gesturing to the waterfall.

"Would you like to taste some?" he spoke loudly over the slapping water but walked off without waiting for an answer, climbing up some rocks to get closer. Meg scrambled behind, following his steps. Being so close to the water spray, along with the rain, made her soaking wet. But she hadn't felt this free in a long time and gladly continued to follow. They were just at the hill's edge. Angus opened the lid and, with one hand leaning on a rock, moved in to fill it. She stepped closer, and just as he turned, she bumped into him and lost her balance. With her arms flailing, she screamed and fell backward. Angus quickly stuck out his arm and pulled her back from going over the edge. Her heart was racing so fast she could hear it over the rushing water.

"You could've killed me!" she shouted.

"But, but," Angus stammered, a puzzled look on his face.

"I was getting you some water to drink!" His face turned a tinge of pink.

"I wanted to come and taste it myself. I thought you knew I was behind you!" she bellowed, then realised they had accumulated an audience below. Several tourists had watched the spectacle, some even taking photographs.

"Bloody hell, woman!" Angus roared.

"Excuse me!" Meg stood up to her full height, which unfortunately wasn't at his eye level but approximately to his chest. "There's no need to talk to me like that!"

He walked past her and slowly climbed down, extending his hand out to her. She didn't take it and instead felt her own way down the rocks. They walked past the enamoured tourists and marched en route to the car in an awkward silence.

She was determined not to speak; he had shouted at her for something that was *his* fault after all. Angus stopped midway down the path, turning to her.

"I'm sorry, I shouldn't have reacted that way. You just gave me a fright. If anything had happened to you, our tour company could've been in—"

"OK, I see, you were worried about me suing the company, nothing to do with me falling and breaking my neck!"

Angus threw his eyes back, exasperated. "I didn't mean that – it's just … Please, Meg, I respect that you're the customer and I want you to enjoy your trip. But I do know what's best and safe for you – please listen to me in future. I'm your guide after all, otherwise I'm not quite sure why you bothered booking us when you clearly think you know better." He continued walking back to the van.

She wanted to throw something at him. How was she supposed to know that she wasn't to follow him up the waterfall? He was putting too much blame on her.

She gritted her teeth, walking slowly behind, feeling like a scolded child, again! She fumed to herself, wondering how Angus had managed to make a business out of being a sour-faced tour guide. He clearly didn't know how to treat people, especially women! She wanted to put him in his place, tell him he had no right, no right at all to speak to her that way. Calling her "woman" as well! How dare he! He must have gotten away with this behaviour all his life – probably raised by a mother who spoiled him and told him he was the bee's knees! She wanted to cancel the tour immediately, but as she descended the path, the reality of things set in. As much as she didn't want to admit it, she needed him. There was no way she would find her father otherwise, especially without Lexi knowing. She kicked a loose stone that bounced down the pathway, fantasising that it would bounce up and hit Angus in the head.

8

MEG

Over the next day, Meg and Angus had kept their distance from each other, Meg taking every opportunity to have as little to do with his grumpy ways as possible. Lexi, blissfully unaware, enjoyed chatting away to both of them, apparently not sensing any tension that might be lurking between them.

The day was bright, and the sun beamed down on the hills. They were heading into a new season, summer melting away and autumn closing in. Meg thought about home … her terraced house and her job. Her next-door neighbour said he'd keep an eye on things which, even though her suburb was fairly safe, reassured her to know someone was there. It was a rare occurrence for her to be on holiday, let alone in a different country. Over the years, her house had taken priority – along with looking after her mother and sister.

There had been little time to explore Australia. But as she had on numerous occasions, she told herself there would be plenty of time to travel. Now was the time to make money, to make hay while the sun shone. When she was older, she could be one of those people who toured around in a camper van.

She gazed out of the van window and admired the rising hills that changed colours before her eyes. The road ahead was a straight highway, with the occasional camper van passing by. Meg wondered if they contained old people who had made their savings in their younger years.

The van continued on the straight road until a small dark spot came into view. As they got closer, a lone man stood at the side of the road with scruffy brown hair and a backpack, his thumb stretched out in hopes of hitching a ride.

"Aw, let's pick him up," Lexi said on approach, looking at Angus.

"No way – this is your trip! We don't know where he's going. Someone else will pick him up." Angus nodded and glanced at Meg in the rear-view mirror for approval.

"I don't know, it might be nice to help him out," Meg said, just as they passed the hitchhiker at the side of the road. She was happy to help a stranded stranger, but if she was being honest, she was more taken with the idea now that she knew Angus objected.

"Angus, stop!" Lexi bellowed, craning her neck back to view the traveller.

With a dramatic sigh and a mutter under his breath, he pulled in at the side of the road.

"Oh, thanks, mate," the cheery face said at the window, a little out of breath from running to the van. Meg slid the heavy door open and welcomed their new friend.

"Where are you heading?" Angus asked in a curt voice.

The hitchhiker sat down on the seat next to Meg and laid his backpack between his legs on the ground. It was covered in stickers, badges, and ribbons tied onto every available space. "I'm off to Skye, but there's no rush – just wherever you're going would be great."

"We're going to Skye too!" Lexi cheered, looking behind her and flashing a bright smile at the man.

"Really? Wow, what are the chances!" He shuffled in his seat and gave Meg a warm smile.

"Yes, but we're not going today!" Angus barked, sideways glancing at Lexi as he manoeuvred the van back onto the main road. "We can take you as far as where we're going tonight. You can hitch a ride further on after."

"Truly, your kindness resonates with the cosmic harmony," Leon said with a serene smile, his hands clasped in a gesture of gratitude. Meg suppressed a chuckle as she noticed Angus's sceptical glance in the rear-view mirror. "I am Leon," he continued, his demeanour exuding a sense of spiritual wisdom as he scratched his head, his wrists adorned with beads and his neck with various pendants and stones.

He appeared to be somewhere between Meg's and Lexi's ages, if she were to hazard a guess. With a worldly air, his tattooed arms peeked from under his T-shirt, adding to his enigmatic presence. She took it upon herself to introduce everyone, stepping into the role of the group's leader.

Leon explained that he was from an island off Skye and was heading home after travelling through Asia for a couple of years. "My mum is going to be in shock when she sees me – thought I'd surprise her!" Leon leaned back, giving Meg his full attention, while Lexi twisted in her seat to try and be part of the conversation too. "I hear your beautiful Australian accents. You're a long way from home."

"We're scattering our mum's remaining ashes. We thought we'd do the trip she took before she had a family. So we're visiting the same places thirty years after her." Meg smiled warmly, noticing Lexi's momentary downward glance.

He shook his head solemnly. "I'm very sorry to hear of your loss. But what a special thing to do, especially together. I'm sure she's here with you."

"Yeah." Meg smiled again, but before she could say anything further, her words caught in her throat. Leon's sympathetic look mirrored the sad faces at her mother's funeral and she instantly was brought back to the pain of that day. Without warning, the familiar overwhelming grief engulfed her. She blinked, and a tear rolled down her cheek. Mortified, she turned to face the window, the emotion not dispersing as she had hoped, only persisting.

"So," Angus cut in, "we were going to head to the Glencoe village then stop for lunch at a nearby café if that suits you ladies?" His eyes searched for Meg's in the rear-view mirror, and she nodded silently.

"Fancy joining, Leon?" Lexi piped up, looking around at their new guest, unaware of the emotional interlude.

"Oh, I don't want to get in the way. You go on and let me know what it's like. I can meet you back at the van later."

Lexi lifted an eyebrow. "Don't be silly, of course you should come – we'd love the company. Right, Meg?"

Meg, who had been looking out the window, quietly daydreaming, turned to them with a dazed look. "Of course."

* * *

After their walk through the charming village with a painful, sad history, they settled in a local café for soup and sandwiches. Once again, Meg's appetite vanished, prompting her to hand her lunch to Leon, who devoured it with the voracity of a horse. Thoughts of Melbourne's vibrant food scene flooded her mind – the giant pancakes with honeyed cream cheese from her favourite bistro, and the rich, creamy coffees. Everything in Melbourne seemed fresh and colourful, with food exuding a zest for life. However, since arriving in Scotland, everything felt a bit grey, tired, and soggy.

"Right, on to the hotel!" Angus declared with authority. "It's a couple of hours away, so make sure you've had your fill." He glanced at Leon, who had finished his meal. "There are biscuits in the van if you get hungry later, Meg," Angus added, gently touching her arm. She abruptly stood up, unused to his kind gesture.

As they traversed more winding roads with breathtaking views at every turn, Leon shared tales of his travels and encounters with people along the way.

Trained as a yoga teacher in Bali, he planned to open a yoga studio back home. Meg found him fascinating; he seemed to marvel at the smallest things, stopping mid-conversation to point to a cloud shaped like a dog or acknowledge hill walkers in the distance, imagining the hills they had climbed and the stories they held. He had a sense of wonder that many adults lose, Meg reflected.

"I paint too, so hopefully I can be an artist in my spare time. I just want to create beautiful things," Leon mentioned casually, before assuming a relaxed posture, crossing his legs with ease.

Meg pondered her own life, particularly her job, and whether it truly fulfilled her. Though content with her position at Simmons Accounting, it left little time for other pursuits. She entertained fantasies of studying yoga or embarking on a nomadic journey to learn a new language. But the idea of coasting through life without a stable job seemed outlandish to her.

As Angus slowed the van, they approached a grey granite building standing alone amidst the hills and sparse trees, its long flag poles proudly exhibiting various countries' colours, flapping in the wind to welcome them. He unloaded the suitcases and casually tossed Leon his rucksack, offering a brief farewell before walking away, leaving Meg and Lexi to bid their new friend adieu.

"We wish you could stay. Can't you spend the night here?" Lexi's hopeful tone was tinged with disappointment. "We could have dinner together. I'm sure there's room in the hotel. If not, you could even share a room with Angus," she suggested optimistically.

"I better not." Leon shrugged, slinging his bag over his shoulder. "Another time, Lex-Lex," he added with a smile, draping his arm around Lexi's shoulder. Meg sensed a certain familiarity in the gesture but couldn't quite place it. She had taken a step back during lunch and their earlier stroll, allowing Lexi and Leon more time to talk. With a polite smile, she edged away, giving them a moment of privacy.

Entering the hotel, she was greeted by a dimly lit space with tartan carpeting covering the floor, mirroring the colours of Angus's kilt. The interior boasted dark oak beams and white-washed walls, evoking a rustic yet charming ambiance.

"Welcome to the Highland Arms Hotel, how can I help you?" A friendly redhead stood up from behind her computer, in a very dated gaudy white ruffle shirt and kilt. Meg briefly wondered if the locals truly embraced kilts as enthusiastically as they seemed to, or if it was all part of the tourist experience.

"Hi, I think our guide, Angus, came this way?" she asked, momentarily transfixed by a large painting dominating the wall with a stag staring fiercely directly at her.

The receptionist's face lit up. "Of course! You're with Angus. He's a joy to have around. We're delighted that his tour company has chosen the Highland Arms Hotel for his guests."

Meg found herself surprised by the receptionist's admiration for Angus, given her own experiences with him. Their interactions had been far from joyful, coloured by his aloofness and sharp remarks. It was as if they were talking about two different people.

"Um, yeah, he's fine," Meg replied cautiously.

The receptionist's expression shifted slightly, her confusion apparent. "Well, yes. If you head through the door here, turn left, and you'll find yourself at the end of the corridor in room number seven. Angus mentioned he's booked dinner for you. Enjoy your stay," she said warmly, indicating the direction to the rooms.

Stepping into the room, Meg's eyes were drawn to their neatly arranged suitcases resting at the foot of each bed. She crossed the room with purpose, her gaze fixated on the window that framed the expanse of barren hills stretching ahead. A peculiar sense of desolation mingled with an undeniable appeal in the landscape's raw beauty.

She chose the single bed closest to the window and perched on its edge, her attention drawn to a deer gracefully navigating the distant terrain. She thought of the painting in the reception, and how something so beautiful could be threatening. They seemed to blend seamlessly into their surroundings, as if the landscape itself had come to life. And then, as if the world had a secret to share, more deer materialised, like ethereal figures emerging from the mist.

As she kicked off her shoes, she sank deeper into the moment. It was her time to absorb the peace that had been hard to come by since they started their Scottish journey. The usual weight of responsibilities and noise from the outside world faded, replaced by the steady rhythm of the murmurs of the land.

9

MEG

The next morning, as they readied for the van, they were surprised to find Leon's familiar silhouette waiting on the pavement, rummaging in his backpack. Upon hearing their approach, he looked up with a cheerful grin.

"Leon!" Lexi laughed with surprise.

Meg could feel Angus bristle beside her. "I thought you were continuing on to Skye yesterday?" he croaked.

Leon stood up with a carefree bounce. "Well, I tried. But it turns out there's a hostel just up the road there." He pointed to a hill track leading into a cluster of trees. "The train stops there too, believe it or not. And there's a great little pub. Lots of backpackers – had a good time there!"

Lexi opened the van door and quickly occupied the back seat, leaving the front seat empty. "Leon, you should've told us! We could've joined you." She pouted. "Our night was pretty boring – just dinner and bed. I'd have preferred a pub night with locals!"

"I thought you were tired?" Angus's voice betrayed a tinge of hurt. "I would've taken you anywhere you wanted."

"Don't worry too much," Leon chimed in, scrunching his

nose. His eyes flickered toward Angus, and a subtle tension lingered in the air. "You didn't miss out on much, Lex-Lex. No locals, just a bunch of merry travellers getting drunk."

Lexi's face crumpled. "That's exactly what I'd enjoy – not stuffy hotels with old people!"

Angus's jaw dropped in surprise, and Meg struggled to suppress a laugh. The shock on his face at being labelled "old" was too amusing. However, she quickly realised that the insult had been directed at her as well.

Leon shrugged, lingering near the van, and glanced at the empty front seat. "I suppose it's a long shot, but can I still catch a lift to Skye?"

Meg sensed Angus muttering something under his breath, though the words were indistinct. An awkward silence settled over the group, all eyes turning to her.

"Sure, come on in," she offered with a sigh.

Noticing Leon had already settled in the back beside Lexi, Meg was less than thrilled about sitting next to Angus for the duration. However, she felt obligated, to avoid appearing rude. Just as she moved forward, Angus tugged her arm, causing her to turn. His grip made her instinctively stand straighter.

"I don't trust him, Meg," he whispered quietly in her ear. "There's something off. I don't like him."

Meg glanced at Angus's hand on her elbow, and he quickly released his grip. "I'm sorry," he mumbled.

She understood Angus's attempt to assert control in the presence of Leon. However, now he seemed to be manipulating her into conforming to his domineering ways. She closed her eyes, taking a deep breath. "He's harmless, maybe a bit frugal with money." She shook her head. "I don't see the problem. He needs to get to Skye, and we're going there."

"Still," Angus said, scratching through his bushy beard.

She felt an urge to stand her ground. "Angus, it's fine.

We'll drop him off today." To her astonishment, she found herself trying to soothe him, then suddenly bristled at her own actions. "Listen, we are paying you, what's one more person in the van? Come on, let's go!" She walked off, leaving Angus with the suitcases.

* * *

She gazed off into the distance from her position in the front of the van, half listening to the animated conversation between Lexi and Leon in the back. They discussed films and music, with Lexi delving into the realm of reality TV shows she missed while being on the other side of the world, a genre that Meg never quite understood the appeal of – a mix of love and hate that puzzled her. Leon absorbed every word, nodding along with a serious expression.

"I couldn't believe he picked Brianna," Lexi breathed, swiping through her phone to reveal images of attractive people from various Bachelor and Bachelorette shows. Meg couldn't fathom why anyone would spend their time glued to the TV when there were so many other things to do, like work or tending to the garden.

"Well, she's bonnie," Leon commented, taking out his phone. "Are you on Insta, Lex?"

Lexi's face lit up as the two of them inched closer in the back of the van. Meg suppressed a sigh and glanced toward Angus, anticipating an eye-roll. However, his attention remained fixed on the road ahead, brow furrowed in silence. The tension between them simmered palpably, suggesting that he held on to his grievances tightly, making any notion of harmony seem remote. If she wanted to pursue her quest of finding her father, she needed to rise above her pride.

"So, Mr Angus, are you from around here?" she asked, attempting to lighten the atmosphere.

"I'm from the village Abergow, and I have a cottage along the coast," he responded, his gaze guarded.

"And have you always been a tour guide, Mr Angus?" she continued, only to be met with his exasperated correction.

"Angus!" he barked.

"Angus," she repeated, forcing calmness into her tone, yet she had half a mind to whack him with her handbag. "Can we just be civil? I understand we got off on the wrong foot, but it's all just misunderstandings. We all want the same thing – Lexi and I want a memorable trip, and you want your company to receive good reviews, right?"

Angus shot her a sceptical look, and she threw up her hands. "We're not here to leave a bad review. As long as you do your job and show us around, and we can all get along …" She backtracked, realising the challenge of conversing with him. "Look, can we just have a nice time? OK?"

"Of course," Angus mumbled, his gaze still locked on the road. He settled back into his seat, easing the tension in the vehicle. They picked up speed, the road widening to accommodate a large bridge spanning over the water. Crossing it, they transitioned from the mainland to the island.

"Hey, I thought we were taking a ferry?" Lexi inquired, peering out the window in wonder.

"There is a ferry, but the bridge is quicker for us," Angus's voice boomed over the rushing wind from his rolled-down window.

"Over the bridge to Skye!" Lexi sang out, laughing.

Angus chuckled, stepping on the accelerator, his expression turning peculiarly affectionate towards Lexi, leaving Meg flabbergasted by this sudden change in demeanour.

Before long, they parked near the water's edge. Angus tapped the steering wheel with a flourish. "Alright, first stop – a castle! After you, ladies," he declared. His cheeriness broadcast to everyone, though his gaze settled on Leon with less enthusiasm. "And Leon."

"Oh yay!" Lexi untangled herself from the conversation with Leon, flicking her blonde hair. Meg had already noticed how fresh and alive she looked since they left Australia. "I wonder if Mum visited here?"

Meg scrunched up her nose, studying her trusty map with her scribbled notes. "I don't see anything marked here; there are castles further up the island." Squinting at the town names to locate their position, she found herself at a loss.

Angus gently took the map from her hands. "Meg, this one won't be on the map … trust me, please," he said, his voice laden with weariness.

Meg bit her lip, torn between scepticism and curiosity. She followed him, with Lexi and Leon trailing behind. They ventured into an overgrown expanse of greenery that towered over Meg's head. The vegetation seemed to engulf them before revealing a scene straight out of a fairy tale – a castle ruin perched atop a moss-covered hill across a tranquil bay. The image triggered memories of her mother's stories, particularly one tale of a prince and his new bride, a marriage born of duty that gradually blossomed into a profound love, defying even death as they were laid to rest together beneath the waves under the castle. She glanced at Lexi, who stood quietly, wide-eyed at the view, likely reminiscing about the stories their mother had shared over the years. She couldn't help but feel pity for her sister's romantic aspirations – a relentless pursuit of the idealised and unattainable. It was clear that Lexi's search for an ethereal love was an exercise in futility, as such love simply didn't exist.

A splash interrupted Meg's reverie, and a slimy head with bulging eyes emerged briefly from the mirrored water before disappearing. Angus chuckled softly and exchanged a knowing look with Meg. The head popped up again, followed by a companion, both creatures gliding gracefully toward the castle. Meg smiled at Angus, suppressing her whimsical thoughts – perhaps the lovers of old weren't confined to the realm of legend but remained watchful seals over their castle through the ages.

Angus playfully nudged Lexi. “Last one to the castle is a rotten egg!” With a mischievous grin, he dashed off, skirting around the bay and ascending the hill. Lexi followed closely, laughter trailing behind.

Meg rolled her eyes and strolled at a more measured pace beside Leon, who intermittently paused to snap photos with his phone. “Have you been here before?” she asked, plucking a tall weed and rubbing the seeds between her fingers, a gesture that took her back to her childhood.

“No, it's my first time. It's pretty cool.” He tucked his phone back into his jeans pocket and locked eyes with her. “Are you enjoying your trip?”

“Yeah, it's been great so far … it's like retracing the steps my mother took. She told us countless stories when we were kids.”

“Lexi mentioned that. I'm sorry again for your loss. You must miss her.”

Meg nodded briefly before steering the conversation in a different direction. “So, are you showing us around here too? You're not far from home, right? Just a ferry ride away?”

“Yes, a bit further up the island, and there's a ferry tomorrow morning. But honestly, I don't know much about this area. There's a lot I'm not familiar with.”

“But why wouldn't you explore this place? Isn't this the bigger island? Where do you shop, go out, and all that?”

“You'd be surprised; our little island has its own attractions.” Leon smiled, pushing aside a tall fern to allow Meg to pass. “As I said before, I did the whole Asia thing. I prefer to travel to distant lands. I can always explore places close to home later, when I'm a bodach!"

"Bodach?"

"An old man," he clarified with a grin.

"Well, you've a lot of years until then!" she said, feeling very much like an old woman. She found Leon attractive, a fact she struggled to admit. As she observed him, she wrestled with the unspoken realisation of the significant age gap between them. She had once dated a man her own age, and had found the experience very sobering. He had spent most of his free time playing computer games and collecting comic books. It hadn't occurred to her then that perhaps they were just not compatible.

Admiring Leon's youthful good looks, she felt a fleeting attraction, which she promptly extinguished. He extended a hand to help her cross a small stream, prompting her mind to wander. When had a man last held her?

She'd had a few encounters, but the most recent had been just before her mother's passing. Gerald from the HR department – he was nice and had asked her out. Cinema and dinner. She had been so anxious leading up to the date that she bought three different dresses, unable to decide what to wear.

When the evening arrived, she settled on a black dress she had worn countless times before. Surprisingly, Gerald seemed to appreciate her choice, so that after three bottles of wine during dinner, the evening took a hurried turn, ending with a brief shag in the back of his car.

He never reached out again, but she hadn't initiated contact either. In the office, whenever their paths crossed in the elevator or hallway, they would suddenly become absorbed in their phones or engage in animated conversations with other colleagues.

Her last brush with passion: a moment void of excitement, replaced by a sense of discomfort.

As she shook off those memories, she was struck by the thought that she might have unknowingly neglected a significant aspect of her life.

"What's the story with the guide guy?" Leon picked up a stone from the small sandy patch of beach and skimmed it across the water's glassy surface.

"Who, Angus?" She snapped out of her thoughts of intimacy.

"Yeah, he seems to have an issue with me."

"Don't worry about it. I think he's like that with everyone. I've even started calling him 'Mr Grumps' to Lexi."

Leon chuckled, handing her a pebble. "Can you skim rocks?"

"Of course," she replied, lowering herself before tossing the stone with speed. Unfortunately, it plunged into the sea with a single splash.

Raising an eyebrow, Leon smiled. "Should we just pretend that didn't happen?" He handed her another stone.

Meg bit her lip and threw the pebble. This time, it barely left her hand before dropping into the shallows. She looked up at him and burst into laughter, feeling as light as a feather. The sea breeze ruffled her hair, and she realised she hadn't genuinely laughed in a long time.

"Come on, you two!" Lexi's voice rang from the top of the hill, the castle ruin looming in the background.

"She's got a lot of energy, your sister!" Leon waved back and walked side by side with Meg, continuing at their leisurely pace.

As they reached the top of the craggy hill, Lexi pointed out the same two seals from before, gliding together amidst floating seaweed. Angus sat perched on a large rock, examining a map and speaking on his mobile phone. Meg took in a deep breath of the fresh, cool salty air and smiled at her sister, who leaned against a remaining stone archway.

"It's pretty magical," Lexi mused, gazing up through the open roof to the grey sky above. "I can imagine Mum being here. What do you think, Meg? Could we maybe scatter some of her ashes at this spot?" Lexi grazed her hand over mossy stones, looking into crevices as if searching for hidden treasure left for a lucky visitor.

"We don't know she was here – I didn't even know there was a castle here."

"She did come to the island, though. Can you really imagine Mum not coming here? This was *so* her thing – a hidden, romantic castle. I can see her stories at this very spot. I can feel her here."

"We were going to scatter her ashes at the castles further up north. We know for sure she went there – remember those old photos she took?"

"Yeah, I guess you're right. I just thought maybe—" Lexi's playful demeanour shifted to one of quiet hesitation. She turned away and wandered behind the entrance walls alone.

Meg stood still. Leon was on the far end of the hill, lying on the grass with his eyes closed in a meditative state. Angus, no longer on his phone, sat on a boulder watching Meg.

"Do you mind?" Meg's tone was curt as she followed her sister, who sat against the outside wall, gazing back over the bay.

"Hey." Lexi sniffed, avoiding eye contact.

"I'm sorry, Lex." Meg pressed her lips together, her tone gentle as Lexi's eyes met hers under her choppy blonde bangs.

"Why are you sorry?" Lexi pulled at a few strands of short grass and tore them apart with her chipped, blue-painted nails.

She sat down beside her and pulled out a black velvet drawstring pouch from her shoulder bag. She placed the small pouch in Lexi's hands. "That's all I have left of Mum, those few ashes."

Lexi held the bag in one hand, uncertainty clouding her face. "Yeah." She placed it in the palm of her other hand and gently opened the pouch, gazing into it briefly before tightening the drawstrings and handing it back to her sister.

"We agreed to scatter these at Castle Creag. We know she visited there …"

"Yeah, sure." Lexi looked back across the bay, an unusual quietness settling upon her, a state Meg had only witnessed after Lexi's breakup with Chris. "I just feel her now. I haven't really felt anything since she passed."

Meg hesitated, cradling the ashes in her hands. "We could scatter a tiny amount …"

Lexi pushed herself up, standing above her elder sister. "No, you're right. I think I'm just starting to feel connected to her. We're following her journey, after all. She's leading us further. This is only the first stop, really." Lexi smiled and extended her arm out to her sister.

"Are you sure?" Meg bit her lip. The last person she wanted to upset was Lexi. This trip was for them to be sisters again, wasn't it?

"Yes, you're right – as usual," Lexi said, giving Meg a reassuring smile before wandering off to explore.

Meg sat alone, a subtle sense of unease settling in the pit of her stomach.

10

LEXI

Lexi strolled along a dazzling white beach, its brilliance nearly blinding her. She squinted at silhouettes of trees in the distance, a sparse cluster that seemed to twist and contort, much like the trees ravaged by past bushfires back home. She had left the tour group behind, their eyes fixed on the horizon in hopes of spotting dolphins. Solace was what Lexi sought in the rhythmic embrace of the ocean.

The desire to lose herself in a different world gnawed at her. She yearned for a moment when she could be on this beach under different circumstances, far removed from the painful farewell to her mother.

With this yearning in mind, she delved into her black leather backpack, hoping to find refuge in music. However, her search revealed a pair of earphones with wires entangled and knotted to a point where she immediately lost interest and discarded them back into her bag.

As her gaze returned to the sea, its waves not as tumultuous as the ones back home, memories of Chris surfaced. She remembered his image, pushing his surfboard into the ocean, glancing back at her with a playful smile. She wanted him even now. Shivering, she remembered his weight on top of her, arching over her, pulling her to him. She wanted to lose herself in his salty skin and his deep kisses.

"Hey, you OK?" Leon's voice cut through the rhythm of the waves. She turned to find him approaching, hands tucked into his back jeans pockets.

The sky above darkened. There was a hint of green in his eyes, a shade murky like the dark sea nearby. The curve of his mouth triggered a faint dimple on his cheek, and she found herself wanting to study him more.

"I'm fine," she replied, her thumbs idly circling her back-pack straps.

"I heard what Meg said," he continued, his tone gentle.

"Um, yeah."

"She's certainly the older sister." He smiled broadly, the dimple fading.

"Yeah, is it that obvious?"

"Likes to get her way? Sure, I know all too well the results of an older sibling."

"You've got a sister?" she asked.

He nodded, a knowing smile playing on his lips. "And a brother."

She felt a subtle shift, a softening of her heart that allowed her to temporarily escape the painful memories of Chris. Leon's easy charm and genuine interest were invigorating. Her thoughts were heard, not dismissed as she was used to. She crossed her arms, staying close, basking in the faint sunlight that provided momentary warmth, which proved short-lived.

"He treats me like his little child," Leon explained, shaking his head. Lexi appreciated hearing about other people's sibling troubles. "Bosses me around, always convinced he's right – no matter how wrong he actually is!"

He scoffed bitterly. “It's frustrating. So frustrating that I avoid being in the same city as him, let alone the same country.”

“I thought you live on a small island?” she asked, hanging on to his every word.

“Yes.” His voice was steady. “But he lives in the city, and I make a point of avoiding it at all costs. Anything our little sister says is warmly embraced, but when it comes to me? Well, I couldn't possibly know a thing!”

There was a quiver in his voice. Leon's attire consisted of a simple white T-shirt, long board shorts, and well-worn sandals. While she, taking no chances against the wild west-coast wind, was swathed in her cosy jumper and denim jacket.

“It's getting quite cold, isn't it? Should we consider heading back?”

“Nah.” Leon responded with a grin. “I’d like to chat a bit more if you don't mind.”

“But you're going to freeze,” she protested gently.

“I’m fine,” he insisted. “It'll make wearing my jumper all the more welcome when I get back to the van. So, shall we sit and talk, or would you rather keep walking?” He extended the offer with an inviting raise of his eyebrow, one that Lexi accepted with genuine interest. They continued strolling along the shoreline, gradually leaving Meg and Angus as mere specks in the distance.

Their conversation meandered through their childhoods, dreams, and adventures, with Chris and their complicated history at the forefront.

“And you both work together?” Leon encouraged.

“Yeah, well … worked together. Now that I’ve left, I don’t know what he’s up to – if he’s with this girl, or single, or even if he’s still in Melbourne. He was pretty impulsive, you see. I wouldn’t be surprised if he packed everything and moved to another city, maybe even along the coast to be closer to the waves."

"Well anyway, he sounds like a twat."

"What?"

"A bloody idiotic twat! To treat you like that. He's insane. You are bloody gorgeous."

Lexi was taken aback, but the compliment made her stand tall. She looked into his stormy eyes with curiosity.

"You don't believe me? Honestly, Lexi, you deserve more than a guy who thinks you're just a casual thing. You need to be valued. You're amazing. I'm just trying to stop myself from doing anything else at this confusing time for you," he confessed, scratching the back of his neck.

"What do you mean?" She couldn't help but smile.

"Well, I would have thought it pretty obvious. I want to kiss you so bad. I've been wanting to kiss you ever since you picked me up at the side of the road."

"You don't need to kiss me to thank me for picking you up." Lexi giggled. "Also, it was Angus who was driving – maybe you should be showing your appreciation towards him." She playfully bit her lip.

"Perhaps, but Angus isn't as pretty as you … or as nice as you. You're just—"

Lexi couldn't wait and leaned on her tiptoes, kissing him on the mouth with force. He took her in his arms briefly, before she pulled away.

His dazed expression made her laugh aloud, his eyes blinking. Behind him, she could see the two dots of Angus and Meg growing larger, getting closer. She gently pulled his hand, leading him toward a small cluster of jaggy gorse bushes. There, they sat down on the edges of the sand and soil meeting together.

Leon's face broke into a look of satisfaction, much like a cat who had just finished a bowl of cream. Their lips met again, and this time he deepened the kiss, his tongue intertwining with hers. There was a sudden explosion inside her, the feeling only intensifying.

Her lips parted from his, and she fixed her gaze on him. "We have only a short time before they come." She waited to see if he understood her suggestion. That dimple of his showed itself again, and Lexi saw his desire. The swell in his jeans couldn't hide the fact. As they melted together, his warm hands on her neck sent shivers down her spine.

"Are you sure?" he whispered.

"Yes," she breathed, her heart pounding with excitement. "Please hurry, we don't have much time."

Leaning over her, Leon continued to kiss her neck, his hand caressing her throat where her mother's ruby necklace sat, its small oval shape neatly nestled on the hollow of her throat. It had stayed there all year. His focus shifted to the rest of her body, his weight pressing down on her. With a deep breath, Lexi released the pain that had been haunting her since Chris left. All she wanted was to forget everything and indulge in this feeling, to swim in it until it consumed her.

She surrendered herself and let it envelop her completely.

11

ANGUS

In the hotel car park, Angus wrestled with their bags and suitcases. With each hotel visit, their luggage seemed to multiply in both size and weight. Lexi's penchant for collecting tourist trinkets and Meg's journal addiction were undoubtedly to blame. At this rate, they'd need to book two extra suitcases for their return to Australia.

Deciding it wasn't his concern, he lifted one of the bags that suddenly burst, spilling orange juice everywhere. It was Leon's bag, and it baptised Angus in citrus. He muttered under his breath as the juice seeped into his clean, white shirt. Groaning, he delved into his bag, searching for a replacement shirt, all while the group was distracted, enamoured by a stag posing for photos nearby.

Changing his shirt and shivering as the cold air hit his back, he chuckled at his own expense. At this rate, he mused, he might as well take a dive into the loch for good measure. He had grown too accustomed to office comforts, tour vans, heated seats and roaring fires.

Before he could pull on his black T-shirt, a hotel staff member materialised behind him.

"Hi, Angus. I heard you were coming today," chirped a petite, pretty brunette with a Baltic accent.

He jumped in alarm, his kilt swaying dangerously. "Good god!" he exclaimed, nearly dropping the bag he was holding. "You startled me!"

The staff member stifled a giggle, her eyes twinkling with amusement. "Sorry. Didn't mean to sneak up on you like that."

He took a deep breath, tucking his T-shirt in tightly. "It's quite alright," he said, forcing a smile. "Just caught me off guard, that's all."

She grinned, a mischievous glint in her eye. "Well, I suppose I have a talent for making dramatic entrances."

Suddenly, Angus recognised her but struggled to recall her name. Jake had once suggested he keep a notepad with every hotel contact in Scotland, a suggestion Angus had scoffed at. But now, seeing her, he realised his friend had a point. Getting on the good side of hotel staff meant a more pleasant stay for both his clients and himself, and a better room often made all the difference.

"Er, how are you getting on?" he replied, hoping it sounded adequately familiar.

"Great since seeing you here." She raised an eyebrow, a long fingernail between her teeth. "Are you staying here long?"

"Just a night, then we're heading further along the coast, to see some more castles."

"Sounds wonderfully romantic," she breathed, edging a little too close.

"Well … it can be, depending on my clients." He took a cautious step back.

"I bet you pull out all the stops." She bit her lip. "A fine Highland man like you!" She laughed, placing a hand on his arm. "Would you like some assistance?"

Angus eyed the heavy bags. "Oh no, I wouldn't dream of asking. I'll just make a few trips—"

"Nonsense." She clapped her hands, summoning a slender youth with freckles and an ill-fitting suit to carry two suitcases toward the hotel entrance.

"How many rooms did you book?" Angus's admirer walked beside him, long eyelashes batting playfully.

"I booked one for them."

"One room?" She tutted.

"I thought I might sort myself out – find a room somewhere, if I'm desperate, there's always the van." He shrugged. Comfort was the last thing on his mind.

"Well, we can't have that. You being cold … and alone."

"This stay is a bit last minute. My clients changed their minds at the start of the trip. We were hoping to spend two nights here …?"

"Well, you can't blame a girl for changing her mind; we must be allowed a little indulgence." Approaching the front desk, she trailed a finger over the polished wood. "Oh, I gather it's for the two ladies outside snapping photographs of Rodger?"

"Rodger?"

"Why, the hotel stag!" She rolled her eyes. "He goes to anyone who offers him the slightest morsel. I caught some guests offering him chocolate once! I really had to intervene then." She widened her eyes in mock alarm. "He does have a reaction to apples …" She tilted her head at the computer screen.

Before Angus could check on what snacks his party was offering the pet stag, the lady manager nodded, her high bun remaining rigid atop her head. "Two nights? A little presumptuous, given that we're one of the most exclusive hotels in the Highlands." She waved a peach-coloured acrylic nail over a black diary on her desk, the same nail shooting upwards towards Angus, menacing. "Very pretty."

"Excuse me?" Angus shook his head.

"The clients you have. Very pretty girls. American?"

"Australian," he replied, feeling slightly uncomfortable.

She nodded. "Yes, they have that look about them."

He remained quiet, unsure what *that* look consisted of and preferring not to encourage further discussion.

"Well, well, well, Angus from Highlander Tours, you're in luck! Not only can you stay an extra night, but I can give you three rooms. You'll be near the staff, on the ground level. The other two will be on the top floor on the far side."

His mouth tightened. "Very good. Thanks very much."

"Happy to be of service, Angus." The corner of her mouth curled. She tapped on the keyboard and clicked the mouse before handing over the keys with a wink. "Do make sure you have your own bit of fun while you're staying. The pubs in town are a good place to let your hair down." She grinned, leaning over the counter.

Meg and Lexi entered the hotel, their faces beaming with delight, immediately infecting Angus with their enthusiasm.

"I get off early tonight. Maybe our paths might cross," she whispered, placing a hand over his. "I'll make sure the bags are sent up to the rooms!" She clicked her fingers and the man from earlier appeared abruptly beside them, startling Angus.

"What was all that about?" Meg asked quietly, her lips pursed, arms folded.

"Oh nothing, she's just a friend." Angus gave her a casual shrug, jabbing the elevator button.

"Looked like you were right in there if you ask me, Angus," Leon chimed in, slipping in behind Angus just as the doors sealed shut.

"Well, I'm not asking you," he muttered. "And the rooms

are booked for the girls; remember I'm not *your* tour guide." He scowled, inwardly cursing his own short fuse. Despite his efforts to remain unaffected by Leon's presence, the urge to eject him from the elevator was almost overwhelming. If it weren't for the girls insisting he stay, Angus would have gladly shown him the door before the lift even reached the next floor.

"Oh Angus, you are a right protector!" Lexi said playfully. "Don't worry about Leon – he just wants to check out the room."

"Well, that better be all. I said to management it is only you two girls staying."

"Management didn't look too bothered about what we do. If anything, she was drooling over you," Meg remarked, her elbow nudging his in the cramped elevator.

Despite himself, he couldn't suppress a chuckle, and Meg blushed.

"And why should that bother you?" he queried as Leon and Lexi exited the elevator, their laughter echoing down the corridor.

"It's just an observation," Meg replied tersely. "Seems a bit unprofessional to me."

"Well, maybe for her. But not for me. I'm a gentleman," Angus retorted, a touch more playfully than intended, accompanied by a wink.

Meg's eyes narrowed. "Oh, please. All men claim to be gentlemen," she retorted, striding off ahead and putting distance between them. He took a deep breath, watching her flip her dark hair. Her scent lingered in the air. She was angry. And not just angry. Jealous. Despite himself, he couldn't help but feel a smug sense of satisfaction as he led them to their rooms.

12

MEG

Lexi and Leon led the group toward the distillery with eager anticipation. "I'm in desperate need of a drink!" Lexi called over her shoulder.

"It's not a pub, Lex!" Meg retorted, deliberately falling behind with a measured pace. Giving in to Lexi's persistent desire for a dram, Meg couldn't shake her own yearning – but for a king-size bed. She imagined herself lounging in a plush robe, fresh from a lavish manicure and pedicure. Her nails had never appeared so unkempt, clearly disrupted by the trip.

Expectations for their Scotland journey had been more grandiose than the reality Meg found herself in. Angus had made it clear that they were fortunate to secure rooms, with her last-minute booking, albeit at a higher cost. Sharing a room with Lexi each night wasn't terrible; it allowed her to keep a vigilant eye on her younger sister. So far, there had been no dramatic calls to her ex or any substance-related mishaps. Nevertheless, she should remain watchful, especially given Lexi's enthusiasm for alcohol.

"Oh well, maybe we'll hit up a pub later!" Lexi's excited exclamation resonated as Leon chuckled, his arm casually draped over her shoulders. As the couple moved ahead, Meg couldn't help the surge of apprehension that washed over her. Watching her sister fall into another man's arms almost immediately after meeting him filled her with a sense of foreboding.

Angus locked the van and wrapped a scarf around his neck. He shoved his hands into his leather biker jacket, still sporting his signature kilt. Meg found herself pondering whether it got draughty up there, especially in the chilly wind. She couldn't help but entertain the thought that he might be a traditionalist at heart, embracing the age-old rumour that Scottish men preferred to go au natural under their kilts.

After a swift tour around the distillery and a few generous samplings of the various hops on offer, Meg found herself perking up. The tour group was a diverse blend of people, including two scholarly Welsh gentlemen, a youthful Indian couple, and a lively, fluorescent-pink hen party. As the tour concluded, camaraderie had blossomed among them, and they all decided to continue the festivities by heading to the nearest pub. As the night unfolded and the whisky flowed, Meg embraced the merriment, donning a penis-shaped necklace and a sparkly crown bestowed upon her by the hen party. The cosy pub was bathed in the warm glow of a crackling fire in the corner, though the slightly ajar door allowed in the cold outside air.

"The best band is coming tonight – courtesy of us bridesmaids!" One of the hen party members looped her arm through Meg's and handed her another glass of whisky. Adopted into the group, she quickly lost track of their names after the first round at the bar. The party's size swelled as the night progressed. In the midst of the whirlwind of festivities, a small group of men gathered in a corner beside the roaring fire. Without any formal announcement, they produced their instruments and launched into a lively folk tune. Meg's feet responded instinctively, propelling her into a dance of utter abandon. She reached out for one of the older scholars, and they spun one another, even though they both lacked the knowledge of the steps. His tweed jacket soon came off in the stomping and flinging and then he rolled up his shirtsleeves to keep up with Meg's energy.

A burly man expertly pounded the bodhrán drum, keeping perfect time with a clean-cut young piper at his side. Sweat poured off her as she twirled and spun with anyone willing and able, the confined space becoming a realm of uncontainable joy. A strong hand reached out and pulled her into a spin. She easily matched the movement, locking eyes with Angus as they danced together in a rhythm only they seemed to share. With his hand on the small of her back, he led her through steps she'd never encountered, but she followed his lead effortlessly. The music escalated in speed, and Angus kept up, twirling Meg around in perfect synchrony. As abruptly as the dance began, it stopped, leaving the crowd cheering in appreciation.

"Wow!" Meg shouted, joining in the applause.

"Wow indeed!" Angus wiped his forehead with the back of his hand, his face flushed from the intensity of the dance. "You're a good dancer, very robust on the dance floor!" he yelled near her ear to be heard over the noise.

"Robust?" Meg mockingly raised an eyebrow. "That's one way to compliment a girl."

Angus rolled his eyes and chuckled. "It is a compliment – to do a Highland ceilidh dance, you need to be able to throw your partner and be thrown in return!"

A tuft of red chest hair peeked out from beneath Angus's dark T-shirt, exposed as he wiped his brow. He had indeed thrown her around the dance floor, making her bounce right back, a rhythm of dancing she had never encountered before – and she had loved every second of it.

"I love a man in a kilt." A slim girl with dark hair approached Angus, lightly touching his arm. "You owe me a dance, Angus," she said, a flirty eyebrow raised. She resembled the receptionist at the hotel, her appearance transformed with flowing hair and a low-cut dress.

Quietly, Meg receded, giving the attractive couple their space as they waltzed. At the bar, she ordered drinks, ensuring everyone from their party was covered. Her gaze shifted to Lexi and Leon, swaying together. An internal sigh escaped her; she had let her focus stray from her sister for the evening, and now it seemed Lexi was smitten with their new traveller friend.

She tried to console herself; Lexi seemed genuinely happy, and perhaps a new romantic interest was what she needed to move on from her cheating ex back in Melbourne. However, she couldn't ignore her deep understanding of her sister's tendencies. Lexi wore her emotions on her sleeve, often prioritising her heart over her head – a pattern Meg had observed too many times.

Leon lived on the other side of the world. She attempted to push aside the unsettling possibilities, but they persisted, a gnawing concern that threatened to spoil the festive mood. The unsettling idea that she might lose her sister to the throes of another impulsive romance made her stomach churn with worry. Lexi had a history of uprooting her life for love.

Lexi handed her wallet to Leon, who smoothly pocketed it before making his way toward the bar. Instinctively, Meg shifted her gaze, avoiding any appearance of overt curiosity. A whirlwind of thoughts raced through her mind as she contemplated what she truly knew about Leon.

"Well, hello there." Leon nudged Meg at the bar, confidently manoeuvring his way ahead of others who were waiting to order their drinks.

"Hey, oh, I think you'll need to queue—" Meg began, but her words fell on deaf ears as Leon paid no heed.

"Great night, huh? I see your man is getting quite the attention tonight." He gestured toward Angus, now engaged in a lively dance with another girl. They twirled and moved in sync, and Meg's stomach lurched unexpectedly. Quickly looking away, she felt perplexed by the unexpected unease. Another whisky was definitely out of the question.

"He's not my man, Leon. He's our tour guide." Meg smiled apologetically at the irritated customers behind Leon, who had been waiting to place their orders. Her accumulated drinks sat on the bar, and the barman was busy preparing the final pint. "What can I get you, Leon?" Meg asked, eager to complete her order swiftly and not irritate the other patrons any further.

Leon appeared contemplative for a moment. The barman, already stressed with other patrons shouting their orders, waited for Leon's decision. "I'll have a double Ardlaig whisky, please."

Meg's attention was momentarily caught by the barman reaching for a bottle on the top shelf, the exclusive and expensive bottles untouched throughout the night. "And Lexi?"

"Oh, she's fine. I think she's had enough." Leon's response was casual, breezy even, as he collected his glass and departed, leaving Meg slightly slack-jawed in surprise.

Something about the situation struck Meg as odd. While Lexi was certainly in high spirits, she hadn't seemed out of control or overly intoxicated. In fact, she appeared to be enjoying herself without being inebriated. Meg brushed off the uneasy feeling and proceeded to distribute the drinks to their party. Just then, Angus materialised at her side.

"Having a good time?" Meg attempted to mask any

sarcasm in her voice, fully aware that a few females were still surreptitiously stealing glances at Angus.

"Great craic! Cheers for the drink." Angus raised his glass in thanks. "I'll get the next round." He winked playfully at her, prompting onlookers to subtly shift their gaze away, affording her a touch more privacy from the crowd of admiring eyes. As Angus took a deep sip from his glass, Meg met his gaze. The warmth in his hair was illuminated by the fire and the dim light of the dingy pub. It brought out hues of red, his light blue eyes dark. His appearance reminded her of some ancient warrior depicted in history books.

"Hey sis!" Lexi emerged from the bustling crowd, enveloping Meg in a tight embrace that snapped her back to reality. "Isn't this the best night ever?" Lexi's eyes sparkled. "Oh, I can't keep anything a secret from you. I've decided to go with Leon and explore the islands … they call it island hopping! I quite like the idea of hopping from one island to another when things get dull." She giggled and cast a friendly glance toward Angus, standing tall beside Meg.

"What are you saying, Lex? Have you forgotten – we're following the same tour Mum did? Why would you want to veer off?" A sudden chill ran through Meg's body, despite the cosy warmth of the pub. This was their trip; they were to reconnect as sisters without men coming into the picture. It was their pact, their way of honouring their mother's memory. And now Lexi wanted to whisk away with the first guy who showed her some attention? She scanned the room, searching for Leon, who seemed to have disappeared since their encounter at the bar earlier. "I can't allow this, Lex. We barely know Leon."

"Excuse me?" Lexi's eyes narrowed, and she stood a bit taller. "You won't allow it? I'm not a child anymore, Meg."

"Sometimes you don't act like an adult either, Lex."

"Leon and I … we really like each other, and I want to be

with him. If I don't take this chance, I might regret it. Just because you're OK with living with regrets doesn't mean I should."

"What's that supposed to mean?" Meg retorted, aware that Angus had begun to subtly step away from the escalating exchange between the sisters.

"Come on – you've had just one love in your life … and instead of being with him, you simply let go. Do you honestly expect me to believe you don't regret that decision every single day? What were you thinking, Meg? How could you not have followed your heart? And now you're trying to dictate my choices, acting like it's made you any happier!" Lexi gave her a dirty look. "You used to sing. You used to be happy." She shook her head, her movements filled with exasperation. Lexi spun around and marched away, leaving Meg bewildered and speechless.

What had come over her sister? Lexi's temperament was known to be volatile, but this? It was as if her determination had eclipsed all reason, making everything else irrelevant – only the intoxicating heights of love, or perhaps more accurately, the idealised notion of it, seemed to matter.

Ryan, of course, was who Lexi meant – Meg's first and only love, from a lifetime ago. She was a completely different person now compared to the naive girl she used to be. It wouldn't have worked out with Ryan; it couldn't have. The practicalities of life would have caught up with them, and at such a young age, their flame would have dimmed sooner or later.

Yet, despite her attempts to brush it off, Lexi's words stung.

In a daze, she trailed behind Lexi through the crowd of dancers and found herself outside. The small pub buzzed with music and chatter behind her, nestled among the quaint houses painted in hues of pink, blue and green. She walked until she reached the end of a pier, at the dark, brooding sea. The light of day waned, gradually being consumed by the encroaching evening darkness.

Lexi leaned against the metal gate of the pier, her back to Meg as she smoked a cigarette.

“It's a nasty habit, Lex,” Meg remarked over the sound of the waves crashing beneath them.

“Do we have to have this conversation every time?” Lexi sighed, turning to face her and exhaling a cloud of smoke.

“Where's Leon?” Meg asked.

Lexi flicked her cigarette and extinguished it on the ground. “He'll be back soon. He mentioned needing to make some phone calls. I'm not monitoring his every move,” she replied, crossing her arms defensively.

Angus burst out of the pub's door, his eyes wide with alarm. “Where's Leon?” he shouted.

Meg looked back at Lexi, but her face gave little away. Angus marched up to them both, and impulsively Meg stood in front of her sister protectively. “We don't know – why?”

“My wallet and phone are gone!” His eyes darted around, as he tugged at his hair.

“You think he stole them?” Lexi moved closer to Meg, her stance reflecting her readiness to defend herself if need be.

“Oh, I'm certain he did – I had my suspicions from the moment I met him! That man is nothing but trouble! And then I let myself get swayed by you two, and look where that's landed me – where the hell is he?” Angus's voice boomed over the waves.

Meg didn't want to believe this. Why would Leon steal from Angus? True, they had not formed much of a friendship over the past couple of days, but surely Leon wouldn't stoop to that level. They had welcomed him to their group and were bringing him back home.

"Angus, is it possible you misplaced your belongings? It's easy to do in the midst of all this. Come on – let's look together," Meg offered, guiding him back into the pub. She desperately hoped that her gut feeling was wrong about Leon, that their trust in him hadn't been misplaced.

* * *

After an hour or so passed, the music had finished and the crowd dispersed into the night air, continuing onto the next pub. Meg and Angus had scoured the whole area for his belongings, asking everyone they came across, but to no avail.

Angus ran his hand through his cropped hair, and blew out his cheeks. "Well, it looks like that's that," he grumbled. His fists clenched in frustration, and he gritted his teeth. "I'll blast him into next year when I see him."

"Why would you think Leon is capable of this?" Meg had pushed the doubts from her mind, for her sister's sake.

"He's been freeloading off you and your sister, hasn't he? Lunches, dinners, and probably drinks, too!"

"We've been over this, Angus … that doesn't make him a bad person. I'm sure he's just penny-pinching – he has been travelling. Maybe he's running low on funds before he gets home," Meg reasoned.

Angus sighed. "Yeah well, I don't think he's anywhere near home, Meg."

"What do you mean? He said he lives on the other island. We've been helping him get back to his family."

Angus fixed her with a pointed gaze. "I've had my suspicions about him since we first met. His accent didn't sound like any islander's – I don't think he's being truthful about where he's from."

"But that doesn't mean he's lying about his family living

on the island. Accents can change over time, especially if he's been travelling," she countered.

Angus sighed heavily again. "He had no knowledge about his supposed hometown. Whenever I tried to engage him in a conversation about the local area, he just deflected. I'm beginning to doubt even his name is genuine."

As realisation dawned on Meg, she recalled her conversations with Leon. He had skilfully avoided revealing anything about himself, particularly his background. Furthermore, she now recognised his subtle attempts to create discord within the group by making snide comments about Angus. But why? Why would he go to such lengths?

They made their way back to the hotel and the darkness seemed to press in around them. They walked closer to each other, seeking warmth against the brisk sea wind.

Meg stuffed her cold hands into her pockets, her focus ahead. As they neared the hotel, its lights started to pierce through the night, and she felt a small relief.

"I'm sorry, Angus," she said, her lip caught between her teeth.

Angus looked concerned, a shadow crossing his face. "It's not your fault. You've got nothing to apologise for. I'm the one who came out and shouted at you girls. You both have big hearts and were taken advantage of," he said, his lips tightening. "Don't blame yourselves. Leon is the one who should feel sorry."

His gaze met hers briefly before returning to the ground. "I've already cancelled my cards, so that bastard won't get away with much. We might need to make a detour though. I'll have to head home and get a spare phone and some cash."

Her heart raced as a thought tugged at her. She realised she hadn't discussed her father with Angus yet, and now might be the time. But how could she? Where would she even begin? To bring it up would reveal her secret.

13

MEG

The next morning, under a clear blue sky, Meg inhaled the crisp autumn air, the scents of leaves and pine filling her lungs. Angus leaned against the van, his raised eyebrow silently questioning her, while Lexi, noticeably subdued, greeted them briefly before retreating to the back seat with her headphones on.

As Angus crossed his arms, Meg's attention shifted fully to him, and she finally noticed his shaggy beard had disappeared. The change threw her – he looked younger, more vulnerable, and his blue eyes stood out like sapphires against the azure sky, reminding her of the small ring Ryan had once given her. The ring, a family heirloom, had symbolised a love that had faded but never lost its clarity, just like those piercing blue eyes now focused on her.

"Your beard?" Meg uttered, her voice tinged with surprise. Angus's smile twitched, and he shifted, scratching his neck self-consciously.

"It comes and goes." He shrugged. "Just fancied a change. Now, is everything OK?" He nodded subtly toward Lexi, huddled in the back of the van.

Meg moved out of earshot, behind the van, and whispered, "He's gone. He stole from Lexi too, looks like he did a runner."

Angus's expression darkened, concern replacing his earlier amusement. "That bastard," he seethed, pacing back and forth, his voice rising. "When I get hold of him … The police won't find him at this rate; he'll be long gone. If only I could teach him a lesson – treating a lass like that too? He's no man!" His dark woollen jumper clung to his bulky frame, tight across his chest. Today, he wore jeans instead of his usual kilt, yet something else about him had altered, although she couldn't quite pinpoint what it was.

"I just want to forget this." She sighed, leaning against the van door. "All I want is to take care of Lexi and continue Mum's trip."

Angus nodded, watching her intently. "Alright, let's head to Abergow. I need to organise my things and get some cash. I can make some calls and find this Graeme guy too," he said in hushed tones. After Meg's discussion about finding her father last night, Angus hadn't asked too many questions. Luckily she hadn't needed to mention that this Graeme guy was her father. The only stipulation was one thing: Lexi mustn't know, at least not yet.

* * *

The journey to Angus's home had been rather quiet, with Lexi barely uttering two words. The van climbed steadily up winding roads surrounded by dense clusters of trees that obscured their view. Meg could catch glimpses of the sea through the branches. Just as she had grown accustomed to the ascent, the van descended rapidly into narrow braes, making her inwardly gasp at each twist and turn, fearing a collision with another vehicle at any given moment.

The trees finally scattered, exposing a few peaked mountains in the distance and a glen below. The sign on approach read *Abergow* and she quietly sighed with relief.

"Home," Angus breathed and turned down a single-track road.

On one side of the road stood a cluster of houses, each one unique in its own way – from traditional stone cottages to modern homes with sleek lines and reflective windows mirroring the clear blue sky. On the other side, a fast-flowing stream carved through the land, surrounded by fields and pockets of woodland clinging to the hillside. Angus's van slowed down in front of a modest-looking grey stone cottage with outbuildings, situated in a large field where sheep grazed.

As he hopped out of the van eagerly, he called out, "Here, my lovelies!" In response, about fifty sheep leisurely approached, forming a circle around the vehicle.

"Angus, they look like they want to eat us!" Lexi shouted from her seat, voicing Meg's thoughts. It was the most she had uttered since they left the island. Angus, surrounded by a sea of white wool, burst into laughter at the two sisters peering nervously out of the van.

"They're hungry, but I don't think city girls are on the menu tonight. I know just what they want." He moved to the back of the van and retrieved two large sacks. He winked at Meg, his eyes gleaming with delight.

Reluctantly, Meg climbed out of the vehicle, her hands held high to avoid the eager nudging of the sheep. Angus led her to a large trough and emptied one of the sacks, releasing a collection of rotten vegetables. His eyes sparkled with joy, and Meg was taken aback by his sheer enthusiasm.

"Your turn," he said, nodding.

Meg followed suit, emptying a bag filled with apples, pears, and lettuce leaves. The pungent odours assaulted her senses, and she couldn't help but cover her mouth to stifle a gag.

"Goodness, what a stench! How did we not notice that smell in the van?" she remarked.

Angus tapped his nose knowingly. "Special bags I get from the grocer in Skye. Every time I'm there, she gives me the waste for my beauties," he said proudly, referring to the sheep.

"You really do love your sheep."

Angus adopted a mock-offended expression. "Love my sheep? These darlings are so much more than sheep – they're my ladies, my friends!"

Meg laughed at his enthusiasm, and watched in amazement as the flock devoured the food in record time. "They sure can eat." Turning to her sister, who stood nearby with an unsure expression, she gestured for Lexi to join them.

Lexi walked over, her hoodie unzipped to reveal a tank top underneath. She had an instinct to zip her sister up to keep her warm, but she resisted the urge.

"They're lovely." Lexi smiled until a sheep grazed against her leg, making her momentarily jump in surprise.

"Well, if you like them, come and meet my goats!" Angus playfully nudged Lexi, dissipating any lingering tension between them.

* * *

"Delicious." Lexi wiped her mouth and leaned back, wine in hand. "I love a man who can cook." She giggled, her cheeks flushed from several glasses of wine.

"Thank you," Angus replied, bowing his head gracefully as he collected the empty plates of spaghetti bolognese and stacked the dirty dishes on the sideboard in his compact kitchen. "All organic; I use my own beef. It's the best way; whatever I can grow and rear on the croft, I'll use or eat."

Lexi pondered for a moment, taking a sip of her wine. "A lot of hard work, though. Surely you get attached to the animals too?"

"You're right in a way, but it's all about getting things into context. These animals live a good life here; they are treated with dignity … even in the end …" He trailed off for a moment. "It's that or I get the meat in a supermarket, which is not something I could go back to. This way I can feed them well, look after them as if there were royalty, and then they can feed me throughout the winter."

Lexi winced. "I don't think royalty would receive that end. I think I'd rather become a vegetarian."

"Maybe." Angus shrugged.

As the night wore on, Lexi went to bed in the guest room while Meg dried the dishes and Angus packed away any left-overs. Topping up her glass with the last of the wine, Angus tapped her on the shoulder, interrupting her thoughts.

"There's no need to be doing all that cleaning, Meg."

She took the glass he extended to her and threw the towel over her shoulder. "Oh, I don't mind. It's the least I can do after that lovely meal, Angus. Thanks for making us welcome in your home."

"I'm just sorry we had to abruptly derail the trip."

"Well, I'm sorry you had your things stolen," Meg replied, wiping down the counter. She sat back down at the table, where the soft crackling of the fire from the adjacent sitting room created a warm and soothing ambiance on the cold, windy night.

"Well, these things happen." Angus sighed.

"If I ever see that Leon again, I'd happily punch him." She thumped the table with her fist, snapping Angus's attention back to her.

"Well well, I've not heard you talk like that before." Angus chuckled.

"No?" Meg coughed and moved in her seat. "I just hate what he did."

"Yeah, well, it's done now." Angus nodded, holding Meg's gaze. "Have you ever actually punched anyone before?" His inquisitive eyes danced around playfully.

"Yes," Meg said quietly. "Though I didn't mean to!"

"What? Really?" His expression was one of borderline alarm and fascination.

A flicker of discomfort passed across her face. She brought the wine glass to her lips, taking a thoughtful sip. "My ex-boyfriend."

"Oh really?" Angus moved his chair further under the table and placed his head in his hand, waiting for further details, which Meg reluctantly gave in to.

"I was different back then," she said, straightening her posture as she tried to shake off the lingering image of Ryan. His scruffy hair, holding his white helmet by his side, the way he used to look at her, perched on his motorbike waiting for her – that vision remained vivid even now.

"He must have done something truly awful?" Angus's eyes twinkled with mischief.

"Oh, you're a nosy one!" She laughed, expelling the rose-tinted image of her first love. She'd been unnerved by the comment Lexi had made at the pub. For all the years after their split, her mind had pushed him to the back, to the dark corners of her mind. But Lexi's few words had made those strong walls buckle; she couldn't quite see what was in front of her anymore.

Angus raised the palm of his hands defensively. "I'm sorry; you're right, it's not my place to pry."

"Oh, it's OK. I was young and full of passion. I thought I was Juliet, and he was my Romeo." She spoke lightly, as if talking about a character from a book or movie she had stumbled on. Ryan was full of possibilities, with his faded denim jacket and scuffed jeans; he looked like he'd stepped out of a Levi's advertisement. His dry, calloused hands strummed his guitar with ease … his passion outside the daily grind of construction work. He encouraged Meg's singing so much that she sang confidently by his side. They were in love and wanted to make the world a better place through their music. Corny as it sounded to her now, she couldn't help but envy her naivety. Things were simpler then. "He played the guitar very well actually and wanted to make it in America. He asked me to go with him." Meg shrugged. "I didn't."

"So you punched him?" Angus wrinkled his nose, not quite grasping the connection.

"He chose someone else …" Meg replied.

"Oh, I see." He pressed his lips together and averted his gaze.

But he couldn't truly understand. How could he, when Meg concealed the real reason behind her actions? After the turmoil at home and her father's departure, she knew that being in love wasn't enough. It had shattered her mother and continued to torment her sister. When their father had left, her mother had done the right thing by sending him away, but it had left her as a mere shadow of her former self. They had been in love, but it was a toxic love. Meg's place was with her mother and her home. At seventeen, she couldn't just leave; her mum needed her. After revealing her decision to stay to Ryan, he had almost immediately taken off with another girl. As painful as it had been at the time, she knew he had wanted to hurt her for breaking his heart. But that act had only reaffirmed her belief that love ultimately turns toxic.

"It was a long time ago, and luckily, I haven't had to punch anyone since … well, until now," Meg quipped. "Have you ever punched someone?" She casually redirected the conversation away from herself.

Angus scoffed. "More times than I'm proud of."

"Seriously?"

He shrugged. "I used to have quite a temper, for no apparent reason. I was young and foolish. But now I realise I just needed some space to discover who I really was, not who others thought I should be. So, I decided to leave this place."

"And … did you leave a Juliet?" She raised an eyebrow.

"Oh no." Angus immediately shook his head, yet his expression appeared to hide something else, a guardedness, Meg was sure. "I had my share of good times, you know, got to know some lovely women, but nothing too serious." He coughed and looked at the table somewhat sheepishly. His eyes flickered momentarily, as if recalling a memory he wasn't ready to share.

She couldn't help but wonder about the extent of Angus's "good times" over the years and rolled her eyes. "A bit of a player then?" she teased.

He rolled his eyes in return and changed the subject. "Shall we sit by the fire?" he suggested, gesturing for Meg to settle on the sofa while he attended to the dwindling flames. Lifting the metal guard, he placed it aside, revealing the flickering flames within the grate. He then reclined on the dark carpet in the fire's glow, arms stretched out behind his head. Together, they watched as the flames caressed the charcoaled log, the room growing dimmer by the minute.

"You have an idyllic life here: the cottage, the land, the animals. It's something I wish I'd grown up with – having life all around me, and freedom," Meg remarked.

"But you had life around you, a bustling city nearby. When I was younger, all I wanted was to escape to somewhere exciting, to be someone new and spread my wings." Angus sighed, his gaze fixed on the ceiling.

"But you came back?"

"Yeah, the city had its way with me – chewed me up and spat me out, so to speak." He chuckled. "Plus, my parents weren't getting any younger, and I was missing too much – birthdays, anniversaries, Christmases. But even with all that, it took a heart attack to make me realise I was running low on fuel." Angus grimaced.

"You had a heart attack?"

"Not quite a heart attack, but a scare. The doctors said I needed to reevaluate my life before it was too late. So, I gave up the stressful job and returned to the area. I bought this wee place and started living the good life," he explained.

She couldn't believe her ears. Angus must be around her own age, and it was quite rare for someone in their age group to experience such a health scare. He must have put his body through unimaginable stress.

"I'm glad for it, though," he said, smiling at her shocked face. "It gave me an 'out'. I had to change. Don't get me wrong, I do miss the city at times," he added, reminiscing. "But I've carved out a life here, and it's mine – something I didn't have in London."

Meg nodded, contemplating her life in Melbourne. Her quiet existence. Was her life idyllic too? She took care of her home and enjoyed her work; even though the hours were occasionally long, they were neither demanding nor gruelling. It was fine. She was content. Yet, an unsettling feeling crept over her as she considered what she truly wanted. Seeing Angus's life, her sister's life, and the life she could have had with Ryan made her hesitate. This trip had exposed something within her, something she hadn't known was hidden. She rubbed her feet together in annoyance and listened to the fire's gentle hiss in the background, trying to quiet her unsettling thoughts.

Angus gazed at her with concern. "Are you OK, Meg?"

He propped his head up with one hand and smoothed the patterned carpet with the other. "You seem different. Is something bothering you?"

"No, I'm fine – I'm great," she stammered, searching for more words that wouldn't come.

They watched until the flames faded completely. Meg listened to Angus's steady, gentle breathing, and eventually, she, too, fell asleep, too tired to go to bed and too content with simply being near him.

14

MEG

She awoke to the clattering of pots and pans and the savoury scent of smoky bacon filling the air. The morning light streamed in, revealing a trail of empty bottles and crisp packets – remnants of a night she hadn't fully noticed. Despite the chill that hung in the room, she cozied up beneath a soft fleece blanket, puzzled as to its origin. As much as she longed to continue sleeping, the tantalising aroma of breakfast finally drew her out from the sofa.

In the kitchen, Lexi buttered toast while Angus expertly flipped bacon rashers, all the while serenading them with a merry opera aria in his rich baritone voice.

"Well, well, sleepyhead, how's the hangover?" he quipped.

Meg squinted, still grappling with the aftermath of the previous night. "Urgh, please, do you have to shout?"

He chuckled and continued his operatic performance in a higher pitch. She rubbed her temples, leaning against the door frame.

Lexi erupted in laughter, her face radiant, hair pulled back, and no make-up in sight. Meg couldn't help but notice how healthy her sister looked. Her blue eyes sparkled as she greeted her with a warm smile.

"Rough night, sis?" Lexi sipped on a glass of orange juice.

"I didn't drink any more than you two!" Meg responded, her tone defensive.

"Well, I did call it an early night, you know? I had the most amazing sleep. Angus, it's unbelievably tranquil here, except for the early morning squawking."

"Oh yes, that's Henry," Angus chimed in. "He's quite the character, always seeking attention."

Meg blinked in confusion. "Henry?"

He scooped the bacon onto a plate and raised his hands. "Yes, he's a funny one, that cockerel. Which reminds me, Meg, could you nip out and get us some eggs, please?" He handed her a small, thatched basket and urged her to hurry before the food grew cold.

She retreated, still feeling somewhat blurry from the night before. Stepping outside, she was met with a flood of icy light that prompted her to hastily shut the door. "It's freezing out there!"

"Put on my jumper then," Angus hollered as he continued to entertain Lexi with his Pavarotti impersonation.

Grumbling, she wrestled into a baggy dark wool jumper that hung down to her knees, nearly concealing her dress. She glanced at the assortment of footwear near the door and grabbed the first available pair – large green wellies. In the direction of the peculiar sounds she presumed to be Henry, she ventured into the chilly air, hoping nature would clear her foggy head.

Angus's fluffy white sheep grazed peacefully in the nearby field as the morning sun bathed the land in its golden glow, gradually melting the dew-kissed grass. She briefly savoured the tranquil scene, agreeing with her sister that it was a serene corner of the world. With reluctance, she pulled herself away and circled the cottage to find a wooden shed nestled beneath two horse chestnut trees. The grass was littered with spiky chestnut seeds, but there were no hens or a Henry in sight.

Approaching the noisy shed, she fumbled to find a latch, swung the door open, and was confronted with a flurry of feathers and cacophonous clucking. She covered her face from the prospect of being clawed or pecked to death while the birds were in mid-flight. After a few moments huddled in a foetal position, she gingerly entered the now much quieter shed, the escapees having fled. To her delight, she swiftly located two eggs nestled in the straw but saw no more. A few hens remained, huddled together and eyeing her cautiously. A pale egg was barely visible under the largest hen she had ever seen, with feathers that occupied the space of two regular hens. Its brown mane and sizeable beak reminded her of giant chickens from the classic cartoons of her childhood. Summoning every ounce of her courage, she reassured herself that Angus wouldn't intentionally send her to face a hen-induced hand-to-beak combat, right? After all, hens were supposed to be placid, friendly creatures, weren't they? She cautiously approached the hen, muttering, “Here, hen-y hen-y!” in a voice that sounded more like she was auditioning for a farmyard talent show.

As she extended her hand, the remaining hens staged a raucous clucking symphony in perfect unison. It startled her, and she jumped and yelped in surprise. The giant chicken, with a voice that could rival an opera diva's, bellowed in a way that would put any horror movie scream to shame. Meg, fearing a feathered uprising, made a hasty retreat, terrified that she'd be pecked to death.

Panting, her heart racing, and marching towards the cottage door, she was alarmed to find the same colossal hen in hot pursuit, with the fluffy cockerel as her loyal sidekick. Just making it in time, she slammed the front door shut behind her, gasping for breath. “That hen has a personal vendetta, I swear.”

Angus wiped his hands on a dish towel and threw it over his shoulder, seemingly impervious to Meg's chicken-related trauma. “Did you manage to fetch any eggs?”

“But those … those hens are c-crazy!” she stuttered.

Angus shrugged, shaking his head exasperatedly.

She gazed down at her rather pitiful collection, her embarrassment growing. “I’m not hungry,” she muttered, grabbing a slice of toast on her way to the shower.

* * *

Emerging from the shower, she felt more like her usual sensible self. However, her relief was short-lived when she discovered that Lexi had embarked on a solitary walk without her.

Angus, sitting at the wooden kitchen table, responded to Meg's unspoken question with a casual shrug. “She mentioned something about wanting to write and explore,” he said.

Meg sighed deeply. As much as she attempted to bridge the gap between her and her sister, she couldn't shake the feeling that Lexi was already halfway out the door, metaphorically speaking. Why couldn't Lexi open up and let her in, considering everything they had been through? It stung. She blinked back the unexpected surge of emotion, hastily tying her hair back and shifting her focus elsewhere.

“I’ve gathered some leads on Graeme.” Angus broke the

silence. "One of the local lads thinks he's a farmer further north in the Glen Tallach region, perhaps we head up there?"

Meg visualised the address in her mum's handwriting. "Is it still in the Glenardburn peninsula?" she pondered aloud, wondering whether her father, who had been thrown out by her mother years ago, had remained in one place or moved many times on his return to Scotland. Her heart lurched at the mere thought. Her father.

"It's just on the outskirts of the peninsula, but some people would consider it still part of the area … it's just lots of hills in between after all!" He scribbled on some paper, propping it up against the kettle. "I'll leave a note for Lexi to help herself to anything. If we catch the midday ferry, we should be back by dinner."

"What? A ferry? You said it's part of the peninsula!"

"Aye, it is, kind of. But it's remote enough that you need to take a boat. If we went by land, it would take us two days to walk there!" He shook his head and chuckled at Meg's seemingly impractical suggestion. "There's no road."

* * *

After a somewhat lengthy car journey to the ferry, Meg was taken aback to discover that the "ferry" was, in fact, a small boat. It had peeling paint and precariously bobbed up and down at the end of the pier. Angus helped a hesitant Meg on board, and they were soon speeding off under a menacingly dark sky.

She gripped the railing, wearing a jacket and hat Angus had insisted she borrow, dismissing her own choices as "impractical" and "what a city person thinks people wear in the country". Initially offended by this wardrobe intervention, she couldn't deny a secret gratitude for the gesture. As much as she prided herself on practicality, her fashion sense hadn't prepared her for the unexpected rain that now drenched them on their journey.

Angus nudged her, handing over a plastic tumbler of whisky. Surprised, she accepted it, hoping the spirit would calm her trembling hands, but it mostly burned the back of her throat. Only then did she notice other passengers sipping whiskies or clutching tins of lager. To her amazement, a corner table next to the captain's steering wheel was loaded with alcohol and a small biro-penned donation box.

"There's even a bar on this boat!" Meg exclaimed. "There's barely enough room for life jackets, let alone a bar!" Alcohol seemed to be a vital part of the Scottish lifestyle.

"Of course," Angus replied with a shrug. "At least we'll have a party if the boat sinks!"

She couldn't hide her alarmed expression as her heart raced, and she felt a sudden cold sweat. "Are you saying there are no life jackets on board? This boat can barely accommodate us as it is. What if it capsizes?" Her eyes darted around the small vessel as she searched for the safest spot to position herself in case they encountered a rogue sea monster or some unexpected force.

Angus placed a reassuring hand on her arm, his grip firm yet gentle. "Meg, there are enough life jackets on board. We're not that careless about safety. Old Jim over there has been steering this boat since he was a young lad." He motioned towards the white-haired captain who casually exchanged jokes with the passengers.

She bit her lip. She couldn't control this situation, no matter how hard she tried. Grabbing the other tumbler of whisky from Angus's hand, she downed it with a cough. To her surprise, he simply nodded in response.

"You Scots do like your drink … a lot!" she remarked

before hiccupping. She had to admit that whisky had a way of loosening her tongue.

"We're not *that* bad." Angus chuckled, shaking his head. "And I don't hear you complaining … or refusing!"

She had to agree. The boat was far from luxurious, and they were getting wetter by the second, either from the rain or the sea spray. As the old vessel sped through the waves, it felt like a gruelling test of endurance, which Meg faced with clenched teeth. Overhead, the plaintive cries of gulls pierced through the sound of the wind, their wings catching the breeze as they circled the boat in search of scraps.

"Whisky is in our blood, you know," Angus continued, a hint of pride in his voice. "We take care of our tourists. Even back in the days when early pilgrims and visitors came to the Highlands, whisky would be offered to weary travellers – even the ladies – to keep them warm for the journey ahead." He winked at her. "Rain has always been very much a part of Highland life, and whisky helps to get through the tough times. It's as natural to us and as part of the land as rushing water down the side of a mountain."

Angus's face lit up with passion for his homeland – a feeling she had never truly considered. Australia had been her home, but the country's history, marred with oppression, had left her questioning her own identity. She had once attended an "Invasion Day" march with Lexi as an excuse to spend time with her sister, but instead the experience sparked within her a long-lasting uncertainty about her own nationality.

Despite the cold and discomfort, she felt a surge of appreciation as the whisky coursed through her veins. The bright cluster of lights approached in the dark landscape, like pearls gleaming in deep waters. The prospect of meeting her father was a constant thought in the back of her mind, but she was prepared to accept whatever would happen. With her mother's letter safely tucked in her breast pocket, carefully protected from the rain in a plastic bag, she was ready to deliver it to its intended recipient. As they drew closer to the lights, she knew she was edging closer to a hidden part of her life, waiting for her to reclaim it after so many years. The secrets that had long remained in the shadows would finally see the light of day, and in that moment, she was willing to surrender herself to them.

15

MEG

Lexi nestled closer to Meg under the warm covers, seeking comfort as their parents' argument raged on in the adjacent room. The two sisters lay still, their small bodies trembling with a mix of fear and hope, silently praying for the shouting to cease. Lexi's cold feet found Meg's, and reluctantly she let her warm them. No matter the time of year, after a hot summer's day or a bath, Lexi's feet would always be cold and grimy.

Meg could feel the desperation in her mother's voice as she pleaded with their absent father. "You're always out drinking, Graeme. You're never here for your two girls when they need you."

Graeme's defensive and slurred response reached their ears. "You blow everything out of proportion. I'm always here. I just need a break sometimes."

"You don't need to drown your sorrows in alcohol to have a break. It's not just about you, Graeme. Your daughters need you."

"I'm not a drunk," he protested, his words failing to convince anyone.

"No?" her mother shot back. "Every week, it's the same story. You stumble home late or disappear for days on your benders. This has to stop, Graeme."

"You don't tell me what to do," he retorted bitterly. "I pay the bills, I bought this house, and I even moved across the world for you. What more do you want?"

"We want a man who is here, not just in body but in mind and spirit." Her mother's voice cracked with emotion. "Your daughters need you. I need you. But you're always somewhere else."

"You don't understand," he muttered cryptically.

Meg couldn't bear to hear any more of the painful exchange. She gently tapped her wide-eyed sister on the shoulder. "Would you like to hear the story of Princess Bonnie?" She waited for Lexi's eager nod. It was her favourite story, and a good distraction for them both. "Well, settle down and I will tell you. There once lived a beautiful princess, her mother and father the King and Queen of the Highlands doted on her so. They gave her all the luxuries they could offer, delighting in her sweet temperament and her beauty. It wasn't long before word got out about the princess's beauty, and soon the palace was inundated with proposals of marriage from all corners of the world; from the sweeping desert to the lush jungle. Princes from all over came to see the princess. But to the King and Queen's dismay, the princess would not have them—"

Before Meg could get to the best part of the story, their mother's scream pierced the air. "Just leave! I don't want to see you ever again. Your children are better off without a drunken father." A door slammed shut, leaving behind a haunting silence, interrupted only by the soft sound of their mother's weeping, which echoed into the early hours of the morning.

* * *

As thunder rumbled overhead, Meg and Angus exchanged panicked glances on dry land. Raindrops pelting them, they quickened their pace along the water's edge, desperately seeking refuge from the impending storm. The wind howled, urging them to hasten their steps. Spotting a warm glow amidst the grey mist, they stumbled upon a welcoming café. Without a second thought, they darted inside, seeking solace from the relentless weather. Once through the door, they shook off raindrops and exchanged relieved laughter, grateful for the sanctuary the café provided.

Luck was on their side, as a cosy sofa by the roaring fire-place became available. Meg wasted no time in peeling off her drenched jacket and basking in the warmth of the flames. Angus, following suit, sat beside her, pushing back his wet hair while eyeing the paper menus scattered on the coffee table.

"Let's make the most of it and grab a bite while we wait out this storm," he proposed, tapping his thighs and heading to the counter to place their orders.

Meg watched him chat with the waitress, a common sight in the Highlands, where people always seemed to be figuring out who they knew in common. Their quick exchange ended with the waitress nodding toward an elegant blonde woman in the kitchen doorway. Her hair was pinned up in a bun, with loose tendrils framing her heart-shaped face. When Angus stood and marched over to her, they embraced for a moment longer than Meg would have considered usual, their smiles beaming brightly.

"Iona, I can't believe it," Angus said, holding her hands and gazing at her with admiration.

Iona waved away the compliment but left her hand resting on his wrist, sliding it up his arm. Meg watched the scene unfold from the sofa, her chest tightening. The way Angus looked at Iona stirred something inside her, and she quickly shifted her gaze to the menu.

"Meg?" Angus called her over, guiding the blonde beauty by his side toward her. Iona's graceful stride gave her the air of a model or someone of noble birth.

Meg stood up, feeling small in comparison to the goddess-like figure before her.

"It's lovely to meet you, Meg," Iona said, extending her hand.

She shook her hand, which was smooth but slightly damp from her work in the café's kitchen. "You have a charming café."

"It really is, isn't it? My cousin owns it. I usually bake for them and send the goods over on the boat. But they were short-staffed today, so I lent a hand," Iona explained.

"But what about your children? Who's looking after them?" Angus asked, clearly concerned.

Meg's heart skipped a beat.

"Mum is taking care of them, Angus," Iona replied, rolling her eyes. "Don't worry about us."

"Oh, good, I should've called in. I've just been a bit busy." His eyes flicked to Meg, making her feel somewhat responsible for his antisocial behaviour.

"Of course you're busy, Angus. But don't let it be so long next time!" Iona shook her head playfully. "Now, what can I get for you, Meg? Would you like some lunch? Maybe a scone with cream and jam? I make them myself." Iona's almond eyes blinked with a touch of mischief, and a wicked smile curved her lips. "Or perhaps the chocolate mud cake? I also made that; it's positively sinful. You must try it, Meg," she said, oozing playful seduction.

"Well, if it's sinful …" Meg replied with a coy smile.

Iona nodded knowingly and left them by the fire. Angus watched her departure and shook his head gently.

"She's lovely," Meg offered. Angus's small smile reflected back at her, and he self-consciously rubbed his bearded neck with the back of his hand. She couldn't help but wonder about their history. Had they once been lovers, now reduced to sharing only stolen glances? Perhaps Angus had relocated to London to heal a broken heart, regretting the loss of his first love. She checked herself. She had clearly spent too much time with Lexi. Her sister's romantic notions were rubbing off on her.

Their food arrived quickly, and Iona joined them at the table. She laughed easily at Angus's jokes, and Meg found herself genuinely liking her too. There was a warmth about her that seemed to envelop everyone nearby, and for a moment, Meg almost felt as though she were falling in love with her.

Reluctantly, Angus suggested they continue their journey if they were to catch the ferry back in time. Meg's stomach churned with anxiety. She had almost forgotten the reason for their trip today, but now the thought of seeing her father left her paralysed. All she wanted was to hide away, stay for another cup of coffee, or perhaps listen to another story from Angus's and Iona's childhoods. However, they needed to press on, and after bidding farewell to Iona, they ventured back out into the drizzling rain.

Following a pothole-riddled single-track road, they made their way out of the village and along the water's edge. The damp air cooled Meg's flushed face as she struggled to divert her thoughts from the impending reunion. Angus continued to chat about the village, its quirks and local stories, but her mind was elsewhere, even if she appreciated the distraction.

As they reached a gate at the edge of the main road, leading onto a grassy pathway with muddy tractor imprints, she gazed off into the mist. Her words caught in her throat. "Does … does he know we're coming?" she asked, trying to maintain her composure while fixing her eyes on a faint light in the distance.

"Erm, no, not exactly. I left him a message on his phone – you know how these farmers are, always outside no matter the weather. I'm sure he'll be glad to see you, though, especially if you mention that he was a friend," Angus replied casually, rummaging in his pocket and retrieving his backup old cell phone. Squinting at the screen, he tapped it a few times and then sighed. "This old thing has already run out of battery! But don't worry, I'm sure he got the message. I'll be there to—"

"No," Meg interrupted. "I need to go by myself."

"Oh, OK." Angus raised his eyebrows but nodded in agreement. "Sure, I'll just wait here then." He untied the worn blue rope that held the gate shut.

She hesitated, sensing that Angus's demeanour had cooled again. "It's just that I won't be long, and it's not a big deal … I don't want to turn it into a big affair. I just need to drop off a letter to him," she explained, her words tumbling out as she slowly made her way down the muddy path. Eventually, she reached a large white farmhouse nestled among old trees. One of them had the same blue rope tied around it, fashioned into a child's swinging rope that swayed in the breeze. A spacious open shed housing a tractor sat nearby, with a cluster of weathered wooden outbuildings.

The closer she got to the house, the worse the mud became, pulling at her feet along the way. She grimaced, trying to avoid the mess, but mud was everywhere. She walked up to the front door and knocked three times, her heart pounding as she waited for any sign of life. All she could hear was her own heavy breathing and the rain dripping from the porch roof above her. What was she even going to say? She usually would have prepared something the night before, but she was caught off guard this morning, and even during the brief quiet moments she'd had on the boat, her mind had remained blank. The only thing that lingered was a memory of her father, drunk and staggering around their kitchen as her mother fed him in between chastising him for his juvenile behaviour.

She waited some more, but there was no answer. She knocked again three times, and in response, she could hear dogs barking and a woman's high-pitched voice.

A woman? She hadn't even considered what she would do if he had remarried. She backed away in a panic as she tried to process her next actions. But just as she was about to melt back into the wet mist, the door opened, revealing a flustered woman with a white apron and floured hands.

"Yes?" She patted her hands down her apron as a Border collie darted past her, barking around Meg.

"I'm sorry," Meg shouted over the noise. "I think I have the wrong house. I was looking for Graeme MacDonald and—"

"That's us, love. Graeme is my husband." The woman pointed her finger downward. "Lochy! Enough of your chat, inside now!" she commanded, making the pup obediently follow. "I'm sorry, I hope he didn't scare you. He wouldn't hurt a fly."

"Oh no. Um, well …" Meg stood still, shifting her weight from one foot to the other, searching for an excuse to leave. "Could I leave something …"

"What's that, love?" The woman's attention turned back into the house. "Stop that, Lisa! I thought I told you not to touch the cakes until I was finished." She stopped mid-telling-off and remembered her new guest on the porch. "Come in, love, Graeme is just tending to the cows. He'll be in for tea soon."

"Oh no, perhaps if I just leave this letter, or I can go and find him …" Meg took another step back. "I won't be long, I just—"

"Don't be silly, come in before you catch your death of cold. It's miserable out here," the woman insisted, rubbing her floured hands together. She gestured for Meg to follow her into the bright, warm glow of the house, leading her down the hall to a traditional country kitchen. A wooden table dominated the space, covered with cake tins and ingredients.

"This is Lisa." The woman pointed to a serious-faced girl with her hair in bunches on top of her head, leaning over a colouring book. Her face looked guilty, with icing sugar smeared at the corner of her mouth. Meg smiled at the little girl, and another little face popped up from under the table.

"And that is Rachel," she said fondly.

Rachel flashed a gummy smile, and Meg's insides lurched. What was she doing here? She couldn't do this.

"Thank you for inviting me inside, but …" Meg started to say.

"You'll take a cup, won't you?" The woman busied herself looking for cups and rattled the kettle on the stove to check if there was any hot water left. "Ah ha, I knew there was enough. Tea?" She asked and poured two cups without waiting for an answer. "It's very unusual, getting visitors. I haven't had a conversation with someone my own age in a long time. Well, unless you count the school run for Lisa, but you know by the time we take the ferry over to drop her off, I'm needed back here, you see!" She hardly paused for breath as she pulled a tin of biscuits from a high cupboard. Little Lisa's interest piqued. "I'm here all morning baking for the kids' fundraiser. They're wanting to go to the pantomime in Glasgow and spend the night, but that takes a bit of work, you see. And money!" she scoffed.

"I can imagine," Meg mused, swirling the remnants of tea

in her cup. But all the while, she was thinking of many believable excuses to leave. Angus would be waiting for her. Maybe she could say her friend was waiting? No, she knew that, even after only briefly meeting this kind woman, she would likely insist Angus come inside too.

The woman nodded knowingly, then, a second later, her eyes scanned Meg suspiciously. "You aren't one of those religious people? Trying to convert us? I'm sorry, love, we have enough to be doing here than changing beliefs. Not that I'm particularly religious anyway, it's just nice to have a routine and see people every week at church!"

"No, I'm not one of those … um … people." Meg panicked, realising she needed to say something. She was a stranger inside this woman's house, with her kids quietly playing together underneath the table. A giggle sounded, and Meg felt four eyes peering from behind the table legs. "I am from Australia, travelling Scotland with my sister," she said, gulping down her tea and thinking of her next words. "I think we have distant family over here, and I think your husband, Graeme, might be related to us."

"Oh, that's thrilling!" The woman's eyes sparkled with excitement. "I've always wanted to go travelling. You know, I had actually planned to go to Australia many years ago. I came up here to visit my aunt; I'm from the Borders, you see, and as soon as I arrived here, I fell in love with the place and met Graeme too."

"You never went to Australia?" Meg responded, trying to show enthusiasm.

"Nope." She paused and looked at the two children; the elder whispered in the youngest's ear conspiratorially. "But I don't regret it. I've had a good life." Her smile illuminated her face as she gazed with love at her girls. "But now you mention it, Graeme spent time in Australia. Before I met him, of course. He's a little older than me, you see. No doubt he met distant family members too. How exciting! You'll be able to catch up when he gets in." She turned around in her seat and craned her head to view the clock on the wall. "He shouldn't be long now. Another top-up?" She collected Meg's empty cup without waiting for an answer.

Meg smiled down at the girls. They coyly hid behind the table legs, and she made a funny face at them. Small, excited shrieks sounded in response, and Lisa, the older one, mirrored Meg's silly expression, while little Rachel tried to copy her big sister. Rachel's big eyes and her clumsy movements reminded her of what Lexi once was like. When Meg found out she was going to have a baby sister, she was so ecstatic that she told anyone who would listen, even strangers walking down the street. She made sure no one was left without the knowledge that she, Meg MacDonald, was due to have a baby sister.

She watched the two little girls weave around the table legs and could see her and Lexi playing together. She couldn't do this to them, not to two innocent children. They deserved a good childhood, and if Meg could protect that, then she must.

"I'm sorry; I must be on my way," Meg exclaimed, pushing back her chair abruptly.

"But Graeme will be here any moment." The woman pleaded, following her down the hallway.

"It's OK; I will send a letter – we're only distant relations, so not to worry!" Meg opened the door herself, eager to flee before she was confronted with her past and the possibility of destroying the future of others.

"Oh, there you are, Graeme," the woman called out with relief to the dark silhouette on the doorstep. "This girl says she's related to you; she's from Australia."

Later, when Meg replayed this moment in her mind, she marvelled at the way time seemed to stretch. Words slowed to a crawl. She couldn't determine how long she studied the man before her, his posture bent to shield himself from the rain while his wife introduced their guest. Meg remained transfixed, unable to divert her gaze. Her attention fixated solely on his inquisitive grey eyes, and a profound sense of relief washed over her.

He was unmistakably not her father.

16

LEXI

Lexi had spent the evening nestled on Angus's couch, re-reading a magazine she had bought for the plane ride over. When Angus and Meg returned home, she chuckled at their drenched figures, shaking water off like dogs after a swim. "Good day for a hike?" she asked, flipping a page, snuggled under a soft wool blanket next to the crackling fire.

Angus shot Meg a look, but its meaning remained a mystery. She decided to play ignorant, dismissing it as perhaps a lover's quarrel. Lately, they had both been acting strangely around her, engaging in conversations but with their true intentions concealed in glances that followed each other silently between Lexi's words. It was becoming tiresome.

"Not the best day for it," Meg declared, sounding like a teacher addressing her classroom. "But we saw a lovely part of the world – a remote village on the mainland that required a boat to reach."

Not really listening or particularly interested in their recent escapades, Lexi gestured behind her. "I made stew with meat from the freezer. I hope you don't mind, Angus?"

Angus rubbed his hands together with enthusiasm and

wasted no time in removing his wet jacket and wellington boots. He then peeled off his damp jumper, revealing a slightly exposed toned stomach.

Meg bit her lip while subtly admiring him from a distance. Lexi raised a suspicious eyebrow and nonchalantly flicked another page of her glossy magazine.

"What?" Meg snapped irritably. Lexi sighed with exasperation, putting the magazine down on her lap, and casually turned her gaze toward Angus, who was busy singing something operatic in the kitchen as he fetched plates.

"You went on a boat, huh? You look a little dishevelled, sis. Did you find yourself rolling around on the deck?"

"Lex, it's a bloody typhoon out there! Of course I'm dishevelled!" She bristled. Lexi's playful inquiry earned her a frosty look. The muscles in Meg's jaw tightened as she shifted uncomfortably on the sofa.

"You really need some company, sis. Are you still single?" Lexi probed. "I can help in that department!"

"I think I can handle finding a man, Lex. No need for your assistance!"

Angus left them, whistling his way towards the bathroom, and Meg's shoulders visibly relaxed. "I've actually contemplated getting a dog," she mused aloud.

Lexi's hands flew to her cheeks, feigning horror. "Oh no, forget finding a guy – now you're getting a dog!" She chuckled, eyes gleaming with mischief.

"What?"

"It's a substitute, you know," Lexi explained, patting her shoulder. The gesture was promptly shrugged off.

"I'm quite content, actually. Good job, lovely house – the works." Meg's words hung in the air, and she winced, possibly realising they might come off as boastful. "I mean, things will unfold if they're meant to, right? Thanks, Lex, but

I'm genuinely happy as is." She fidgeted, avoiding eye contact.

Lexi tilted her head from side to side, considering. "Fair enough, I guess I just worry sometimes that you're one cat away from spinsterhood."

Meg turned to her sister, incredulous. "Seriously, Lex? Are we stepping into eighteenth-century England now? You do seem to have a fondness for the absurd."

"I genuinely believe that a life without love is no life at all," Lexi announced.

"I'm pretty sure you pulled that from a book."

She wrinkled her nose. "Maybe it was a movie."

"But I do have love – I have you, and maybe a puppy soon," Meg countered.

"Or a cat, if you intend to be properly enrolled in spinsterhood," Lexi quipped. "Come on, you guys need to get a shag over with; you'll feel much better after!" Sensing the rage building up in her sister's body, Lexi raised her hands defensively. "OK, OK. There's no need to be so het up. It's obvious you both like each other."

"Shhh!" Meg's eyes widened, her head ducked, and she peered over Lexi's head to see Angus still in the kitchen, taking out plates from the cupboard, lost in his own singing. "Don't be so outrageous, Lexi. We're just friends. He's showing me around," Meg whisper-screamed.

"Oh, please. I see the way he looks at you, and you look at him."

"No, Lex, you're mistaken." Meg's red face darkened.

"And he's always gazing at you as if he's undressing you slowly …" Lexi sniggered.

Meg stood up abruptly as Angus came in with two plates of dinner. "What are you two chatting about?" He handed a plate to Meg, and Lexi made room for him on the sofa.

"Oh, just discussing what a wonderful day Meg had with you. She says you're the best company, Angus."

"I didn't say 'the best'," Meg mumbled quietly, but a slow smile sped across Angus's face. Lexi savoured the awkward silence that enveloped them. For once, she felt in control. She had been growing weary of the way both Angus and Meg looked at her, especially Meg. That particular expression on her sister's face, the one reserved for her ever since she'd found her unconscious, often stirred blind fury within her.

Though Lexi didn't want to be unkind to her sister or mock her infatuation with Angus, it seemed unavoidable. Despite Meg's good intentions, Lexi knew she had been closely monitoring her for a relapse. So, she kept her distance. If she could just avoid both of their judgemental glances, it would make things easier. Angus's distrust in her since Leon was evident in the accusatory glances he kept shooting her. He even asked if Leon would be back. Checking with her if he had messaged or called her. No, he hadn't.

Lexi knew it was only to get his money back. Of course, he did not want to see Leon under any other circumstances than that. Her stomach churned at the thought of Leon's betrayal. Angus's money was gone, and to make things worse, Leon had torn her down when she thought she was getting back up. He'd robbed her of everything, even her mum's gold chain with a ruby. She rubbed her neck, thinking of it. Meg seemed oblivious to the missing item, or maybe she had simply decided not to mention it. It was a small trinket that she'd found among her mother's things the day after her passing. She had put it on, hoping to catch a glimpse of her mother's features in the mirror, but instead was faced with her own pale and blemished complexion. Not much of her mother had been passed down to her, apart from her hair that was thick and dry like straw, and all the bleaching had only made it worse. Being compared to Meg made her so uncomfortable that she went to great lengths to change herself.

Meg was the first to speak. "So, um … Lexi, want to do something tomorrow?"

Lexi took a small sip of her tea, trying to buy herself time to think of an excuse. The words emerged from her mouth in a weak and muddled fashion when she finally spoke. "Um … tomorrow? Actually, I've plans for tomorrow. Er … how about the day after?"

"You have plans?" Meg blinked, her plate of food still untouched on her lap. Both her and Angus regarded Lexi with a peculiar expression.

"Yeah, I met someone today … and I'm going to see them again tomorrow," she replied breezily, anticipating the forthcoming barrage of questions.

Meg remained quiet.

"So, let's plan for another day, then? Maybe see a castle? I did promise to meet them tomorrow …" She tapped her cup with slight agitation.

"There's a gala event in the next village?" Angus suggested, scraping the last morsels of food from his plate with relish. "I thought of going, Meg, if you're interested? I'm sure it's not Lexi's thing anyway." A mischievous smile played on his lips as his eyes flickered towards Lexi.

"Boats and posh people? Nah, not my style," Lexi remarked with a casual shrug.

"Well, that's settled then!" Angus chuckled. "Although I'm pretty sure there's more to it than just boats and posh people. It should be fun."

"I thought we were carrying on with our journey?" Meg watched Lexi closely, a frown line appearing between her brows.

"We will," Angus assured her. "I'm sorry for the delay. I'm still waiting for my credit card and a new phone to arrive.

Hopefully, they'll be here in the next few days. As soon as that happens we'll head off north. Promise. Maybe we can revise our plans? I'll get the map."

Lexi winked at Meg, eager to escape the brewing tension between Angus and her sister.

"You don't need to go," Angus called after Lexi as he spread out the map on the floor and knelt next to it.

But Lexi slipped out of the room, leaving them alone in front of the fire. Whatever was happening between her sister and Angus, she didn't want to be caught in the middle of it. And if she could sidestep further discussions about her personal life, she would be happier for it.

17

MEG

Meg sat by the crackling fire, her gaze fixed on the dancing flames. Since arriving at Angus's cottage, she'd developed a peculiar fascination with fire. Her town house lacked the cosy warmth of a real fireplace, leaving her with nothing more than a wall-mounted heater. On cold days, she'd wrap herself in a blanket, crank up the artificial heat, and watch a faux fire on her small television screen. It all felt sterile and artificial now, a far cry from the comforting embrace of a genuine hearth.

Tonight, her mind wandered freely, deliberately avoiding thoughts of her sister, who seemed to prefer solitude over connection. The trip had taken unexpected turns that were far from Meg's meticulously planned itinerary. Leon's sudden appearance, just as she thought she was making progress with Lexi, had thrown her off balance. And now Lexi had found someone new to captivate her attention already. It was all too much, and she couldn't control the whirlwind of emotions swirling inside her.

She turned her gaze to Angus, who was hunched over a map on the floor, muttering to himself. Drained of energy and still processing the day's events, she recalled the intense anticipation she'd felt earlier. As they'd journeyed back, the crashing waves had provided a chaotic backdrop to her racing thoughts. She'd shouted over the tumultuous sea, sharing a slightly altered version of her encounter with Graeme with Angus. It wasn't that she wanted to lie to him, but she couldn't risk him revealing the truth to Lexi, potentially shattering everything further.

She rested her head on a cushion, welcoming slumber, until an unexpected knock at the door jolted her awake.

“Who could that be?” Angus muttered, rising from his seat.

Still groggy from her slumber, she couldn't help but feel a tinge of unease. Visitors to a remote Highland cottage in the pitch-black night were the stuff of horror movies. She watched as Angus opened the door, but the dimly lit entrance concealed the identity of their guest. Loud voices and greetings filled the air as Angus welcomed the stranger in, who shook rain from his coat and took off his tweed cap in respect.

The newcomer, named Ronnie, had balding fair hair streaked with grey and a warm smile. He addressed Angus before turning his friendly gaze toward Meg, who offered her hand in greeting.

“Oh deary me, I’m very sorry – I’m disturbing you. You have company.” He smiled at her warmly. “Good for you.” He turned to Angus.

“Come dry by the fire, Ronnie,” Angus said, a little awkward. “This is my client, Meg, from the tour group. Remember, I started working for Jake?”

Ronnie settled into a wooden chair near the fire, struggling to remove his damp green jacket. “Oh yes,” he said, his thumb to his mouth in contemplation. “Jake … Jake … The Badger's son?”

“Aye,” Angus confirmed.

"And how is he? I mean, I know how the Badger is, just called over there last week." Ronnie produced a small pipe from his pocket. He glanced at Angus, who nodded in silent permission, indicating his familiarity with Ronnie's habit.

She decided not to delve into the peculiarities of people named after animals and instead let the conversation ebb and flow around her. Ronnie's familiarity with Angus through their mutual acquaintance, Jake, sparked a lively exchange of pleasantries. Meanwhile, Angus, his voice resonating over the sizzling kettle, seamlessly carried on their discussion as he disappeared into the kitchen to prepare tea.

As she sat there, the exhaustion of the day weighed heavily on her, and she wished she could follow Lexi and retire to bed. Ronnie, however, regarded her with a curious look. "And how do you like it here, Meg? What brings you to Scotland?"

She hesitated, trying to find the right words without revealing too much. "Well," she began cautiously, "we're here … We're scattering my mother's ashes along the coast. She came here when she was young, and it stayed with her, made quite an impression. My sister and I thought she would want to rest beside the magical places she spoke of."

Ronnie nodded, puffing thoughtfully on his pipe. "That's a special tribute to your mother. You must be a thoughtful girl."

She blushed and fidgeted. "Oh, I don't know about that," she said modestly. "She just raised us on stories from here, and it seemed fitting, really."

"There are some unique places here, alright." Ronnie leaned back, crossing his arms and propping up his pipe, his foot tapping rhythmically as if he was seated at a spinning wheel. With each tap, he continued, "They can strike up the imagination. Although there is some truth behind it. Sometimes the layer between the other world and this is so thin, you can put your hand through it, but it can pop like a bubble if you're not careful."

She listened in silence, her thoughts wandering while the distant chuckles of Angus echoed from the kitchen.

Ronnie, now leaning forward with his hands resting on his knees, pressed on. "Your mother must have seen something to make such an impression."

She hesitated, her gaze flicking over her shoulder to make sure Angus was still engrossed in tea-making. "I don't know about that," she replied cautiously. "She told us a lot of fairy tales. I think she wanted to believe in something more, but we're not those sorts of people."

Curiosity gleamed in Ronnie's eyes, and he asked gently, "What people might that be then?"

She struggled to find the right words, her thoughts circling the strange occurrences she'd witnessed recently. "Um … I don't know – people who see things … believe in things."

Ronnie leaned back, laughing softly to himself. "My dear, you don't need to believe in a thing to see it. I know many people, myself included, who cannot explain or quite understand something – but it doesn't make it any less real."

She shrugged, her thoughts involuntarily turning to the image of the sea eagle from her dreams, its piercing eyes locked with hers. She had pushed the unsettling graveyard incident to the back of her mind until now. "I think people want to believe in something, so they imagine things that aren't really there," she ventured.

"I wouldn't say I believe or don't believe in things." He raised an eyebrow. "I'm a churchgoing man, but have witnessed things that no sane person could convince me otherwise."

“Oh, ghost stories already, Ronnie?” Angus interjected with a chuckle. “You're barely through the door!” He handed Ronnie a steaming cup of tea, and the trio continued their conversation, the crackling fire dancing shadows up the wall as the night outside grew darker.

Meg sat back, sipping her tea, a shiver running down her spine as she braced herself for what she might hear.

“I think your guest might need to hear what happens around here. You've got to keep your wits about you,” Ronnie said, his eyes scanning them both as he cleared his throat. Then, with the room's attention on him, he began, leaning forward, “It was a cold, dark night in winter.” His voice was soft. “I had gone to see old Charlie up the hill. He doesn't get out much since his fall. So we had a good natter for most of the night, about the people who used to be here. How the village had once been full; full of families, summer picnics, and the best ceilidhs around.”

He continued, his words painting a vivid picture of days gone by. “Now, it's all old people and quiet solitude. Life has left here,” Ronnie lamented. “I thought to myself of how people left, and the people that did stay don't want to be involved with anyone anymore. They keep to themselves, watch TV, stay inside. I used to know who lived in each house along this lane.” He pointed behind him, his voice still gentle. “But now, how can we connect?” He shook his head. “My mind was distracted that night, grieving that it wouldn't be long until our way of living will be extinguished for good. Our old traditions lost. Our stories. Our connection.” He shrugged helplessly. “Then, just as I’d almost arrived home … I saw a light at the side of the road.”

Meg leaned forward, her eyes wide with curiosity, her tea forgotten.

“Now, as you know, Angus, that is a single-track road,

one side with trees, the other side an old stone wall. The wall is made with the same stone that makes the bridge on the same side. It's said the bridge took many years to build, that the stone came from a quarry nearby, and they ran into every difficulty during its construction. Accidents, deaths, loss of money and time. Everything that could go wrong with the bridge, did. Some said it was the stone that was cursed."

Ronnie's voice dropped to a near-whisper, making the hairs on the back of Meg's neck stand on end. She couldn't tear her gaze away from the old man, his pipe held tightly in one hand. "So I am driving back slowly along the road," he continued, "then I see lights on the stone wall. I approach it slowly, thinking how strange for kids to play that late at night. But then I knew better. Before me were tiny people. The size of children, but not children. Some with faces as old as mine, just sitting on the wall, talking amongst themselves, some gazing at my car."

Meg's eyes widened further, and she exchanged a glance with Angus, who had been silent throughout the story. He sat with his ankles crossed, head slightly lowered, listening intently, a small smile playing on his lips. Ronnie's tale was unlike anything she had ever heard before, and she couldn't help but hang on to every word.

"I stopped the car, not knowing what was going on, thinking the two cups of coffee from earlier were playing tricks on me." Ronnie chuckled. "I started to roll down my window, then that's when a voice came to me. 'Do not talk to them.' Well, I didn't think any more about it. I floored it to the end of the lane, and marched right in the house for a dram to steady my nerves. I haven't seen them since."

A heavy silence fell over the room. Meg and Angus exchanged a perplexed look, both unsure of how to respond to this inexplicable tale of tiny people by the roadside.

Meg placed her cup down on the floor, interlacing her hands together, trying to find a rational explanation for Ronnie's story. "Perhaps," she started cautiously, "you thought you saw something."

Ronnie's expression remained unwavering, and he replied with conviction, "No, dear. I saw something as clear as you are now to me."

She continued, her curiosity piqued, "Well, you said yourself, you were thinking of other things. Your way of life, as you said, is changing. You were grieving over a friend who sounded frail, and it made your mind …"

Ronnie let out a scoff, clearly not buying her attempt to rationalise his experience. "If that's how you want to process these things, my dear Meg, then so be it. I know what I saw, and that's not the only thing. I've seen many things over the years. Not that I wanted to, but I did nonetheless. These things appear to us at times where we may need to listen; they're telling us something."

Realising that her scepticism wasn't welcome, she changed her approach. "What do you think they were telling you?"

Ronnie lit his pipe again, the small glow of the ember reflecting in the smoke as he puffed it slowly. "I'm not sure," he admitted after a moment. "But sometimes, you've got to let it go. It will come back if it needs to."

"Will you have some dinner? There's stew in the pot," Angus offered, clapping his knees with both hands as he stood up.

"Oh, dinner you say?" Ronnie looked a little uncomfortable. "I don't want to impose."

Angus waved a hand dismissively, chuckling gently and went to reheat leftovers. With a polite goodnight, Meg bid Ronnie farewell, leaving the two men to their discussions about local affairs. She headed to her room, her tired body yearning for rest. As she lay down in bed, she silently hoped that her dreams wouldn't be filled with more fairy stories or cryptic messages. This trip had left her feeling wearier than she'd ever imagined, and at that moment, all she wanted was to sleep for a thousand years.

18

LEXI

Lexi threw on her denim jacket, grabbed an umbrella from the stand by the front door and left before the cottage stirred. She marched out into the fresh air, the cold stinging her nostrils as she breathed in. She walked briskly, closing the gate behind her, and admired Angus's small farm. His sheep grazed quietly, paying her no mind as she ambled along the fence line and across the road. She nimbly hopped over a small stream, mirroring her actions from the previous day, and leisurely made her way through a cluster of charming cottages until she arrived at the unremarkable white square building. Its peeling paint and faded blue windows greeted her, as did its makeshift roof, seemingly enduring one too many harsh winters. She couldn't help but think of it as the village eyesore as she settled onto a bench by the main entrance, just as she had done the day before. Familiar eyes soon met hers.

"Hi," greeted a young man in a white and blue uniform, his head popping out of the door. His brown eyes assessed Lexi.

"Hi," Lexi replied warmly.

"Here again?" He walked towards her and sat in the space next to her.

"Yeah, why not. I thought maybe I could hear some more stories or help in some way?"

He grimaced, scratching his chin. "She didn't have a good night. Maybe talk to her later?" he suggested.

Lexi's face fell. "Really? But yesterday, she was very talkative …"

He shrugged. "It's just the nature of things, I'm afraid. You can never tell."

She abruptly stood up, her relaxed demeanour vanishing for a moment. She turned away, her gaze returning to the path she had come from. Clusters of bright amber and crimson red foliage adorned the road, both above and underfoot. Leaves fluttered down, one by one, landing gently on the ground. Time was ticking away.

"Mark, it is Mark, right?" she asked.

The man nodded, tapping his almost completely hidden name tag under his pocket flap.

"I won't be back tomorrow." Lexi raised her hand. "I'm not sure how long I'll be here. But if it's OK, I'll stay. I promise not to bother her. If she comes out, we can chat. If not, she can carry on her day without seeing me." Lexi offered a pleading look.

"OK," Mark conceded, shaking his head. "Please don't upset her. We don't always know what can trigger her."

"I will be on my best behaviour," Lexi assured him, offering a playful salute in an attempt to lighten the mood.

Mark quickly stood up, glancing at his watch. "OK, time to organise the teas. See you later, Lexi."

She waited in the cool breeze, as more clouds gathered overhead, bringing with them a stronger wind. She shivered, regretting not having a coat warmer than her meagre denim jacket to protect her from the elements.

Going back on her word to the nurse already, she briskly walked to the little shop further up the street and bought a cup of watery coffee that scalded her mouth on first sip and took it grudgingly back to the cold bench. Pulling up her jacket collar, she placed her paper cup of scalding liquid on the armrest and lit a cigarette. These were her guilty pleasures in life – a cigarette and coffee. She wondered if anything could be better. Well, perhaps the coffee.

Lexi had been smoking since she was a teenager, but regardless of how long she'd had this "bad habit," she always felt like a naughty schoolgirl. She sighed at the absurdity of it all and exhaled a puff of smoke into the chilly air. She was an adult now, who cared?

Meg had always commented on Lexi's habits – in fact, every aspect of Lexi's life. Her criticisms had worn her down over time, pushing her to become a completely different person from her sister in every conceivable way.

Her tense shoulders relaxed as the nicotine began to soothe her temper.

"May I have a cigarette?" asked a woman with grey hair elegantly pulled back, standing with her arms crossed, towering over her.

"Of course," she replied, reaching into her pocket and handing over a cigarette.

"Thank you." The woman sat down next to her. She wore a long purple cardigan that covered her dark red loose pants. Her colourful appearance was a warm contrast to the dark, cloudy day. "This is just what I need – after enduring that awful place," she remarked, nodding at the shabby building.

"Why do you say that?" Lexi frowned, genuinely curious.

"Oh, never mind. You don't work in there?" The woman tucked a stray hair behind her ear, not particularly concerned whether Lexi was an employee of the retirement home behind them.

"No, remember we met yesterday? We spoke about your career as a theatre playwright ...?" Lexi reminded her.

Mrs Archer raised her eyebrows and exhaled a cloud of smoke. "No, love, you must have me confused with someone else."

Lexi bit her lip, remembering Mark's warning that Mrs Archer wasn't herself today. The last thing she wanted was to upset her newfound acquaintance, especially after the inspiring conversation they had shared the day before. For Mrs Archer's sake, Lexi needed to tread carefully.

"Just now you mentioned it being a bad place. Can you tell me why you feel that way?" Lexi asked, trying to keep the conversation light, more as a topic of discussion with a stranger over a cigarette than anything else.

Mrs Archer crossed her legs and leaned towards her, casting her eye back to the building. "They gave me pills. They're trying to control me, take my money, keep my family from me. They don't think I know." She jabbed a thumb to her chest. "I know!"

Lexi sat there, dumbfounded. The lady before her was a stark contrast to the charming one she had met yesterday. If it weren't for the brightly coloured wardrobe, she might have assumed they were different people altogether.

"Why do you think they're trying to do that?" Lexi crossed her legs as well, mirroring the same body language. "I'm sure they are just looking out for you, they want you to get better."

Mrs Archer shook her head. "No, dear, you don't understand. You don't know this place." She cast a sympathetic look at her. "At least I've still got my wits about me. I haven't let them win."

Lexi's shoulders slumped as she leaned back against the wooden bench, struggling to reconcile the person beside her with the vibrant Mrs Archer from the day before. The Mrs

Archer she had encountered earlier had been brimming with life, her face animated and playful. Lexi had spent most of the previous night meticulously replaying the stories Mrs Archer had shared – tales from behind the stage, the dramas, and the tears of the London theatre scene. The allure of glitz and glamour had left Lexi craving for more. Mrs Archer had even dropped hints about an affair with a famous actor, tantalising clues to his identity that Lexi had mulled over throughout the morning. Yet now, those breadcrumbs would remain forever untraced.

"Let them win what?" Lexi asked, grimacing as she sipped the last of her coffee, which tasted like pond water.

The old woman shrugged again. "My family is being kept away. I know they are. I don't trust that nurse." She carefully stubbed out her cigarette on the bench, her narrow eyes fixed on the nursing home's front door.

"Who? Mark?"

Mrs Archer studied Lexi for a moment. "You know the nurses?"

She sighed inwardly. Today wasn't the day to delve deeper into the matter. She might end up causing more trouble for herself, Mrs Archer, and the staff. Lexi dropped her cigarette and pressed her foot down on it, then clasped her cold hands between her legs. "Do you have any family?" She quickly changed the subject to a lighter tone before saying her goodbyes.

Mrs Archer's face lit up. "I do have family – a boy and a girl, Samuel and Marianne. Samuel is such a good boy; he went to Oxford, made me so proud. Marianne used to help me at the theatre; she loved being on stage too." She smiled to herself. "Such a beautiful dancer. She was even in *Cats*, you know?" Mrs Archer nodded. "Nothing like their father, though – thankfully. He was a layabout scrounger," she muttered to herself.

"But you told me you loved your husband?"

"What?" Mrs Archer snapped.

"I'm sorry, I thought you had mentioned being happily married," Lexi backtracked, her mind muddled by the previous day's conversation. "I must be getting you confused with another local lady here." She hoped this feeble excuse would suffice. Today's conversation had left her feeling jittery and self-conscious, as though she were a silly little girl asking foolish questions. "Never mind; it was nice chatting."

Lexi, about to stand, was stopped by Mrs Archer's cool hand on hers. The old lady's face relaxed, her eyes briefly darting downwards as if a forgotten memory was gradually unfolding in her mind. Her slow smile returned, her eyes filling with tears as she suddenly sobbed, her body shaking as her hand covered her mouth. The sound startled Lexi, and it was so heartbreaking and haunting that she put her arm around the old woman, doing her best to offer comfort. She hadn't had much experience with people crying, except for maybe a friend in the bathroom at a nightclub, but this was different. Mrs Archer didn't flinch; she closed her eyes and remained on the bench, a stillness enveloping her, with Lexi close by. The wind whirled around them, blowing leaves off the tree above. Slowly and peacefully, some brown, crisp leaves floated down around them, creating a safe cocoon from the outside world.

Lexi handed over a packet of tissues she had stashed in her jacket pocket for her own unexpected bouts of crying, usually when she thought of Chris. It was something she still hid from Meg; the pain he had inflicted on her was hard to process even now. But she kept her pain locked away, especially from her sister. When Leon had left, she couldn't bear to endure another one of Meg's "I told you so" looks. She hadn't fallen in love with Leon, not really. But he had cracked her shell, making her exposed once again.

She could have loved him. If he had waited.

She trailed off, gazing at the quiet road ahead. Despite their proximity to the village shop, only one car had passed by. She had never been in such an empty place before; it was peaceful but lonely. With the nursing home behind her and the desolate landscape surrounding them, she couldn't help but feel a melancholy in the hills. Or maybe that was just her own imagination.

"Please don't be sorry; I didn't mean to pry or make you upset," Lexi said, contemplating how impolite it would be to get up and leave a weeping woman.

"No, I'm fine. I want to remember him. My husband, Richard …" She smiled, wiping the last tear from her blotchy eyes. "He was a theatre producer. We met when I was writing one of my last plays. We had such a connection. As soon as I saw him, I thought, 'This is it.' You know?"

Lexi hoped to feel that way one day, but if she was being honest with herself, she hadn't even come close. Listening to Mrs Archer's love story made her whole body tingle; it was the special magic of romance that so many searched for and only few found. Fate drawing two people together who were meant to be – what a wondrous thought! She had always imagined her perfect man as a dashing prince from her mother's fairy tale stories. The damsel would be in danger, all hope lost, but her love would arrive just in the nick of time to save her. Maybe she was about to be eaten by the castle dragon or marry a cruel old king, only to be rescued by her hero. As much as Lexi could be persuaded to think there was no man out there for her, especially by her sister, she just couldn't accept it. He was out there somewhere; she just had to kiss a few frogs first.

"He was such a rascal," Mrs Archer continued, unaware of Lexi's distant longing. "Always playing tricks on people like he was a little boy. He kept me young, by my side when others left. It was just us two. He had always wanted to live in the Scottish Highlands, such a change from Okinawa. So we did, packed up and came here."

"Japan?" Lexi asked, intrigued.

"Yes, he was unique, my Richard. Exotic and a true story-teller … I treasure the memories," she said, her eyes glazing over again, making Lexi panic. She really did not want to be scolded by the nurse.

"OK, it's getting cold out here," came the deep voice behind them, startling her. "I think it might be wise to come in now … I have a cup of tea and a scone with your name on it, Annabel," Mark said gently, and to Lexi's surprise, the woman stood up eagerly.

"I must say, I'm parched. Could our visitor come in for a cuppa too?"

Mark shrugged in quiet defeat. Mrs Archer looped her arm through Lexi's, making her feel like they were two mischievous teenagers scheming a plan. "I feel so much better, talking to you. Oh, pardon me, darling, I don't think I got your name?"

"It's Alexandria, but call me Lexi," she replied, not for the first time to the old lady, and gave Mark a cheeky wink as they passed him.

19

ANGUS

Angus perched on the flat rock by the sheep pen, a ritual of his early mornings. He often awoke before dawn, and after checking his croft he would watch the sun lift over the hill, sipping hot coffee.

With the arrival of colder months, he noticed his energy gradually waning. It was a peculiar adjustment, one he had grown accustomed to. Rather than resisting this change, he had learned to embrace it, finding peace and tranquillity in the quiet moments of the morning.

The sun gently filtered through scattered clouds, slowly illuminating the fields before him with its warm, golden light. He stretched his back against the cold rock, unused to his new sleeping arrangements; since the girls had come to stay, he had opted to take the couch, giving them some space and privacy. He couldn't help but chuckle at the thought of himself, a solitary crofter, now sharing his home with two girls from Australia. But each day they shared, he grew to enjoy it more, making him see that his days on the croft had been a little lonely at times.

Finishing the last dregs of his strong coffee, he rose to his feet and surveyed his land. As much as he relished the slower pace of life, he had no intention of stopping work altogether. The sheep and hens had ample space, leaving a considerable section of empty land leading to the bottom gate. The idea crossed his mind to introduce pigs or perhaps expand his vegetable patch, which would keep him occupied over the winter months. The thought of introducing pigs brought a smile to his face. He wondered if Meg might enjoy accompanying him to see piglets. It could be a fun day together, especially since her sister seemed so preoccupied. He needed to pack in as many activities as possible for them before their trip home. Although the thought of the girls leaving made his throat tighten. Showing them around had rekindled his passion for his job as a tour guide and his love for his homeland. He just wished he could make their stay a bit more upmarket, especially for what they had paid. The idea of suggesting a partial refund from Jake had crossed his mind, but he hesitated. After all, the unexpected chaos caused by Leon had complicated matters.

Maybe if he focused on finding this Graeme MacDonald it might make up for their disaster of a holiday? Although he was sure he had already exhausted all his contacts. No one knew this elusive man.

He zipped up his coat to shield himself from the biting cold wind and headed back to the cottage. Inside, he found Meg at the kitchen table, engrossed in her notes.

"Morning. Coffee?" Angus offered, moving toward the percolator to prepare a fresh batch.

"Yeah, that would be nice," she said quietly. Her hair was pulled back into a bun, and she appeared a little paler than usual.

Angus couldn't help but notice the soft wisps of hair along the back of her neck, a subtle detail that unexpectedly sparked a desire to reach out and caress the spot with his hand. He shook himself, clearing the unwanted thoughts; he had clearly been alone for far too long if just any woman's presence stirred up such feelings.

But was Meg just any woman? Their shared experiences and the time they had spent together made him realise how starved he had been for female companionship. Determined to remedy his loneliness, he resolved to plan a trip to the city at the earliest opportunity. Perhaps reconnecting with old friends during a long weekend in London would provide the social interaction he craved.

As good an intention as it was, his body tensed at the mere thought of London and all its allure – the constant flow of people, the urgency of everything, and weekends that always felt too short.

The coffee pot hissed and bubbled on the cooker. He carefully poured black coffee into two small cups, one of them marred by a tiny chip along its side. Despite its imperfection, he held a special fondness for these cups, their chunky handles and faint blue stains evoking memories of the sea. Crafted by his mother years ago during her tenure at the pottery shop, they had been a cherished gift one Christmas. Each sip transported him back to those simpler times, yet now, amid the familiar comforts of home, his thoughts inexplicably drifted to the bustling streets of the city.

Could he ever find complete contentment, or would he always long for what he didn't have?

"After you get your packages in the post, I thought we could carry on up the coast. I believe there's another castle, one that you can reach only when the tide is out?" Meg suggested, her head ducked over a map.

Angus nodded. "Aye, a tidal castle. Plenty of those around."

"But this one I'm sure Mum went to ..." She scrutinised her notes, tapping her pen absentmindedly on her lower lip. "Although it's difficult to be sure where she went!"

"Do you not want to find Graeme MacDonald?" Angus placed the cup without a chip next to her arm.

Her eyes remained fixed on her notes. "It's not that I don't want to find him, Angus. It's just that I've been thinking … Maybe it's not worth the effort. I mean, we've already spent so much time searching, and we're no closer to finding him. It's frustrating, you know?" she replied, taking the small cup in her hands, her thumbs stroking its rippled surface. "And besides, our main reason for coming here was to scatter Mum's ashes. I don't want to lose sight of that goal in pursuit of something that might not even pan out. So, maybe it's best to focus on what's truly important right now."

"I'm sure you don't mean that. If I had long-lost family, I'd be keen to find them. One setback doesn't mean we give up – let me try," he insisted, in a change of heart that left him confused. Since their day out at the farm, Meg had seemed more tired, her usually strong-willed attitude fading.

"No, Angus – I just don't want to dredge up things." Her voice tightened and she sipped the coffee.

"What do you mean, dredge up things?" He frowned. One minute it had been vital that he found this Graeme MacDonald, but now she was giving up when they were closer than ever. If he did a little more digging, he was sure he'd find him. "Are we not looking for your relative?"

"Yes," she replied irritably. "But I don't want the trip to be focused on this. We came here for Mum – to scatter her ashes. We need to do that." She pushed the cup away, signalling that the conversation was over.

"OK." Angus shifted in his seat. "Whatever you need."

"That's what I need. I don't want to talk about it again." She rubbed her arms, as if she was cold and giving herself a hug. "Are we good?"

He nodded solemnly. There was nothing else he could do. The trip was proving a failed attempt on his part. He couldn't hold his part of the bargain – so much so that the client had given up all hope. He cringed at what kind of review Meg might leave them, but the thing that really hit him was her disappointment. He simply didn't want to let her down.

Silence fell over them, apart from the ticking clock on his kitchen wall, which made him look up. "Shall we head to this gala then?" he asked with a hopeful smile.

20

MEG

Meg gasped at the spectacle before her. Speedboats, yachts and row boats cruised along the waterfront, while spectators lined the rocky foreshore. Angus parked the van a distance away, unable to find parking near the site. "We should've left earlier, but there's nothing for it – we'll need to walk," he said, shoving his hands into his jean pockets and zipping up his jacket to shield himself from the harsh wind.

Meg emerged from the van, greeted by a sea of people and a hive of activity. Cars were haphazardly parked along the main road, hastily left in lay-bys or abandoned on the grass.

Walking side by side, their arms nearly touching but keeping a comfortable distance, they moved towards the festival. Her attention was drawn to a woman on a small stage, her voice echoing witchy harmonies. Beside her, a guitarist wove melodic chords, and another musician dressed in gold played an instrument resembling a pipe. Women in floaty dresses made of patchwork fabrics swayed in time to the music.

Along the shoreline, vibrant stalls burst into view,

displaying handmade crafts, tapestries, trinkets, and makeshift bars served cold beers and sweet ciders.

Angus nodded to a passerby. “Looks like the whole of the Highlands are here today. Plenty of tourists too, I guess. For the last social event of the year, people want to see a human being before they're indoors all winter!”

“Not all winter?” Meg gasped. “Surely there’s things to do? I’d lose my mind being stuck indoors!”

He grinned in response. “Me too. There’s nothing like a hike in a storm to get the blood pumping. Plus, it makes the dram in the pub after all the more worth it! Though you won’t have all that in Australia, I’m sure you go to festivals all the time?”

“No, never.”

“But you have so much around you?” Angus raised an eyebrow in astonishment.

“We do,” Meg shrugged. “But I never was particularly interested in festivals or attending big functions.”

“Trust me, if you lived in a place where you virtually saw no one all winter, you’d be out making the effort!”

Their leisurely stroll took them through clusters of people, more tents emerging in the distance. Meg marvelled at the abundance of human life in this seemingly hidden part of the world. Everyone was out, and for a moment, she yearned for her sister's presence, wishing they could share an experience untainted by the grief of their mother.

Numerous families occupied the rocks, huddled around flasks of tea and picnics. Children leaped from stone to stone, nets in hand, exploring rock pools, while their parents strolled behind, engaging in leisurely village gossip. The water was a lively display of boats, each waiting their turn for a race. Before Meg could fully immerse herself in the scene, a woman's shrill voice echoed across the water, announcing, “The raft race will commence in thirty minutes.

Please make your way to the red flag on the north side of the beach."

Further along the grassy foreshore, additional food stands appeared, their tempting aromas of sizzling hotdogs and smoky barbecue wafting through the air with the intoxicating sweetness of freshly baked jam-filled donuts.

"Donut?" Angus nudged her.

She nodded eagerly and gravitated toward a coffee stand, only to change her mind at the last second, opting for alcohol instead. She bought two cups of cider, her eyes locking with the lady behind the counter, and a smile instantly graced her face. "Iona!" Meg noted Iona's beauty seemed even more dazzling than their last encounter.

"Well, hello there, Meg. I thought you might have departed by now?" Iona's eyes held a curious spark, but not unkind.

"Not yet. Angus has been nice enough to let us stay with him." Meg took a sip of the tangy hot cider, which quickly numbed her throat.

Iona's expression briefly shifted to one of alarm, her composure wavering before a smile returned to her lips. "Oh well, hopefully, you can continue your journey soon."

Meg nodded in agreement. Waiting for Angus's bank card to arrive by post felt like an eternity, especially since they were living in the middle of nowhere. She was starting to lose faith that it wasn't sitting in some dusty depot. Her eagerness to leave and refocus on her mum grew stronger, but she couldn't find much else to say to Iona. Instead she bid her farewell and made her way through the throngs of people, feeling somewhat irked by the encounter.

Angus appeared, a paper plate piled high with hot, sugary donuts. Meg's mouth watered, and she dismissed the nagging feeling that having donuts and cider for a late breakfast might not be a good idea.

Further down the shore, they ambled along in the flow of people. A gunshot in the distance signalled the start of a rowboat race, and the crowd erupted in cheers as the rowers synchronised their efforts. Meg took another long sip of the warm cider, relishing the heat as her hands grew colder by the minute.

"Oh, it's Meg, right?" came a voice from behind her. It was the friendly woman from the farm, now sporting a bright orange life jacket and carrying her toddler in her arms, with the older girl standing close, her arm wrapped around her mother's leg.

"That's right!" Meg smiled at the two shy girls. "It's Rachel and Lisa, isn't it?"

The two girls remained quiet, the smaller one hiding her face in her mother's shoulder.

"Now you two are hardly shy … you were just jumping up and down wanting donuts!"

Meg chuckled. "Oh, sorry," she added, looking down at the half-eaten treat in her hand. "I might not be a good example here for kids."

Meg introduced Angus to the woman, realising she hadn't learned her name.

"It's Sue, don't worry, honey," Sue reassured, "you did leave very abruptly that day, but it was nice to meet you. Did you find your family?"

Angus lapsed into silence as Meg shifted the topic, eager to divert attention away from the sensitive issue of her father. Sue, preoccupied with her young daughter's requests for snacks, remained oblivious to the tension lingering in the air.

"We're in the raft race – well, I am. Little Lisa and Rachel will be waiting with their daddy on the sidelines of course," Sue explained.

"I want to come!" the eldest girl bellowed, her fists clenched, startling them all.

“Now don’t start this again, you can come next year when you're a bit older,” Sue replied, waving off her daughter's pleas. “A bunch of us mums are joining in. We're each rockin' different eras of the pop princess herself: Madonna!” Sue added with a cheeky wink at Angus, like they were in on some juicy secret.

“And which one are you?” He squinted, attempting to decipher a costume beneath Sue's bulky life jacket.

“Oh, I'm Cowboy Country Madonna!” She laughed, plucking a glittered fedora hat from where it had slipped down her back, fastened with a neck tie, and smacking her thigh with glee. “Ta-dah!” She struck a pose, her enthusiasm contagious.

“Very imaginative!” Meg chuckled.

“Oh, you haven't seen Mary – she's Dominatrix Madonna! We couldn’t find leather or PVC, so she wrapped herself in black bin liners,”

As swiftly as the rowboat competition had begun, it catapulted into its grand finale. The announcer, with resounding pride, declared the triumphant victors, who stood in a line, wearing big smiles and even bigger orange life jackets. Amidst the jubilation, Meg's attention was abruptly seized by a glint of metal. Dressed in a black suit with a white collar, the local priest bestowed shimmering medals upon each neck, his gestures warm and congenial as he exchanged handshakes.

She remembered a moment of fleeting triumph like that. Her sister had fashioned a makeshift medal from tinfoil, scavenged from their mother’s baking cupboard. With a yellow felt-tip pen, she’d attempted to imbue it with a golden hue. It was the day Meg sang at the school’s talent show – a poignant melody about being far from home and the promise of returning, one their father often sang to them. On that scorching afternoon, her father had ceremoniously placed the homemade medal around her neck, proclaiming, "To the true winner of the talent show," as if initiating her into knighthood.

It didn't bother Meg that the actual winners were a group of awkward boys, a year younger and rapping like Ice Cube. She hadn't minded at all because she had succeeded in making the one person proud that mattered most – her father. That night, he fired up the barbecue in their backyard, and they each got a whole dollar to treat themselves to an ice cream from the corner shop.

Even with her mixed feelings about her dad, she couldn't help but grin, shaking her head at how memories could pop up in the weirdest of places.

As more people came towards the stage, the gaps closed, and the crowd turned into a lively bunch of spectators.

Sue, now on a determined mission, shimmied through the crowd towards a woman with white lace gloves, a leather jacket, and a scrunchie perched atop a permed hairdo.

Meg, intrigued, nodded towards Sue's new friend. "Which Madonna is that?"

Angus, head tilted thoughtfully, shrugged. "So, what do you think?"

"Of the competition? Or of Madonna's music?" she replied, finishing the last of her cider and suppressing a burp. Savouring the sweetness on her sugary fingers, she, in an uncharacteristic move, wiped her hands down her thighs, forgoing the usual search for a wipe.

"Neither!" Angus laughed. "What I'm actually asking is, do you like it here?"

Her mouth twitched. "Sure …"

As the speaker announced a break before the next race, the crowd surged closer to Angus and Meg. Amidst the commotion, a man in a handkerchief cap and apron, speaking into a microphone, declared half-priced donuts at the nearby stand. The crowd erupted with excitement, and Meg and Angus found themselves swept back by the enthusiastic surge, the swell of bodies pressing in from all sides towards the even busier festival activity.

The air thickened with the mingling scents of hot meat. She felt sick. A surge of panic gripped her chest, an unwelcome visitor she hadn't anticipated. Her breaths grew shallower as the walls of people seemed to converge, creating a suffocating tunnel of bodies.

She glanced at Angus, her eyes wide with distress. His concerned gaze met hers, and without a word, he reached out to pull her from the sea of people. Holding her hand, he guided her away from the noise to a small horseshoe bay. The dark sand nestled against a hill carved out as a backdrop.

Her chest heaved as she took gulping breaths, her eyes darting nervously around. The unexpected intensity of the crowd had triggered something deep within her – an unease that clawed at the edges of her consciousness.

"Are you OK?" Angus asked, his voice a steady reassurance.

She found herself speechless, unable to articulate the sudden onslaught of fear. She looked at her trembling hands.

"OK, OK, you just look like you had a shock there," he said kindly, taking off his backpack and unrolling a blanket for them to sit on.

With his assistance, she lowered herself onto the ground, her breaths shaky. His reassuring hand rested on her back as she held her forehead.

"Just breathe, take your time. There's no one here, just space."

A few moments passed, during which Angus pulled out a bottle of water from the backpack. "I would give you an energy chocolate bar." He shrugged, scanning the backpack. "But I think donuts and cider would cancel out anything an energy bar could do for you." He eyed her. "So are you claustrophobic, then?" he gently probed.

Meg frowned. "I didn't think so. Well, sometimes on planes, or in a lift, or in a car."

"So … yes?" Angus grinned, reclining and admiring the tranquil waters. "It's hard to believe all that chaos is just around the corner."

As her breathing gradually steadied, she sipped the cool water and, taking a cue from Angus, allowed herself to lie back. "I do love the stillness of things here. Not the donut queues." She chuckled.

"Would you ever move? Live away from Melbourne?" Angus asked, his voice hushed, his hair – slightly longer with each passing day – resting on his backpack.

She pondered the question. Australia was her home, and the idea of leaving her sister was inconceivable, especially now since their mother was gone and was soon to be scattered to the seas in a foreign land. More than ever, she must remain constant. The promise she had made herself all those years ago must prevail.

Just as she opened her mouth to speak, Angus nudged her, his eyes wide and pointing upwards. A large bird circled them, so enormous that Meg could hear its wings beating against the wind. It moved towards the sea in front of them and very gracefully swooped down with what looked like very little effort, peeling away from the water with a fish clasped in its claw.

Angus's hand grazed against hers. "A sea eagle," he whispered, his face close.

She watched in silence as the eagle hovered for a fleeting moment before gracefully taking flight in the direction of the hills that loomed behind them. A peculiar sensation washed over her. Hadn't she dreamed of this exact scene? Except, in her dream, she wasn't sitting beside Angus on the blanket; it was her mother.

“Truly incredible creatures, aren't they? That poor salmon didn't stand a chance,” Angus remarked with a quiet chuckle.

She swallowed, but her mouth was dry from the cider. She had to tell him about the dream, surely he’d understand. She needed connection, grounding when things seemed so out of her hands.

On the verge of sharing her strange déjà vu experience with Angus, suddenly his piercing eyes locked onto hers. In that singular moment, his hand extended, lightly grazing her cheek. He drew her nearer. She found herself ensnared, much like a deer caught in the unyielding glare of oncoming headlights. She couldn't resist, nor did she wish to. His lips met hers with a gentle, lingering tenderness, and his fingers brushed aside her hair as he pulled her closer.

A whirlwind of thoughts whirred through her mind. As swiftly as their conversation had transitioned to this unexpected intimacy, she found herself unable to pull away. This wasn't part of the plan, yet she hesitated to step fully back from the new world she was plunged into, her heart pounding with a mixture of uncertainty and desire.

21

MEG

"Meg! Meeeeeeeeeeeeg!" Sue ran towards them, frantically waving her hands. "Hey, you guys, over here!" she boomed, her face flushed as she approached. "I thought I saw you walking in this direction!" She put her hands on her hips and doubled over, gasping for air. Her cowboy hat slid behind her head but hung loosely fastened around her neck. "We need you both now – the race is about to start!" She clapped her hands eagerly. "Penny and Amy have dropped out last minute, they went home with a tummy bug, it's been going around the village —" She waved her hand, as if trying to stop herself from giving away too much information. "It doesn't matter, anyway we need you two – now!"

Meg looked wide-eyed at Angus, hoping that he could make some excuse for them both, but rather disappointingly, he got to his feet quickly. "Of course!"

"But it's out in the water?" Meg backtracked, wondering why this trip involved so many boats. It wasn't that she was afraid of water as such, but the thought of being squished on a rubber dinghy with a group of Madonnas, to be submerged under the sea, sent her into a panic.

"Of course it's in the water, it's a regatta!" Sue shook her head, humoured by Meg's slow grasp of events. "Now, follow me quick!"

* * *

She sat on the edge of a makeshift raft, clutching her life jacket as she double-checked that the belts and buckles were secured. One of the moms handed her a flower and a blonde wig. Unsure of which Madonna she was supposed to be, she put the stringy item on her head.

"Very nice," Angus remarked beside her, donning a long, flowing black wig that cascaded over his shoulders. His beard and bare arms protruded from beneath the luminous-orange life jacket. He winked at her, and she couldn't help but burst out laughing.

"I don't know who looks more ridiculous!" She hooted, relaxing a little until all of a sudden, a gunshot was fired, and they were off!

Having never rowed a boat before, she'd been given a two-minute lesson by the team. With all her concentration and strength, she focused on keeping in time with Angus, who appeared to be a natural.

"Heave!" Sue called from the front. "Come on, girls, let's show Tilhoe who's boss!" she bellowed, looking over to their right, where another raft of women sped next to them.

Meg and Angus laughed through the chants of the crowd and the cries from the other teams.

"Cheaters!" screamed a rather overly competitive small woman from the other raft. She stood up for a moment until their boat wobbled, watching them through slitted eyes. "You've got to go around the buoy!"

"Whoops!" Sue said under her breath. "Calm down, we didn't see it!" she called back to the other team, who shook their heads in such a serious manner that Meg was gobsmacked. “Ignore them!” Sue bellowed. “Heave!”

Meg's arms were burning, and her feet were freezing cold, immersed in the sea water. To her horror, the raft was slowly coming apart the more they moved; made only from large blocks of polystyrene and rope, it was unravelling around them.

“Almost there!” Sue barked, taking her role as coxswain very seriously.

“It's not going to make it!” Meg cried in alarm as the rope under her bum loosened.

“Heave!” Sue ignored Meg's pessimism as the end was in sight. “We're going to win! Come on, girls!”

Angus caught Meg's eye and screwed his nose. His foot, which was inside the raft, clamped down on a knot of rope, barely holding the raft together. She clenched her bum down on top of the fastenings too, hoping to stave off any unravelling for the last remaining minute.

“The Tilhoe Rafters and The Virgins are in the lead! Who's going to win the Glenardburn cup?” an excited voice boomed from the speakers by the beach, echoing across the water.

“Come on, get your backs into it!” screamed Sue, eyes wide as they reached the finishing line mere metres in front of the Tilhoe Rafters.

The crowd cheered, and Meg breathed out, exhausted and exhilarated. She hunched over, recovering her breath, her limbs aching all over. And just as soon as they all congratulated themselves, the rope unravelled and the ramshackle raft fell apart instantly, plunging them all into cold water. They bobbed in the waves, laughing.

“Cheaters!” the small woman called again as the speedboat came to bring them into shore.

“We didn't cheat, Sally. God, lighten up, woman!” Sue

shook her head as she was helped into the motorboat, which collected the contestants one by one. The angry woman and Sue kept on either side of the boat, eyeing one another with suspicion until they were ferried over the short stretch of water to the beach. The crowd cheered and patted their backs, but as soon as their feet touched dry land, the opposing team briskly walked up to the organisers, murmuring their grievances to a woman with the mic. Seconds dragged, as Meg watched breathless. Then, as quickly as she resigned herself to wait longer, the speaker turned on the mic, and the crowd hushed.

"The winners are: The Virgins!" she announced, clapping her hands and gesturing for the team to come up on stage to receive their medals.

Sue whooped, and Angus picked her up, whirling her around. Cheers erupted around them. Meg was dizzy with excitement. She had never won anything before! Her elation carried her up the steps to be congratulated by the speaker and the local doctor. As the priest, a figure of quiet authority, began handing out medals with red ribbons, a strange feeling settled over her. Much like witnessing the sea eagle in person, that déjà vu crept up behind her, standing over her like a shadow. She could see her young self wearing that tinfoil medal with pride, her father patting her head gently.

She lingered at the back of the line, her eyes fixed on each teammate as they received their awards. The priest's hands, weathered with time, cradled each medal before gently placing it around the recipient's neck. As the line inched forward, the strange familiarity grew more prominent.

When it was finally her turn, the priest's tired eyes met hers, and at that very moment, it all became clear.

"Well done!" he said, smiling down at her.

Her throat tightened, and she shivered in the cold wind swirling around them. Yet, in her mind, that same hot summer evening unfolded. The handmade medal against her chest, the stain of the felt-tip colour on her skin, her father's admiration.

Now, on the brightly lit stage, she accepted the congratulations and pats on the back, but beneath the surface, a mounting tension gripped her. It had been years since she'd last glimpsed those hazel eyes, yet she could recognise them anywhere.

Her father stood right in front of her, handing her an award, and what's more – he didn't even recognise her.

22

MEG

She knocked back another strong drink at the bar, cheers surrounding her. She coughed and slammed the glass down, her head swimming. Could it be that she was back on that raft, bopping over waves, slowly unravelling into the dark water?

"Another?" Sue asked, getting the attention of the barman.

"I can't."

"Nonsense! We're celebrating! I couldn't believe the look on Tilhoe's faces!" Sue reminisced about their earlier win, and soon another eruption of cheers came from their group.

With Angus at the far side of the pub, huddled around a small table with an old high school classmate, Meg edged away from the bar, seizing the smallest chance of escape. The air inside was thick with the scent of perspiring bodies, and the stifling warmth was making her queasy. All she craved was solitude, and a chance to process the day.

She bit her lip, trying to edge closer to the door. As soon as she sensed Sue's attention elsewhere, she bolted.

Her eyes adjusted to the gloomy light outside as she zipped up her jacket. With an intake of breath, she set off on foot, heading back to Angus's place. It wouldn't take long if she walked quickly, and she needed alone time.

The country pub was perched behind her on the edge of the village, overlooking tranquil water. The same water that only hours earlier had been a hub of activity.

The glow of the building behind her faded, along with its sounds of joviality, growing fainter with each step. She let nature's gentle sounds envelop her as she stood on a rock by the water's edge. Her whole body shook, her fingernails tightly clamped to her palms, her knuckles white. She couldn't avoid the shock that seeing her father had imprinted on her. Seeking him out had been one thing, but facing the living, breathing person in front of her was an entirely different challenge.

And there she stood, dumbfounded, unable to utter a single word. The Meg she knew would have candidly spoken her mind. Yet, she allowed him to slip away, affording him the luxury of ignorance while she grappled with the harsh truth.

How could her father have become a priest? The irony struck her – preaching about goodness while abandoning a family on the other side of the world without a backward glance.

He'd paid them little thought over the years. He didn't know his own daughter right in front of him.

But what did she expect? He had been absent from their lives for so long, missing everything: birthdays, graduations, those Christmas days when they eagerly unwrapped presents lovingly bought by their mother, even when money was tight. And how their mum would cheer, capturing the moments with the click of her camera, the flash buzzing loudly as their bleached images showed them barefooted in front of a tiny Christmas tree.

The memory of the last time she had seen him haunted

her, always resurfacing when she yearned for their family to be whole. But that memory had a cruel way of jerking her back to reality. The last time she saw him was the last time she would see him drunk, too. It occurred on Lexi's eleventh birthday, and Meg had felt uneasy from the moment she woke. An elderly neighbour had casually mentioned spotting him, but instead of sharing this news with anyone, Meg kept it to herself. It had been years since he had been a part of their lives, years since her mother had told him to leave, leaving him to gamble and drink his life away on the fringes.

Meg had stood outside their front door, her insides clenched with anxiety, her body trembling. She'd been wearing ripped jeans and a striped cropped T-shirt that exposed her belly button. The confused look he had given her that day; he hadn't recognised her then, just as he didn't know her now. He left without even stepping through the front door, while Lexi was serenaded by schoolmates with "Happy Birthday" and blew out the candles on her cake. Their mother cut giant slabs of chocolate mud cake, the icing melting over her fingers. The joy experienced inside those doors, Meg didn't want to be contaminated. She'd kept watch, and kept him out.

No one knew. No one but Meg.

She'd been protecting her family.

Just as she now needed to protect her sister.

Her sister was her priority, her concern. Her father had left them in pain. Lexi was only just getting back on her own feet again.

She couldn't go through with this anymore. Whatever her mum may have wanted to tell him, it was too late. After all, she didn't know him either. He had moved on, embracing religion, something utterly foreign to her. Even her mum hadn't been religious; they had never attended church when they were girls. Their father had never taken them to church either. The question loomed in her mind: was he even a Catholic?

With a forceful kick, she sent a loose stone hurtling into the water, watching it soar through the air before splashing onto a cluster of rocks along the shoreline.

Then there was Angus. His desire to truly know her sent electric shivers through her body. At times, she had been tempted to let her guard down, to trust the growing connection between them, but it always felt like an insurmountable feat.

Their kiss lingered in her thoughts, a moment that defied reason amidst the chaos of her current situation. How had she allowed it to happen? It wasn't just a simple kiss; it was some magnetic force that drew her in, a torrent of emotions she couldn't resist. She had been there, leaning in, her heart racing as his hand grazed her neck. His lips met hers, and it was as if the universe had conspired to create that very moment. It was a swift, passionate exchange, so natural and unbidden that it left her head spinning and her heart aching for more.

The sky darkened overhead, and thunder rumbled ominously. She gazed up just in time for a deluge of rain to drum down upon her. As the sky grew even darker, she pushed forward, finally reaching the outskirts of the village. She embarked on the final leg of her journey to Angus's croft. The once salty sea air had now been replaced by the earthy scent of pine trees lining the road. It was just her, the pounding rain, and the cleansing sensation it brought, washing away her troubling thoughts.

23

LEXI

Lexi's peaceful slumber was rudely interrupted by Henry, the farm's resident rooster, whose relentless squawking pierced the morning air. She half expected to find him perched right outside her window, delivering his wake-up call with all the subtlety of a rock concert.

With a grumble, she reached over and pushed aside the curtains, fully prepared to scold Henry for his audacious intrusion. Yet, what she saw was anything but the usual farmyard scene. Instead, the sky blazed with vibrant shades of pink, casting a warm, golden glow over the distant hills.

"Red sky in the morning, shepherd's warning," her mum used to say. Lexi had always treated these old sayings as quaint relics, never paying them much mind. However, with her mother no longer around, she found herself pondering the significance of these well-worn phrases. Might they be something she'd pass down to her own daughter someday, should she ever have one?

She quickly dressed in a woolly jumper, her denim jacket, and her trusty pair of jeans. Since arriving, she'd rarely worn anything else. Tying her hair up in a ponytail, she tried to look presentable, rubbing away the sleep from her eyes. She hadn't worn make-up in the last few days, her face felt fresh against the crisp morning air and she welcomed the break from her concealer routine, especially with her unpredictable skin acting up. Her former self would be horrified to see her like this. Back in the café days, she wouldn't dare step out without her full make-up armour. Who knew who she might run into? Chris often complimented her beauty, especially when they started serving coffee to the very early risers. But now, looking back, she had always been behind a shield of make-up: some artfully drawn eyebrows, a touch of shimmer on her cheeks, and a daring pink or red lipstick.

After unlocking the hen shed, releasing a chorus of clucks, she skirted around the house and headed for the nursing home.

"Hey, Marky Mark!" Lexi winked and waved to Mark, who was engrossed in a serious conversation with another staff member at the reception desk. He looked up, his eyes bright, and waved her on playfully.

The worn carpet of the hallway gave way to a spacious canteen area, bustling with activity. Several white-haired residents moved about, their movements slow and deliberate, as they sipped tea and nibbled on breakfast at various tables.

"You're early," Rosa, the cook, called out from behind the counter, her black hair pulled tightly into a bun, her face glistening with sweat from the ovens.

"I'm a morning person. Thought I'd see if herself was around," Lexi replied, feeling surprisingly at home after just a few visits.

"Well, if you don't see her, I could use you in the kitchen! Got plenty of dishes that need scrubbing." Rosa chuckled, hands resting on her hips. Lexi rolled her eyes and smiled, sauntering off in the direction of Mrs Archer's room. At the blue door with the tag A. Archer, she knocked twice.

“Come in,” called a cheery voice from within.

Inside, Annabel was standing by the window, bathed in soft morning light. She was in the midst of tying a vibrant yellow scarf around her neck, the fabric complementing her flowing deep blue wool cardigan perfectly. With a satisfied nod, Annabel grabbed her handbag, the leather gleaming in the sunlight.

“Great! Do you think you have everything?” Lexi's initial enthusiasm waned as she immediately regretted her choice to go au naturel today. She couldn't help but notice the effort Annabel had put into her appearance, and at that very moment, she felt Annabel's gaze sweep over her ripped jeans, dishevelled hair, and faded jacket.

“Is that what you’re wearing? We’re going to the … *theatre*!” Annabel whispered the word. Her eyes widened dramatically and moved back to her wardrobe.

“It's only a matinee , and it'll be dark!” Lexi protested.

“Even so …” Annabel pulled out a dark tweed flared coat and held it up, despite Lexi's glum expression. “I think we need something else, too,” she declared, crossing the room to a coat stand adorned with various hats. Her eyes sparkled with determination as she grabbed a black beret and casually tossed it toward Lexi, who leaned against the wall, nibbling on her fingernail.

“It's fine, Annabel,” Lexi began as Mrs Archer helped her into the heavy coat. “I think I’m a bit young for tweed?” She started to protest but then caught a glimpse of herself in the mirror; she couldn't believe how different she looked. “I haven't seen this much tweed since … well, since never.”

Annabel dismissed Lexi's concerns with a wave. “Darling, tweed is timeless. It's like the little black dress of the countryside. Trust me; you're going to turn heads!”

“I don’t really want to turn heads,” Lexi muttered, trailing behind, the words so foreign to her. She loved attention. At least, she used to. As they strolled through the canteen, Rosa and the gang shot them curious glances. Lexi held up her head, focusing on the front door.

"Make sure to bring her back here for dinner, OK?" Mark, holding the front door open for them, teased, a hint of authority under his cheery tone.

"Absolutely, sir!" Lexi saluted with a playful twirl, ushering Annabel towards the bus stop. "This feels like high school mischief, doesn't it?"

Annabel chuckled, her eyes glinting mischievously. "Oh, the thrill of rebellion! I haven't felt this alive in years."

* * *

"She's been doing very well, actually," Mark admitted over the phone late one evening. "She even pitched taking the residents to the theatres in Glasgow. Can you believe it?"

"That's genius!" Lexi cheered over the line. After spending an afternoon with Mrs Archer, she had reluctantly spent the next day away, making sure to dedicate time to Meg after her not-so-subtle hints about her absence.

"I'm not sure about it, though." Mark sounded worried. "There are forms I'd need to check over, and then there's the issue of accommodation …"

Lexi groaned. "Go on, be a rebel – it'll cheer up everyone!"

The theatre escapade had turned into a rollercoaster ride of emotions. Lexi witnessed a baffling play about love and jealousy that left her more confused than a cat at a dog show. But Mrs Archer clung to her like they were conquering Everest together, not lounging in plush velvet chairs. "It was like the Oscars in there, Mark! She cried, she laughed, she practically demanded an encore." Lexi chuckled down the line, her mind swimming with ideas. “Mark, I've been thinking …”

“Oh dear.” He laughed. “Never a good sign!”

“Hey!”

“She has been asking for you – you've made quite the impression. On everyone, as a matter of fact,” Mark said, his voice slightly muffled over the line.

Lexi blushed to herself. The past few days had gone by in a whirlwind, so much so that it was as though she’d known Mark and everyone at the nursing home for years. “She talks about her children often. I wonder if we could arrange something – maybe if I let them know she's asking for them. Or we could plan a surprise visit!”

Mark's response abruptly halted Lexi's idea before it could fully take shape. “No, that won't happen,” he said flatly.

“But surely she would love that?”

“I don't doubt it, Lexi, but we can't get involved in everyone’s personal lives. She's free to call them, text, email, write to them, even!”

She clenched her teeth, her mind echoing Mrs Archer's unsettling words.

My family is being kept away. I know they are.

Annabel mistrusted the staff. Could there be some truth to it? What motive would they have to keep family at bay? She rubbed her eyes, her growing suspicion casting a shadow. She ended the call; her stomach churned with unease. She chewed at her already short fingernail, a sharp pang of discomfort shooting through her.

She still had to complete the journey with Meg and scatter her mother's ashes, but she found herself utterly consumed by the old woman and the nursing home. It wasn't in her nature to idly stand by. A persistent notion gnawed at her, refusing to be ignored. It was as though she was fated to meet Annabel and offer more than a simple outing.

Someone needed her help, and her deep-seated need to assist was impossible to ignore.

24

MEG

Her eyes sparkled with excitement as she bounced in her saddle, her gaze fixed on the endless expanse of the beach stretching out before her. Lexi rode closely behind, her horse's mane whipping in the wind as they galloped along the shoreline. The two gentle stallions had been generously loaned to them for the morning by Iona's sister, Jane, who ran a local riding school. Jane handed over the reins briskly, her attention already drawn to two children on ponies nearby.

"They could use a good run, and I've heard you know what you're doing," Jane said with a no-nonsense tone, before turning her focus back to the young riders. Her short blonde hair framed a ruddy complexion, which Meg considered was due to days spent outside.

Meg had allowed her mind to wander for most of the morning, hoping some thoughts would distract her enough from the fact that Angus and Iona were spending the morning together.

Jane's mention of "business to discuss" had stirred a hint of suspicion in Meg's mind. But then she reminded herself of the simple truth: there was no reason for her to be concerned about Angus. They were free agents, bound by no claims or expectations. He was free to do as he pleased, and Meg refused to let jealousy or insecurity get the better of her.

She urged her steed toward the water's edge. The beach – stretching out for what seemed like endless miles – provided the perfect canvas for her and her spirited mare to race along the shore. The rhythmic thumping of hooves on the wet sand echoed the beat of her heart – a sensation she hadn't felt in years.

Glancing back, she saw Lexi approaching. She pulled on the reins, coaxing her mare to slow down with graceful ease. Guiding her horse into the shallows, she let the cool water lap at its hooves, fond memories of her teenage years flooding back. Riding had been one of the few activities she and her sister had shared.

"It's been too long," Lexi muttered, her teeth clenched with caution as her horse joined Meg's. She wasn't as skilled a rider as her older sister.

"But it comes back, you know. I feel like I was riding just yesterday – it's like riding a bike … only it's a horse!" Meg chuckled.

"You were always the better rider." Lexi admitted defeat, no longer trying to control her horse. It followed Meg's lead, venturing further into the cold sea. Lexi squealed as the water reached her dangling feet over the sides of the saddle. "Make him stop, Meg!" She panicked, and Meg couldn't help but snigger quietly.

"Just pull on the reins, like this!" She demonstrated with ease on her own horse. "It's easy! And you were never worse than me at riding, Lex, honestly. You just gave up before even trying." She watched as her sister followed her instructions. "That's it, now follow us." She led her horse out of the water and onto the soft sand.

"He's just following your horse anyway." Lexi pouted.

After the girls had eventually returned the horses to the stable, with reluctance on Meg's part and what appeared to be relief on Lexi's, they bid farewell to Jane and headed back in the direction of the cottage.

“Iona seems to be getting cosy with Angus. You might have competition,” Lexi said casually.

“Not interested,” Meg replied flatly.

“Are we really doing this again? Why are you so afraid to admit anything, Meg? We won't think any less of you,” Lexi whispered the last few words, making her bristle. Her little sister always knew how to get under her skin by continually prying into her love life, or lack thereof.

“Who's 'we’?” Meg asked.

“Everyone!” Lexi said, wringing her hands, then puckered her lips. “You don't need to be so prim and proper, Megan MacDonald.”

“Can we please drop this subject? I have no intention of 'hooking up' with Angus,” she replied, her cheeks growing hot even in Lexi's presence. Over the past few days, she had often thought about their chaste kiss before the raft race and what might have happened if they hadn't been interrupted. “So, tell me more about this Mark?” Meg casually inquired, hoping her sister would finally provide more details since she had overheard her on the telephone.

Lexi scoffed. “That's not how it works, sis. You don't tell, then I don't tell!” She tapped her nose.

She let the conversation dwindle off, lost in her thoughts about the last few days. Now might be the best time to tell her sister about their father. They were alone on the quiet road back to Angus's, with the sea roaring on one side and soundless forestry on the other. But what could she say? “Oh, remember our father who abandoned us long ago? Well, he's here, and he's a priest! He'll be having a service this morning, let's go! Oh, and remember your birthday? Well, I sent Dad away, and it was my fault he never came back to see us. Surprise!" Meg shivered at the weight of the secrets between them. This trip was turning into the worst holiday of her life, and that was after enduring a spa week in Thailand that ended with her head down the toilet the whole time due to food poisoning.

When she got back to the solitude of her own home – her clean, fresh, home – she was locking the door and not emerging until she had to. The mere thought of returning to the simple life she had in Melbourne, where the rhythm of her days was dictated by her own choices, brought a sense of comfort. The familiar hum of the city, the routine of her job, the cosy evenings in her apartment – it all seemed like a haven compared to the tangled emotions and secrets unravelling in the Scottish countryside.

They turned back onto the last stretch of the beach, with Angus's croft just in sight, perched on the distant hill. Edging closer with every step they took. Time was ticking. Meg could hear it, like the clock on her kitchen wall that seemed to follow her even now.

Lexi's steps were light as she skipped over the soft sand towards the water. A gentle breeze played with her hair as she stooped to pick up a pebble and cast it into the deep. Her gaze fixated on the spot where the stone disappeared beneath the waves. "I think I'm OK about Mum," she said gently, turning to face Meg.

In that stark light, Meg saw their mother looking back at her.

Lexi bit her lip. "Not that I'm glad she died or anything like that," she backtracked. "But I'm at peace with it, you know?" She collected another pebble and threw it into the sea. The gesture made Meg think of Leon at the castle.

"So are we going to continue on with the trip?" Lexi

linked her arm with Meg's. “Scatter the rest of Mum's ashes?” Her wide eyes searched Meg's.

“Sure,” Meg replied simply.

The best outcome would be to leave this place, leave their mother's ashes in Scotland, leave her newly found father, and, above all – considering her tumultuous history with men – retreat from Angus before they crossed a point of no return.

25

LEXI

As Lexi stepped inside, a gust of wind howled through the open door and slammed it shut behind her. She shivered. “I thought it was only autumn! I could swear it’s the Antarctic!”

“Aye, it can be quite cold up here,” Mark replied, signing off paperwork at the reception. His foreign tones had acquired a Scottish lilt, which Lexi found rather adorable.

“But seriously, it's like it's going to snow any minute! At this rate, I'll need to wear another two jumpers and an extra winter coat!” Lexi complained, to which Mark simply chuckled and shook his head.

After a night of mulling things over, spurred on by a chat with Angus, Lexi had had a bit of an epiphany. When Angus mentioned how close he was with his folks and how he always kept an eye on his little troublemakers, it hit her hard. Even though she'd lived in the same city as her mum, she realised she’d hardly made time for her. Now that her mum was gone, it stung even more. The occasional home-cooked meal used to tempt her to swing by, but that was about it. Compared to her sister, who practically had 'world's best daughter' stamped on her forehead, Lexi felt like she'd completely fallen short.

Even though she could never get back the time she wasted with others instead of her mother, she saw a chance for a family to reconnect. Mrs Archer often spoke of her children, and Lexi realised she needed to act. After years of missing out on her own mother's company, she felt compelled to help Mrs Archer reunite with her kids before it was too late. If Mrs Archer wasn't going to contact them, then Lexi would.

She coyly sauntered up to the reception table, perching herself somewhat ungracefully on the paperwork, and accidentally knocked over a cup of coffee.

"Lexi!" Mark's voice boomed as he gathered the now dripping-wet, stained documents.

"Oops." Lexi winced and gritted her teeth. "I hope that was nothing too important?"

"Well, it isn't now!" Mark said in exasperation as he scooped up the soggy papers and placed them on another counter away from Lexi.

"Oh good, only you shouldn't leave your coffee near paperwork if it was. That would be silly." Lexi chuckled.

"What do you want, Miss MacDonald?" Mark said through clenched teeth.

"Oh dear, I really must be in trouble now."

"No, no." Mark sighed, rubbing his forehead. Giving up on the paperwork, he gestured for her to sit in a small wooden chair on the other side of the desk. She clasped her hands, realising they were clammy, and ignored the strange feeling of butterflies in her tummy. She had to broach the subject with Mark. He knew the details of Mrs Archer, and she needed him on her side if she was to get her strategy underway, even if their initial interactions had perhaps started off on the wrong foot.

Lexi began, “I really want to do something special for Mrs Archer, and since I am leaving soon—”

“You're leaving?” Mark locked eyes with her. “I didn't know … I mean, I knew you were just visiting, but we were just getting used to seeing you around.” A frown line appeared on his otherwise smooth face, and Lexi noticed a small freckle beside his eyebrow. His dark eyes, framed by refined eyebrows, examined her intently.

“We can't gatecrash Angus's house anymore. Plus, we're due back in Australia – I need to start …” Lexi paused. What was she going to start? She had impulsively quit her job and didn’t want to go back to the cold house she shared with strangers. Nothing in Melbourne seemed to be calling her home.

She shifted in her chair, under Mark’s gaze. “Anyway, I thought I might contact Mrs Archer's kids,” she continued. “Maybe they don't realise that their mother misses them.”

“I’m sure they don't need someone they don't know telling them that,” Mark began, but he stopped abruptly and sighed. “As lovely as the thought is, we cannot interfere. If Annabel wants to see her children, she can call them herself. There's nothing stopping her.” The corner of his mouth twitched. “It's sweet of you to think about Annabel like this, but as I told you before, we cannot get involved. I cannot get involved with those people again.” He shook his head.

“What do you mean?” Lexi asked quickly, her interest piqued.

“They are best left alone. Come on, let's have a cup of coffee, eh?” He stood up, ending the conversation.

Her mind was buzzing with questions. Had he already contacted them before? Whatever he was hiding, if Mark wasn't going to help, she might be better off pursuing this on her own. She declined his offer and instead went off in search of Mrs Archer.

As she ventured further into the building, she was immediately struck by the stark contrast in temperature. Stepping into the canteen, she was met with a suffocating wave of stifling heat that engulfed her, and her skin prickled uncomfortably. The overpowering scent of industrial-grade disinfectant mingled with the musty odour of old upholstery assaulted her nostrils. Beads of sweat formed on her brow as she hastily shed her jacket, the fabric sticking to her clammy skin. Underneath, she wore a simple tank top, a garment she typically paid little attention to. However, in this environment, she couldn't help but clutch the jacket close to her chest.

With each visit, she noticed something new in disrepair; the building was falling apart at the seams. Dark damp patches clung to the ceiling, and the door handle to the canteen hung by a few loose screws. She couldn't imagine sending a loved one to somewhere so sad and crumbling around their ears. Mrs Archer shouldn't have to live in a place like this; no one should.

She waved to Rosa, the dinner lady, who leaned against the kitchen hatch, eagerly waiting for her daily catch-up on the outside world, or so she claimed. Lexi, being a tourist and knowing no one in the area, couldn't provide the local news Rosa sought, but she tried her best to accommodate her. However, before Lexi could respond, a sudden eruption of cheers from the corner of the canteen startled her. She turned to see Mrs Archer with three men, all engrossed in watching a technicolour musical on TV.

A man in a wheelchair tapped his hand on the armrest. "Look at these actors; they sing, they dance – that was talent."

"Pure talent!" His friend, dressed in a smart tweed jacket and younger than Mrs Archer, nodded in agreement. "Give me Gene Kelly any day!"

"Or Fred Astaire!" Mrs Archer chimed in.

"I'm rather partial to Ginger Rogers myself!" scoffed the man in the wheelchair, and playfully nudged Mrs Archer on the arm.

"Of course you are, Jim!" Mrs Archer shook her head.

"But really, nowadays, it's all about the prettiest?" He scoffed, his eyes blinking at the TV screen.

"Well, I never, that's truly an old-person thing to say if ever I heard it!" Mrs Archer declared, her tone mock-horrified.

"Well, it's true! And if you didn't notice – we're all old here, Anna!" He laughed.

"Speak for yourself, you old codger!" Mrs Archer raised her eyebrow, folding her arms.

The man in the tweed jacket sat upright, admiring Mrs Archer. "I'm sure you were a good dancer, probably still are, judging by those lovely legs," he said with a smile, making Lexi shudder at the compliment. But Mrs Archer positively glowed, then she spotted Lexi and waved. "Lexi, love!"

"Are you ready to go?" She moved toward the group, having planned an afternoon walk in the nearby woods and a cup of coffee in the village café.

"Yes, I just need to get my coat." Mrs Archer began to slowly rise.

Lexi gestured for the elderly woman to remain seated and went in search of her bedroom, throwing a backwards glance at the man in the tweed suit.

"And my hat too! The yellow one, please." She waved jovially.

When she let herself into Mrs Archer's room and collected the requested items, she noticed a small address book on the cream dresser, beside some make-up and a black gem necklace. She bit her lip and casually skimmed through the pages with one hand. She caught sight of her reflection looking back from the mirror ahead, then noticed a couple of small photographs tucked into the mirror's edge.

One photo showed a little girl in a ballerina tutu, hair pinned up, arms stretched in mid-pirouette. The photo above that featured a lanky teenage boy wearing a suit too big for him. His shy smile and stance were the complete opposite of the woman who stood next to him. Annabel, hand on hip, was wearing a red and black dress with a flamboyant red ruffled hat, poised next to him. She looked in her prime, oozing charm and with a captivating aura that Lexi could still see in her.

She found the familiar names in the address book and copied them down, along with another name that had been mentioned to her before, although she wasn't altogether sure who it was. She couldn't let this opportunity slip, especially when she knew she wouldn't be in the country much longer. There was no time to waste.

* * *

Mrs Archer looked out the window with quiet contentment, lost in her own thoughts. Lexi shoved her hand into her coat, pulling out a deep red leaf. She had collected all manner of different-coloured fallen leaves and stashed them in her pocket, unsure of what exactly she had planned to do with them.

Mrs Archer squinted at Lexi's wristwatch, suddenly breaking out of her daydream. "Is that the time? I must go home soon!" she said with urgency, taking a gulp of her coffee.

"Hey, calm down – I'm sure it can wait another ten minutes, whatever it is," Lexi reassured her.

Mrs Archer wrinkled her nose and raised her eyebrows, the expression reminding Lexi of the old 1960s comedy shows her mother used to have on in the mornings. "Maybe you're right; I could miss the beginning …" The old woman tried to hide her disappointment.

"What's the rush? What are you doing?" Lexi leaned over the table, intrigued. Annabel had never wanted to be back at the nursing home sooner than she needed to be.

"I have a schedule to keep," she said, tight-lipped, then sighed fully at Lexi's inquisitive look. "Well, if you must know, Hamlet is on the TV, and well … I said I would watch it."

"With the old codgers?" Lexi chuckled in surprise.

"I presume you mean Jim and … I forget the other man."

"You mean to tell me you've already forgotten the handsome man that was with you?" Lexi pouted her lips suggestively. "Especially after his nice remark about your pins."

Mrs Archer smoothed her forehead with her fingers, then traced the line around her face. Lexi immediately saw she had struck a nerve and was all the more fascinated. Mrs Archer raised her eyebrows with indifference, an act that Lexi certainly was not buying. But she thought better than to make fun of the old woman.

"They seem to be my friends now. We appear to have the same interests … who am I to judge?" She chuckled, and Lexi saw a sparkle in her eyes that she hadn't seen before.

* * *

Lexi stretched out on her bed, staring at the scribbles on the piece of paper in her hand. Her heart thumped so hard she could hear the blood rushing in her ears. Why was she so nervous?

It didn't matter; she had made up her mind, and now was the time to do it. It was like ripping off a bandage, she instructed herself and quickly dialled the numbers on her phone before another distracting voice invaded her thoughts.

"Hello?" a man's deep voice answered.

"Hi, my name is Lexi … um, sorry to trouble you. I just wondered if you are David?" Her pulse raced.

"Yes?" the man said cautiously.

"Great … um, I was calling, um—" She wasn't sure where to start. It had sounded better in her head, but the words were stuck there with no intention of coming out.

"Look, if this is a sales call – I'm not interested in whatever you've got to sell. Good—"

"No, no, no! Please don't hang up," Lexi replied quickly. "I know your mum, Annabel Archer."

She was met with silence.

"Hello? David, are you there?"

"You mean Mrs Adams?"

Lexi's brow furrowed in confusion. "Mrs Adams? Uh, no, I mean Annabel Archer, your mother."

Silence lingered for a moment before David sighed. "Well, that was her name before she remarried several times," he said bitterly. "Who did you say you were?"

The conversation wasn't going exactly according to plan. Lexi panicked. Why hadn't she come up with a script or something? "I'm Lexi," she blurted out, trying to explain. "Your mother and I … we're … we're friends!"

"And she asked you to call me?" David sighed a second time, his impatience to leave the conversation becoming glaringly obvious.

"Well no, not exactly. But she said recently how much she missed you and your sister … so I … I just thought I'd get in touch and—"

"Let me stop you there," David said curtly. "My sister and I see our mother. We have busy lives, as our mother well knows. So thank you very much, Alex." Lexi bristled. "We will see Mother when we have time," he said in a sarcastic tone and ended the call abruptly.

Lexi sat in stunned silence. Had she overstepped? Disappointment and frustration lingered over her. This David turned out to be distant and indifferent, killing any hopes of a warm family reunion Lexi had hoped for. She had messed up everything. The chance for Mrs Archer to reconnect with her children was lost. Did they not realise they had only a short time left with their mother, something Lexi wished she still had. If she knew her mother wanted to see her, she'd drop everything – just for one last moment with her. She blinked back tears, refusing to let her own emotions overshadow the task at hand. Determined, she glanced at the hastily scribbled numbers and took a deep breath before dialling the next one.

"Hello?" an older lady's voice answered.

Lexi was confused; this didn't sound like a thirty-year-old daughter of Mrs Archer's. She peered at her scrawl; she had dialled the wrong number. Arse! What should she say? She chastised herself once again for not planning her speech. If this had been Meg, she would have drafted a script for each person and highlighted the points she wanted to make! Now was not the time to think of Meg! Lexi gritted her teeth.

"Hello. I'm a friend of Annabel's," Lexi began, testing the waters.

"Annabel?" the lady croaked. "Is she OK?"

"Yes, yes, she's fine," Lexi rushed to reassure. "It's just that I've noticed she has been a bit lonely."

"I haven't heard from Annabel for so long," she said wistfully. "I rarely hear from my sister. She's always doing something, always busy."

She was her sister! Lexi's heart leaped with excitement. "She is quite a vibrant person—"

"Oh, yes. She made us proud. Such a firecracker, even

when we were little … I have contacted her over the years, but don't hear much …"

"I'm sorry to hear that," Lexi said awkwardly. "All I know is she wants to reach out to family, but I think she might be too stubborn …" She regretted the words as they left her mouth.

"Hmmm, a bit stubborn alright." The woman chuckled.

"And I thought, if I contacted you – perhaps you might visit her?"

The woman murmured something Lexi didn't pick up on, then. Some words like "A long time ago".

"I'm sure whatever it was, it's water under the bridge," Lexi said, without knowing the details. It didn't matter. After all, they were sisters, and surely they must talk.

"Thanks for your call, Lexi. Annabel is very lucky to have someone like you looking out for her. But I spent too long chasing her; she knows where I am. Bye now." She hung up.

She flopped back onto the bed, screaming into her pillow. The universe was reminding her of her supposed incompetence just when she had hoped to leave things better. Seemed like she couldn't do anything right. And now with them on the verge of leaving, she guessed she'd be following Meg back to Australia like a lost lamb. Thankfully, her sister was unaware of Lexi's recent escapades; otherwise, she'd have shared her unfiltered opinions.

She sighed, gazing out of the window as the pink sky surrendered to dusk. In the quiet room, shadows danced on the walls as she replayed the conversations in her mind again.

The solitude wrapped around her like a suffocating cocoon, nudging her to confront the messy tale of Mrs Archer's family and her own life, dangling precariously. As the room plunged into darkness, she was left grappling with the questions echoing in her mind.

26

MEG

Meg hovered outside the cottage in the chilly breeze. She couldn't keep her distance from Angus without it starting to look odd, so she seized the chance to divert her thoughts away from her father and her complicated love life. She called the Melbourne office and spoke to the receptionist, who, to her surprise, couldn't seem to recognise her. With a flushed face, Meg absentmindedly twirled a strand of her hair as she rattled off her regular desk location, her boss's name, and even her tradition of bringing in cakes every Tuesday.

"Sorry about that." Mr Simons' voice softened, and Meg could almost picture the reassuring smile on his face as he said, "Poor Patricia had a bit of a mental block earlier, but of course, she knows who you are, Megan."

"That's OK, Paul," Meg said, still not entirely comfortable addressing her boss by his first name, even if he had encouraged it for many years.

"What can I do for you, Megan? Oh, how's Ireland?" he asked warmly. "You know, I think I have roots over there. I wish I paid more attention to what my late father told me."

"Yes, very good," Meg replied, pausing. "But I'm actually in Scotland."

"Aren't they virtually the same place?"

"No, they're quite different." Meg resisted the urge to explain that they were entirely different countries, surprised that her boss, as intelligent as he was, didn't seem to have a grasp of basic geography.

"I thought I'd check if there's any work you need me to do," Meg said, twirling a strand of her hair. "I have internet, I could do some jobs remotely for you."

Mr Simons gasped. "Haven't you got enough to do over there than work?"

Meg welcomed the chance to escape her current situation with work, immersing herself in numbers to avoid thoughts of Angus and their brief, taunting kiss. She willed the memory away with all her might.

"I just thought maybe you might be needing an extra pair of hands, especially since we have the new contracts from Addison and Sons. I know I left at the worst moment, especially after gaining new clients, so this could be the perfect time to dive into new processes."

"Megan, you're a treasure. Take your leave, enjoy yourself!" Mr Simons chuckled. "You might as well extend your holiday too, I know you've taken little time off since you became an employee; we're all under control here. Nothing to worry about."

Meg fidgeted with the hem of her coat. "Are you sure? I really don't mind?"

"Not at all, get away with you. Enjoy yourself. Oh, and have a Guinness for me!" he said jovially. She was about to correct him again that she wasn't in Ireland, but her boss hung up before she could.

She perched next to the hen house, watching the hens eagerly peck at the grass for insects. The sun dipped behind the hills, leaving her in a gloomy haze. She needed to confront her issues and regain control. Normally, she excelled at this, but the weight of her current problems had left her paralysed. She herded the hens back inside the coop, a task she had become quite skilled at, even naming several of the distinctive chickens and sheep.

"Now it's your turn, Isabella." Meg coaxed a white, fluffy-feathered hen attempting to flee, guiding her to the shed with practised ease.

Returning to the house, she was enveloped by the warmth and delicious smells in the air. As she removed her wellies and placed them by the door she could hear the rhythmic clatter of utensils against the pan, and Angus tossed the contents in a steaming wok. She braced herself for what she might say, but her words were stuck in her throat. Should she mention the kiss? Her stomach churned as he smiled at her, his checked shirtsleeves rolled up to reveal his strong arms. Her legs turned to jelly.

Lexi burst into the room, her denim jacket buttoned up, and her thick scarf wrapped tightly around her neck. She pulled off her bobble wool hat. "So, what are we having tonight?" She rubbed her hands together with relish. Meg, delighted to see her sister, was almost tempted to hug her for the timely interruption.

"I don't know! It smells delicious, though. I could get used to having a personal cook," Meg said with a cheerfulness that took her by surprise.

Lexi produced a bottle of red wine. "Stopped off at the village shop. They had red wine and white wine to pick from. Like actually 'red wine' or 'white wine'. No variations of grape," she explained, opening the bottle and taking a tentative sip, before shrugging and locating some glasses.

"Are we celebrating something?" Meg asked, surprised that her sister had put her hand in her pocket for anything.

The last time had been at the airport when Lexi had offered to buy her some chewing gum.

"No." Lexi shook her head. "At least I don't think so! Unless you both have something to tell me?" Her smug grin met Meg's horrified expression. But she decided not to rise to the bait.

"No, nothing new – only maybe this could be our last hurrah since it's our last night at Angus's," Meg explained, giving Angus a warm smile.

"Eh?" Lexi gulped down more red wine and coughed. "Already?"

"I told you this days ago! I said we were leaving tomorrow, and you just said, 'OK, sure, whatever!'"

At times, she could throttle her sister. It was up to her to plan everything. If they relied on Lexi to do it, they would never leave. "Lexi, we are going, OK?" Meg felt her temper rising; all she wanted was to leave. What would happen if they bumped into their father at the local village shop? Would her sister even recognise him? It was a chance she didn't want to take.

"OK, OK!" Lexi put her hands up, placing her glass on the kitchen table. "Where are we staying?"

Meg relaxed her shoulders. This was good – Lexi wouldn't fight her on this. They would finally leave. "I haven't decided, but there are two B and Bs further up the coast that seem to have vacancies. I thought we'd play it by ear, see how far we get tomorrow, and I'll call them up."

"Or …" Lexi's eyes widened, her lips pressed tightly together. "We could do something really different. Why don't we go bothying!" Lexi cheered, picking up her glass again.

"What do you know about bothying?" Angus's smirk filled Meg with anxiety about what might be asked of them.

Lexi sat upright. "I heard some men talking about it in the shop. They bought a fishing net and said they were sailing to some place with a name I can't pronounce … and that they were going to do a trip. Bothying!" Lexi's hopeful face looked up at Meg's, and then she crossed her arms like a petulant child before Meg could answer. "I want to go. Let's go bothying!"

Angus laughed and shook his head in wonder but kept his opinions to himself. He spooned out the food, and they all gathered around the kitchen table.

"Well?" Lexi eventually asked while twirling hot noodles on her fork.

"We need to go up north; we have little time left to go bothying," Meg said, sipping the wine and suppressing a gag at the taste of a mouldy basement.

"Don't be a stick in the mud, Meg. Let's do something fun and random!" Lexi insisted.

"We *are* doing something random!" Meg retorted.

"Oh, please, don't say that deciding on what hotel we'll use tomorrow is an act of spontaneity."

Meg actually did mean that, but she wasn't going to admit it now. "What do you call this whole trip? It's been spontaneous. We're spending our holiday in our tour guide's house because you had to fall in love with a scoundrel who was thieving all over the Highlands!" Meg roared. Seeing the hurt look on Lexi's face, she stopped herself from saying any more. "I'm sorry, I don't know why I said that," she stammered and glanced at Angus, seeking some support, but he was fully absorbed in his meal.

"You've been edgy for a while, Meg. What's happened? You're usually so … together." Lexi's red eyes narrowed in her sister's direction.

"I'm fine. I just want to get on with the trip, Lex."

"Yeah, sure, after we've gone bothying?" Lexi persisted.

"Bloody hell, Christ – OK!" Meg snapped. "We'll go bothying! We'll go bothying!"

Lexi, pleased with herself at winning yet another point in their private game, stood up and rummaged in the fridge for juice.

"What's bothying?" Meg whispered to Angus.

"Oh, it's like camping – off the grid stuff." Angus smiled broadly. "It's really fun."

"I'm sorry I asked," Meg mumbled to herself in defeat.

* * *

The cottage was freezing the next morning. Meg threw the curtains open to see that they were still in an icy darkness, the sun hiding behind the hill. With very little time to get ready, the girls were soon standing as an audience to Angus packing the car.

"Surely it's a bit early to be going already?" Meg shifted her weight from one foot to the other. Even wearing a thick coat, the icy wind made its way into every nook and cranny, chilling her to the bone.

"No, it's not!" Angus chuckled. "It's a good idea to get out of here sharpish. I've got a big day planned for you girls!" He clapped his hands together with vigour. "Don't you have daylight savings over there in Melbourne?"

"Oh no, the clocks went back!" Meg scrutinised her phone for its lack of updates.

"Yep, that's us getting into winter now," he said brightly and threw in the last of the bags in the back of the van.

"Darkness? More darkness?" Lexi moaned. "More cold too?" She blew on her hands and screwed up her nose.

"This was your idea, Lex – remember! You wanted to do something *spontaneous*," Meg snapped.

Lexi shrugged. "It seemed like a good idea yesterday. But now, it's cold … and dark," she repeated as she squinted at the faint hue above the hill.

Angus scoffed, rolling his eyes to the heavens. "Oh, bloody hell, girls, enough of the whingeing. Get in the van; that's all you need to do!" Sarcastically, he bowed and opened the van door with a flourish.

Heading towards the most westerly point on the mainland, as advised by Angus during their journey, the roads steadily narrowed. Anticipation settled in Meg's stomach. What would happen if another car approached?

Lexi, engrossed in her phone in the back seat, returned to her usual antics with a swipe. Meg inwardly let out a sigh of relief; they were moving on, away from her father. All she had to do was keep open-minded for the next day, letting go of negative thoughts. Easier said than done, she mused and snapped another photo with her phone. The landscape was barren and seemed to stretch as far as the eye could see. There was something about it that moved her; it was both eerie and beautiful.

They came to the end of the road, where a white lighthouse stood on the cliff edge. Parking the van, they followed Angus with quiet anticipation. Down a rough path carved into the hill by centuries of sheep wanderings, they walked around a small pebble beach. Turning a corner, they discovered a young man and three kayaks.

"Hey, Callum!" Angus saluted and patted the man on the back.

Callum, a sturdy figure with the build of a rugby player, stood confidently. His nut-brown hair tousled in the breeze, and his attractive features lit up with a warm, reassuring smile. "As instructed – three kayaks at your disposal, Gus!" he said, glancing at the newcomers with curiosity.

"Hey! It's Angus in front of the ladies, mate," Angus muttered.

"Oh, I see – are you trying to impress these lovely lasses?

I should've known. If only they knew you back in the day." Callum chuckled.

"Oh, I'd love to know what Angus was like." Lexi leaned closer to Callum in that casually flirtatious manner Meg knew all too well.

Callum raised his hands. "I'm sorry, looks like I'm sworn to secrecy – can't break the code. Plus – he's a hard man on the field, and I don't want to be beaten to a pulp!" Callum nudged Angus playfully. "Anyway, sports aside – where are you planning to go?"

"I thought we'd paddle over to Tildarn old church ruin, park up, and head on foot through the glen to that bothy by the old train tracks." Angus looked up to the fluffy white clouds. "Hopefully, the weather holds up!"

"I know it well – take the odd punters there if the weather's good too. A bit remote, not in the tourist books, so a nice little secret." He tapped his nose to Lexi, who looked all the more transfixed with her new acquaintance. "Well, I better get on, nice to meet you, ladies." He smiled, shook Angus's hand, and headed back up the hill to the lighthouse.

"Well, well, well, who knew we'd see a dish like that on a remote beach." Lexi's eyes followed Callum until he was a dot on top of the hill. "What's his story, Angus, single?"

"Lexi!" Meg groaned. "Seriously, you can't get your mind off men!"

"Whatever for?" Lexi blinked in disbelief. "There's nothing wrong with keeping my eyes open – you never know where that special love of your life will be. He could be on a sprawling beach with dreamy dark eyes and luscious lips." She crossed her arms, her voice low. "At least I'm not too afraid to follow my heart." She cast her eye over to Angus, who had disengaged from the conversation and with a focused expression was meticulously inspecting each kayak, his weathered hands running over their smooth surfaces.

"That big love could be right in front of you," Lexi whispered.

Meg could have pulled her sister's plaits there and then like she used to do when they were little. "Meg pushed me!" Lexi would bellow, crying to their mother, if their game of hide and seek spiralled out of control, as it often did when the two sisters played together.

Happy with the equipment, Angus whistled through his teeth, glancing again at the sky above. "Well, I don't know about luscious lips, but I'm sorry, Lexi,' he said. 'Callum is very much smitten. Back with his high school sweetheart, and a nice lass at that. She owns a clothes shop in the town over; you girls should check it out if you have any time left."

Lexi's eyebrow twitched with both disappointment and disgust. "I think not," she mouthed to Meg when Angus's back was turned.

The kayaking turned out to be much more enjoyable than Meg had anticipated. Paddling silently under low clouds reflected like a mirror beneath them made them feel as if they were floating from one fluffy cloud to the next. Meg followed Angus, watching the back of his head move side to side, scanning the shoreline and then gazing out to the horizon. If she were to compare him to the man she had first met in Edinburgh, she would swear they were different people. His uptight and gruff demeanour had added years to him, but now, his relaxed shoulders and smiling eyes that found her even over the still water made her pick up the pace just to be near him.

She wondered about life as a local here, exploring the land. Despite missing elements from home, they paled in comparison to her new surroundings.

Was this what had attracted her father to this area?

She secretly wanted to see more, and something about that frightened her …

27

ANGUS

Angus waded back into the water to help the girls out of their kayaks. He pulled the boats up over the grassy bank, hiding them in the bracken. Bundling the life jackets together and concealing them from view, he organised the girls and set off for the next leg of their journey. The wind had picked up, whipping around them as they trekked through the glen. Small mounds rose and fell around them, and the occasional wild stag could be seen in the distance.

"What are these?" Meg pointed to a stack of rocks, her inquisitive eyes examining the spectacle.

"Cairns." Angus nodded. He appreciated Meg's interest; not much escaped without her wanting to know more. Lexi, on the other hand, was on her phone, mostly just searching for a signal. Angus smiled; Meg shared his curiosity. With each passing day, he discovered more of her personality traits that he warmed to. He chuckled at her blank expression. "These marked an old path, guiding communities carrying their deceased for burial."

Meg's horrified expression prompted him to explain further. "See the island we passed in the kayaks? That's a graveyard, a holy isle. People would walk for miles, carrying their dead, the cairns marking their journey, where a boat would finally carry them to their final resting place."

"Can we go to the isle?" Lexi brightened. "I love graveyards!"

"I'd rather not. There are too many graves there; they couldn't bury any more people." As much as Angus wished he were a cosmopolitan man, a significant part of him remained a superstitious Scot. "I don't want to stand on anyone's grave," he said quietly.

Lexi squinted up at Angus in wonder, then scoffed. "You had me there for a minute. It's not as if they can feel you standing on them."

"No, maybe not, but it's a matter of respect. If you don't respect these things, you could unwittingly become involved in something complicated." He scratched his jaw. He struggled to explain this concept to people who hadn't grown up with the shared stories he'd absorbed as a boy. And that island had many tales tied to it.

"But Edinburgh had graveyards, we visited some there," Lexi pointed out, her brow furrowed. Meg remained silent, but Angus noticed her face paling.

"You can't honestly be that superstitious, Angus? That's a bit silly for a man of your age," Lexi said, blinking as she scrutinised him, her gaze fixed on him like he was some tropical bird.

"You grew up with fairy stories, right? But your mother sugar-coated them. Presented them as happily-ever-afters for little girls. That is not a fairy story. True fairy stories are not sweet. They are a warning. There is so much more meaning behind them than most people believe." He kicked a loose stone. "For instance, if anyone saw a banshee, they'd run from her. Her wails or screams served as a warning of impending death in a family. And if you came upon The Wild

Hunt raging through the glen, led by a headless horseman, it meant disaster, war, or death. Fairy stories are so much more than love; they are a guide. Love stories are all very well, but there's darkness in everything, and light. But your mother wanted to keep you safe, I get it, but it wouldn't have hurt you to be a little more cautious."

"Please don't bring our mother into this," Lexi bristled. "She saw beauty in the world, and in people."

"Yes, and that's a lovely way to be. But you need to be wary, Lexi." He grimaced. "Life is not smooth; not everyone is kind. A lot of people try to get what they can from you. I would've thought you'd have realised that by now? After Leon, and what your ex did."

"How dare you! I can mind my own battles!" Lexi threw her hands down by her side, standing tall.

"Well, you may think that – but it seems you can't, and other people get dragged into your problems too!" Angus glanced at Meg. "I said I didn't want to give Leon a ride; I knew he wasn't good from the start. But you wouldn't listen."

Lexi stormed off, her face flushed.

Meg called after her but quickly sighed and gave up, watching Lexi's blonde hair disappear behind a large boulder. "You can't blame that on Lexi; I was fooled by him too," she said gently.

He watched Lexi melt into the bracken behind them. "Bugger, I didn't mean it." He backtracked, turning back, about to follow her.

Meg touched his arm gently. "If I know Lexi, she'd prefer a little time out right now." She smiled weakly.

"I'm sorry, Meg. That was uncalled for. I don't know why I said that."

She shrugged. "I know why you said it. I know you weren't being unkind."

"I can't leave her like that."

"She'll follow. She wouldn't dare stay in a place like this by herself, particularly after you mentioned a headless horseman!" She smiled.

He rubbed the back of his neck, pacing. He knew he should apologise – his mother had always taught him that, especially when he hadn't meant to hurt someone. He saw Lexi almost like a little sister, as much as a lone child could imagine what having a sibling might be like. But her real sister should know what was best. He had already stepped on toes and didn't want to do it twice in five minutes. With a shrug, he marched onward. "You don't believe me either?"

Meg pressed her lips together, appearing to consider the question. "No, not when it comes to fairy stories. But I understand your meaning, and I agree – they were symbolic, to educate kids before they went off into the world. It makes sense."

"Do I sound a bit silly to you, also?" he asked, faltering on a loose stone, then kicking it out of his way.

"No, Angus," she said quietly. "I'd have thought you'd know that." She kept up with him, yet her eyes remained on the uneven ground.

"I'm sorry, Meg. I was lost in my own world there." He sighed, slowing his pace. "It's just funny, I hadn't thought of something in a while – and then Lexi reminded me of something … someone." He let the words come, and hoped his emotions wouldn't betray him. Something in Lexi's manner made him think of Claudia. The slight ridicule in her voice. He hadn't noticed it until now.

Meg nodded, casting her attention back to Lexi's frame some distance behind them. With her hands in her pockets, she navigated the uneven path, intermittently dodging puddles.

Angus regarded her for a moment before speaking. "You are pretty straight, Meg."

"What do you mean? I'm not a lesbian, if that's what you're implying!" Meg responded with a hint of alarm.

Amidst the frosty atmosphere left by Lexi, Angus burst into laughter. His posture immediately relaxed as he hooted through gasps. "That's not what I meant, but I must say I'm relieved to hear that." He wiped his eyes, still chuckling. He marvelled at how Meg could be utterly serious one moment and unexpectedly playful the next. It was a side of her he found increasingly captivating. "What I meant is that you know who you are. Take it as a compliment; what you see is what you get with you."

"Well, I'm not entirely sure that's a compliment," she replied dryly.

"It is, trust me." He briefly placed his hand on her arm in reassurance. "Some people spend their lives unsure of anything, following everyone else."

She sidestepped a larger puddle on the path, skirting around the edge of the murky water before rejoining.

Feeling more open than he had in months, he found himself sharing more than he usually would. Meg's unjudgemental presence next to him made it easier to speak. "You know, there's something about this place, and your company, that makes it easier to talk."

She looked up at him, curiosity and warmth in her eyes, and he continued, encouraged by her silent support. "I had a girlfriend, a partner named Claudia. She was an associate from another firm when we met. You could say it was an instant attraction," he began, then pressed his lips together in contemplation. He glanced back at Lexi, who trailed behind, absorbed in picking heather at her own pace. "We moved in together, and I was planning to propose. I was just searching for the perfect ring."

He scratched his head, glancing over at Meg. "Sorry, this may not be the conversation you were looking for."

“No, please continue … if you'd like,” Meg said gently.

“It took me a while to find the ring. Claudia was very sure of her style – her taste. I knew that when I stumbled upon the right ring, I'd recognise it.” His voice softened. “Turns out she was quite certain about her style, but her feelings toward me were far less so. I should have realised it when she expressed her desire to live in the Highlands with me, near my parents – yet when we began to make it a reality, a house found, she pulled out of it. She said she didn't want to live in the countryside after all.” He gritted his teeth, the familiar sensation in the pit of his stomach when he thought of his heartbreak. “In the end, I had to break it off. There's nothing worse in a relationship than when you doubt the other person, doubt yourself.” He couldn’t believe how freely the words came. He didn’t even know he had been feeling this way. He hadn’t uttered a word to his parents or even Jake. But it was natural, being this close to Meg and telling her everything. “It's like you're reaching, and they're settling, always with an eye looking elsewhere.”

“I'm sorry, Angus,” she replied, her eyes downcast.

“Don't be. If I had ignored the signs and continued to deceive myself, I'd still be in that situation.”

“Is that why you came up here?”

He nodded. His parents had been thrilled to know their only son was coming home, with hopes of grandchildren on the way. “We had put an offer on a house. She said she loved it, and we could raise goats and a family there. I genuinely believed it all.” He scratched his head, again surprised by how easily the words poured out of him. “When it didn’t happen … I came to see how much I wanted that life – so I couldn't forget. Then the health scare happened, and it finally compelled me to make the journey.”

“It was meant to be, Angus,” Meg reassured him. “People

weave in and out of your life. The most important thing is to stay true to yourself, and happiness will follow."

"Are you happy, Meg?" Angus needed to know. It hadn't been his intention to bare his soul like this, but he wanted to understand Meg's perspective. There was something beneath her exterior that both intrigued and gave him pause. "After that man left you to go to the other side of the world, were you happy with the outcome?"

She opened her mouth, her expression one of such shock that he stopped walking abruptly. "I'm sorry, that didn't come out right. I love speaking to you, but sometimes, I feel a bit tongue-tied around you, and what I do manage to say comes across as harsh. It's none of my business. I apologise for asking." He cringed inwardly, feeling more ridiculous than he had in a long time. It reminded him of the crush he used to have on his English teacher, Ms Levers. And, just like Meg, she would look at him with the same sympathetic eyes, as if he were a misbehaving puppy rather than a lad with real feelings.

"Hey, wait up!" Lexi's voice interrupted their conversation as she ran toward them, waving her arms. Her hair fell loosely around her face, and her nose was pink from the cold.

Angus observed the subtle relaxation in Meg's tense features upon seeing her sister. Perhaps, he thought, what he felt toward Meg was merely a one-sided sentiment.

"Are you OK?" Meg asked her with concern.

"Yeah," she said with a small smile.

Angus absorbed Meg's gentle calmness and the loving nature she showed her sister – one he wasn't so sure was returned to her. Her kindness shone, but there was so much more beneath the surface. All he wanted was to speak with her, truly speak, and get to the bottom of things. He knew there was more to her than she allowed him to see, and still it didn't waver his interest. He wanted to know more.

Reluctantly, he tore his attention from Meg and turned to Lexi. She stood by Meg's side, looking like a little girl. What he had said hadn't come from malice but, dare he think it, love. But what could he offer this young woman in the twenty-first century? He couldn't offer her protection, but he felt a deep connection. He gazed at her almost innocent look, much like a child who, after some moments, had completely forgotten their previous quarrel.

"I am very sorry for how I spoke to you, Lex," he said and held out his hand. "Please forgive me?"

Ignoring the formal gesture, Lexi looped her arm through his instead, and silently they walked on together.

28

MEG

The three continued along the path in silence. The gloomy, dark afternoon light enveloped them, obscuring their surroundings. Angus, with a fishing rod on his back, stopped by the water's edge. Skilfully assembling the pole, he tied a bright red and yellow fly hook to the line, the only colours standing out in the encroaching darkness. He cast the line swiftly, reeled it in, and repeated the process back and forth with ease – a rhythmic dance of angling.

Lexi and Meg perched on a rock, watching intently.

Lexi muttered, "We should've brought some food. I could really go for a packet of biscuits!"

Angus shot Lexi a stern look. "Quiet. You'll scare the fish away!" he scolded, then returned his focus to his fishing.

"At this rate, we'd be better off trying to catch fish with our hands; it might be quicker," Lexi scoffed.

Angus narrowed his eyes in her direction.

"Or maybe we'll have to resort to cannibalism – Meg, you've got the biggest bum, we might have to sacrifice you to save the rest of us."

"I'll have you know that I wouldn't let you anywhere near my rear end, even to save your life!"

"That's just mean – I'm your little sister, and you wouldn't save my life?" Lexi protested.

Meg shook her head and laughed. "You had a huge breakfast a few hours ago, and you devoured two packets of chips on the journey – one of them mine!"

Angus hooted with amusement, his hands gripping the fishing rod. He reeled it in quickly, engaged in a battle of wills with the fish until it finally surfaced.

Meg gazed at the sky, where ominous clouds gathered, growing darker with each passing moment. The air felt heavy; a storm was looming. The dark loch evoked memories of her mother's stories – tales of a kelpie that haunted a quiet loch, assuming the guise of a handsome man to lure lost young maidens. Upon contact, the man would vanish, revealing the sinister kelpie beneath, dragging the innocent maiden to her watery demise. She envisioned sitting by a fire outside their Australian home on a cold winter's night, telling ghost stories. However, it was the image of her father's slight figure that lingered in her memory, sipping hot chocolate and keeping her close, under a blanket during the more unsettling parts of the tales. No Lexi, or her mother. Just the two of them. Could it be an old fable designed to caution women against trusting men? Was her father warning her from a young age? She bitterly dismissed the thought.

After a sizeable catch, Angus stowed his gear and urged them forward.

"I don't trust this weather – let's hurry!" he declared, striding forward with determination. Lightning flashed. Thunder roared. The sisters hurried to keep up. Angus pointed to a small stone building a few hundred yards ahead, nestled among trees and ferns. They skirted around a much larger loch and reached the door just as a deluge fell upon them, bringing rain and hailstones. Lexi slammed the door shut behind them, and they were greeted by a cold stone floor and a simple wooden bunk bed. The dim, empty space was far from a warm welcome in the face of the extreme weather outside, and Meg's heart sank. They were to spend the night in this cold, damp room. She tried not to let her disappointment show on her face, but her expression mirrored Lexi's equally downcast demeanour. Angus rummaged around in a cupboard, then cheered when he found a pot.

Striking a match, he ignited a fire, setting kindling in place and patiently awaiting the flames to embrace the wood. "Not a bad spot, girls – they left wood and equipment! I've been to a few where there's nothing!"

Lexi and Meg exchanged a glance, standing awkwardly as Angus got to work. He unrolled sleeping bags, laid out a yoga mat, and positioned a tin kettle over the growing flames. Kneeling by the fire, he skilfully tended to it. Meg couldn't help but smile; he was at home in this rustic setting.

"You must have been at the top of your Boy Scouts class?" she asked, removing her wet coat and boots.

"Not at all!" He snorted. "That's what you city kids do to give your parents a night off. You forget I was brought up here," he said with a hint of humour. "One of the first things my dad showed me was how to make a fire."

"What, before teaching you how to ride a bike?" She wrinkled her nose, a playful smirk spreading across her face.

"Make fun all you like. But it's a useful skill; it serves you well in life. I don't see any of you rushing to get stuck in!"

The fire crackled, and the flames began to displace the damp chill. Lexi and Meg knelt down, savouring the warmth, their admiration for Angus growing as he prepared tea. Meg's hand brushed against his leg as he handed her a tin cup. The hot, sweet liquid flowed down her throat smoothly, and she let her hand rest on his leg, almost unconsciously. The warmth enveloped her, and Angus's playful gaze locked onto her. She secretly wished they could be alone here, even just for tonight, bathed in the soft glow of the firelight. She self-consciously withdrew her hand before Lexi noticed the subtle display of affection.

Lexi shivered and extended her fingerless-gloved hands toward the heat. Lost in her own thoughts, she murmured, "Actually, Dad took us camping. He showed us how to light a fire too … but I was quite young, really."

"Dad didn't take us camping, Lex," Meg said flatly, she had known her sister to embellish details from time to time, but would not allow her to make up such a false story.

Lexi squinted at her, confusion etched across her face. "He did, I remember he did."

Meg shook her head firmly. "Lexi, he didn't. Maybe once, if even that … but he wasn't around much to spend time with us."

"He did, Meg!" Lexi retorted, leaning forward. "We camped in the backyard; he took us several times—"

"He didn't, Lexi." Meg rolled her eyes, a faint chuckle leaving her lips.

"I remember, Meg – I may have been young, but I remember Dad took us out camping," Lexi asserted as she got to her feet. "Why do you always do that? Why do you never have a good thing to say about Dad?"

"Because he left us, Lex – he got up and left us!" Meg's voice trembled.

"Mum asked him to go. He would've stayed," Lexi countered.

"Mum was protecting us. He was a drunk, a gambler – a lowlife who cared more about his own self-destruction than his family," Meg retorted. She had no time for the make-believe version of her father that Lexi was pushing. If Meg wasn't careful, her sister would romanticise their father, along with her failed relationships.

Lexi shook her head vigorously. "You don't know anything. You're just angry because he let you down. Mum said you were thick as thieves, you were his little shadow—"

"That's enough, Lex. I don't want to talk about it anymore." Meg shifted, a bitter taste in her mouth. "He had his chance. Mum looked after us; we have to look after ourselves. We can't wait around for a fella to fix us, Lex."

Lexi paced to the front door and glared back at Meg. "I do look after myself, I'm a grown woman!"

Meg followed her sister, her temper flaring. "You don't look after yourself. I'm always the one cleaning up your messes! You can't just be level-headed for once; you have to pursue these god-awful men who you know are going to treat you like crap. I was so close to taking you to hospital, Lex!"

"Well, why didn't you? I said I was sorry, but that doesn't mean you can control me – control my life!" She lifted Meg's wet jacket and shoved her hand into the breast pocket, producing the letter wrapped in a plastic bag.

Meg's throat tightened, freezing her in place. "Lex, what are you doing?"

"You're hiding something from me," Lexi stated as she hastily opened the bag, pulling away from Meg's reach. "You think I haven't seen you with this?" She pulled the bag off, letting it fall to the ground, and feverishly ripped the envelope open.

Meg moved toward her, tears welling up in her eyes. "Stop! Don't do this!"

Behind her, Angus gently placed his hand on her arm, making her freeze like a statue, watching her sister's emotions unfold before her. Lexi turned her face away as she read the letter.

"You can't read that; it is private!" Meg pleaded, knowing her words were falling on deaf ears.

Lexi turned back to them, her face illuminated by the fire's glow. Tears streamed down her cheeks, and her confused look met Meg's. "Why do you have a letter from Mum? When did she write this? Why would you keep this from me?" she asked, her voice husky.

"It was Mum's. I found it at the house the last time I cleared her things. I don't know any more about it," Meg explained.

Angus stroked her forearm, offering comfort that Meg knew she didn't entirely deserve.

"Why would you keep it from me?" Lexi's frown deepened as she continued reading. "It's a love letter. Who was she in love with?"

Meg sighed. "It was for Dad."

Lexi turned the envelope to see the vague name and address. "Dad? He's here? I thought we were here to scatter Mum's ashes." A small smile crossed her face. "Dad is here?"

Meg swallowed hard; this was it. She had to decide now whether to open her sister up to the possibility of heartbreak for the foreseeable future or nip this in the bud now. They could grieve for their mother and go home; they would be happier. Lexi would be happier.

"Well?" Lexi's impatience cut through Meg's thoughts like a knife.

All her nerves bundled up inside her, her stomach knotting, her teeth gritting, her whole body shaking with sensations. She turned to Angus, his hand still tenderly caressing her skin. His sympathetic eyes met hers, but she shook her head. "I'm sorry," she whispered.

"What?" Lexi demanded.

"Dad is here," Meg breathed. "I was going to send it, but I couldn't. The address on the letter was too vague. I thought I could use help to locate him. So that's why I got Angus; he was from the same area—"

"Angus knew this whole time?" Lexi shouted, eyes wide, glaring at them both.

"No, I didn't know anything," Angus interjected, his shocked expression evident as he removed his hand from Meg's arm.

"OK, so we came here to say goodbye to Mum, to do something together as sisters. And you mean to tell me, in actual fact, you were looking for Dad, sneaking around behind my back? Were you ever going to tell me?" Lexi's cheeks reddened with rage, her fist tightening around the letter.

"Of course, I just wanted to check if he was here before I said anything." Meg tried to find the words, but feared the time to placate her sister was long gone. "I didn't want to discover he was still a drunk or dead! I couldn't do that to you … we only lost Mum last year. I needed to make sure," she said quietly, unable to look Lexi in the eyes.

"No, what you wanted to do was control everything. You wanted to control Ryan because you couldn't control Dad. Is that why you control me, Meg? You should look to your own life before you interfere in everyone else's!" Lexi's grip tightened, and the letter crumpled further in her hand.

Meg walked back to the fire, away from her sister's ferocity. She stared into the flames, trying to feel the warmth, but no heat penetrated her. She was cold, cold right down to her soul. "There's more," she said, steeling herself to look back at her sister and seeing a little girl. Lexi's face told a thousand stories – hurt, anger, but also a hopefulness that broke Meg's heart. She couldn't protect her; they had to face this together. "I met him. He's alive, and he looks just the same as I remembered. He's a priest."

"A priest?" Lexi leaned against the door, her eyes fixed on Meg.

"Father MacDonald?" Angus murmured, a revelation lighting up his features. "From the raft race?"

Meg nodded, feeling a burden lift, but Lexi's pain mirrored in her eyes was almost unbearable. "I'm sorry, Lexi, I just—"

"Wait a minute." Lexi stood up straight, her voice quiet and calculating. "You were going to pretend he was never here? You wanted to leave and go north. If it was up to you, we'd be on our way back home, and I'd know nothing about this?"

"Please, Lexi, understand I was just trying to—"

"Don't give me that! I cannot believe this. You would deny me seeing my father again. How dare you! What gives you the right?" She threw the letter on the stone floor. "I will never forgive you. We lost one parent, and you decided that we'd lose the other too? I will never forgive you for this," Lexi said once again, her words dripping with venom. She grabbed her jacket and slammed the door behind her.

Angus approached Meg, interrupting her breath. His attention, however, was on the fire; he tossed a log onto the flames. As he crouched to pull on his boots, Meg watched him, stunned.

"Angus, I'm sorry—"

He shook his head, tying the laces with deliberate motions. "This is between you two. I'm just a guy you needed to lie to."

Meg moved closer, tears welling up. "It wasn't like that."

He kept his gaze low. "It's OK, Meg. I get it now." His words were clipped as he donned his jacket, following Lexi and leaving Meg alone, the door closing with a heavy finality.

29

LEXI

The rain fell relentlessly on Lexi as she forged ahead through the muddy hills. Her vision blurred with tears, but she pressed on, determined to put as much distance between herself and the bothy as possible. Her soggy feet squelched in her wellington boots with each step, but she brushed off the cold that seeped into her bones. Her mind was fully absorbed by her sister's actions, and the result was fresh, hot, angry tears streaming down her face. Meg had interfered in her personal life for the last time. How could they ever move forward from this?

She fretted as she continued to wade through the boggy marshland, dodging puddles that were forming at an alarming rate among the heather. Her thoughts were a whirlwind of confusion, memories, and unanswered questions. Why couldn't Meg let her live her own life? Was this just another attempt to control her, just like in their childhood? The sting of resentment mingled with the cold dampness that clung to her.

Breathless, she found a cluster of large boulders and huddled under a ledge to catch her breath. The sky rumbled overhead, startling her, followed by a flash of white light. The rough, cold stone underneath jabbed into her, and she shuffled to make herself as comfortable as possible, with little success. She gazed out onto the miserable hillside, but the thickening mist limited her view to just a few yards ahead. Oh, how she wanted to hit something, to scream at something, or someone.

What she would give to be back in her own home, where she could lock herself away from the world. But no, she was stuck on a barren hill in the Scottish Highlands, getting soaked through. Even if she were back home, her cold Victorian share house hadn't been the cosy home she'd wished for. Somewhere warm, a light on for her, someone waiting. She didn't have any of those things. Perhaps Melbourne was just not a good fit anymore?

She sighed under the relentless rainfall, which kept her confined under her makeshift shelter. She was keenly aware of just how alone she was, without anything to call her own – no mum, no home, and no sister. Sheer frustration boiled inside her, and, without Meg, she was essentially homeless. She gritted her teeth and allowed the fury to flow through her. She nudged herself into the flat rock, craning her head back to avoid the large drops of water continuously falling from the sky. She shivered in the bleakness. She wanted comfort, needed comfort.

Her thoughts drifted back again to her ex, and without thinking, she took her cold, damp phone from her breast pocket. The screen illuminated with missed calls from the nursing home. She glanced at the few phone signal bars on the top left of her screen and silently prayed that she could phone Mark or Mrs Archer. Before she pressed the button, the phone vibrated with an incoming call again from the nursing home.

"What? What happened?" Lexi's voice trembled with urgency.

"Are you OK, Lexi?" Mrs Archer's warm voice came

through the line, tinged with confusion. "I tried calling, but there was no answer. I just wanted to see how you were doing, love."

A soothing warmth flowed down the line, instantly easing her anxiety. "For a second …" Emotion caught in her throat. "I thought when I saw all the missed calls that something had happened to you—"

"Oh, for goodness' sake." Mrs Archer chuckled affectionately, a comforting sound. "I'm as fit as a fiddle. I just wanted to thank you."

Lexi frowned as a raindrop dribbled down the tip of her nose. She wiped it away, only to have another form in its place. "Thank me?"

"Mmm, yes. You are a cheeky rascal for contacting my sister."

She pressed her lips together, half expecting a scolding. But it never came.

"My big sister came yesterday. She spent time with me and the boys, watching a show on television. I swear I did not recognise her at first; she caught me unawares. I thought, 'Who is this old woman?' Then, it's as if the years fell from her, the more time we spent together. Even the boys thought so."

Lexi suppressed a chuckle at the term "boys", considering the youngest of their friend group couldn't be under seventy. She leaned back against the cold stone, relief washing over her.

"We had a good catch-up. I forgot how much fun we used to have together. You know, we would often go to the dances when we were younger, and people would remark that we looked so similar, so much so that we used to play tricks on our dates," Mrs Archer said mischievously. "We were a force to be reckoned with!"

"You sound like a naughty pair. I'm so glad you're talking

again. And I'm sorry I contacted her without telling you …" Lexi scrunched up her nose.

"Yes, well, I was a little angry to begin with," Mrs Archer admitted. "But my sister said you were looking out for me, and I was lucky to have someone who cared so much, even though we haven't known each other for long …" The old woman paused, her voice trembling. "We have a special connection, don't we?"

Lexi grinned. "Yes, we do."

"I just wish you could meet her." A trace of sadness laced Mrs Archer's words.

"I will."

"But you're going back home."

Lexi smiled weakly to herself. "Honestly, right now … at this very second – I don't know what I'm doing."

Silence lingered on the line. "Is everything OK, Lexi? Come over, we'll cheer you up. We could take another trip to the theatre, and I could tell you about more secrets behind the stage!"

"Is there more? I thought you'd already spilled all the gossip."

"The mind, Lexi." Mrs Archer sighed. "Sometimes it's overflowing with memories, but the next moment, it's as if half of them have slipped away." She spoke softly.

"I want to thank you too," Lexi began, suddenly realising that it hadn't been a one-sided act, that in helping Mrs Archer, she had also helped herself. "For taking me out of myself, even if just for a little while."

"Well, that's one thing I can do. There's a spare seat around the telly with me and the boys, and my sister would love to see you. If you get time …"

Mrs Archer was beckoned by someone in the distance, and bid her farewell with an air of excitement. Lexi, left alone, felt a serene calmness settle around her. Thunder rumbled above, but she paid it no heed. Mrs Archer had lost everyone important in her life, and if it hadn't been for Lexi's inquisitiveness, she might have remained alone. She had followed her instincts, and thanks to her actions, two sisters were reunited.

A nagging thought whispered in her ear, and she tried in vain to dismiss it. Hadn't Meg, in her own way, done what she'd done to protect her? Meg, a steadfast pillar in Lexi's life, the only stability that remained when everyone else had departed.

As the rain relentlessly drummed on, a profound realisation settled within her. If she was truly honest with herself, she had contemplated letting Meg go, just as she had with her apartment, her job, and even her mother. The persistent question had lingered: was it Meg's turn to slip away?

As a crack of lightning inched closer, she couldn't help but shiver. What choices would Meg make if she were in Lexi's shoes, both in life and in this very moment, sheltered under the rocky ledge? Were there shared threads of uncertainty binding them together? Perennially in her sister's shadow, she found herself incapable of reaching a firm decision. The prospect of Meg departing felt more ominous than the idea of Lexi walking away. With these unresolved thoughts lingering, she chose to weather the storm, allowing the tumultuous thoughts in her mind to settle like the rain-soaked earth around her.

30

MEG

Meg's hands trembled as she picked up the crumpled letter from the floor, the paper slick with the wet footprints it had absorbed. She inhaled, a desperate attempt to steady herself, but the tears, salty and unrelenting, betrayed her composure. The letter slipped, ink bleeding onto the dark stone.

She couldn't contain it any longer. A scream clawed its way up from the depths of her chest, raw and unrestrained. It tore through the silent room, leaving echoes that startled even Meg herself. It wasn't just a scream; it was a release, an unravelling of the tightly wound emotions that had held her captive.

Her body convulsed with the force of her outburst, and she felt the hot, prickling sensation behind her eyelids as tears streamed down her face. The room seemed to tilt, and she staggered, grappling with the weight of her emotions. In a frenzy, she searched for something – anything – to distract her from the suffocating darkness that threatened to consume her.

Pacing the floor, her footing faltered, and with a violent crash, the pot of steaming water – that had been over the fire

– toppled over. The scalding liquid splashed into the air, dancing before plummeting to the stone floor, carrying the already drenched letter with it. Meg, desperate and half blinded by her own tears, lunged to salvage the pages. The boiling water seared her hands, but she clutched the sodden papers with urgency.

Her mother's words, now a smudged blur, faded before her eyes. Collapsing against the bunk bed, she felt the sting of pain in her scalded hands. What had she done? Lost in the grief that overtook her body, she feverishly went to the open fireplace and tried to salvage some flames that lingered after the exploding pot of water. Her hands shook as she found Angus's lighter and lit the kindling of wood again. Nothing. Everything had been soaked. She collapsed on the floor, her fists clenched tightly. She had let down her mother.

Staring blankly at the small window beside the door, she glimpsed a faint glimmer of grey light outside amid the cascading raindrops and relentless winds that rattled the building. In that quiet moment, she yearned for a sign from her mother, clutching on to any hope that she lingered in the afterlife, guiding her through the storm. The rain persisted, and the only response was the mournful whistle of the wind. She laughed bitterly, acknowledging the harsh reality – her mother was not there. She had died and left, and here Meg stood, a rational woman clinging to a fading hope.

She couldn't bring herself to passively await something that would never surface. Everything that had unfolded until now had seemed random or a consequence of her own actions. She wouldn't surrender to the longing for something beyond her reach. Instead, with a resolute decision, she acknowledged the conflict between what she wanted and what she needed.

She had no choice; she needed to act. Donning a jacket, she stomped into her boots, preparing herself for the wildness that awaited her outside. But when she left the bothy, she didn't feel the elements, as everything became clear in her mind – she must find Lexi.

She crossed a fence with deliberate steps, balancing on the wire to avoid its jagged spikes, and her gaze lingered on the expansive, sodden marshland. Rain and fog seemed the only inhabitants of this desolate landscape. The mystery of the fence's existence in such a remote place briefly crossed her mind, but she pushed the curiosity aside. As she ventured further, deliberately choosing a different path than Angus, she felt the fading light around her. Each passing minute made it more imperative to locate Lexi.

Her progress grew slower with each step, her boots sinking into the boggy ground. Anxiety gnawed at her, and the treacherous mud seemed to threaten her very resolve. She hesitated, realising she would have to turn back soon if she ever hoped to find her way back to the bothy in the dark. But she couldn't afford the luxury of waiting for Angus to locate Lexi. After all, it was her actions that had led them into this precarious predicament. Determined, she pressed forward, calling out Lexi's name as she trod on.

Suddenly, as abruptly as it had begun, the wind ceased, and an eerie silence settled over the land. Her heart pounded in her chest as she scanned the surroundings. The dim light played tricks on her eyes, casting shadows that danced with uncertainty.

In the midst of this unsettling calm, something caught Meg's eye – a wellington boot partially submerged in the mud. It looked just like Lexi's. Panic surged through her, and she screamed her sister's name at the top of her lungs. The folklore of the kelpie, haunting these lands, flashed through her mind again, and as much as she called upon her rational mind, her thoughts spiralled into the darkest possibilities.

She scrambled frantically to the boot, pulling it out of the mud with desperate effort. Her hands submerged in the cold, wet soil, she pulled again, and the earth finally released it. As she glanced around for more evidence of Lexi, the mist seemed to play tricks on her senses. Her sister might be anywhere – in a place she didn't know, or worse, trapped somewhere, crying out for her help. If only she had been honest with her sister from the start, this wouldn't have happened. The weight of potential loss tightened around her chest. She couldn't lose Lexi.

She screamed over the mist, hoping her voice would break through the unsettling quiet that enveloped the landscape.

Suddenly, Lexi's head popped from behind a boulder. “Meg?”

Startled and breathless, Meg shifted her gaze from the abandoned boot to her sister's face. Relief washed over her, yet the mysteries of the foggy marshland still lingered, leaving an unshakeable sense that danger might not be far away.

Lexi hopped out from behind her boulder cover, one foot clad in a welly boot, while the other dirty pink sock hovered in the air. “It took my boot!” Lexi scratched her head, perplexed.

Meg rushed towards Lexi's hideout, pulling her sister into a tight hug, tears welling up in her eyes. “Oh my god, I thought … If anything happened to you, Lexi, I'd never forgive myself!”

“What?” Lexi pulled away, a puzzled expression on her face. “You thought I had disappeared?”

“I can't even begin to explain what I thought,” she replied, pushing away thoughts of menacing kelpies and childhood fairy tales that had haunted her. She wrapped her arms around her little sister, comforted by her familiar scent. “I'm so sorry, Lexi. I'm the worst sister. You have every right to never speak to me again. I love you, and I'd do anything for you."

The atmosphere on the misty hillside shifted, the tension gradually dissipating like morning fog under the touch of the rising sun.

Lexi freed herself from the embrace. "I know that, silly. I know you were looking out for me. I just wish you didn't put all that on yourself." She met her sister's sad eyes. "What's wrong?"

She found herself standing at the precipice of truth, a truth she had long buried beneath layers of denial and guilt. As Lexi gazed at her with those searching eyes, the weight of her secrets pressed down on her shoulders, threatening to crush her.

The words, once suppressed, now clawed their way to the surface. "You were right about everything," she confessed. "I've not been happy. I never wanted Dad to go. I was angry at Mum, at myself for letting him go." Each word carried a piece of her soul, a confession she had guarded with fierce determination. Her gaze dropped to the ground, unable to meet Lexi's eyes directly. "And I have something else to tell you." The admission hung heavy in the air. "Dad came to the house after Mum had kicked him out. I didn't trust him. It was your birthday, and I thought he would cause a scene …"

Lexi gently grasped Meg by the shoulders, the unspoken understanding passing between them. "Let that be the end of interfering, Meg, OK?" Lexi's voice was not unkind but carried the weight of a plea for honesty and acceptance.

Meg looked at her sister, confusion etched on her face. "Didn't you hear what I said? I stopped him from coming back, just when we all needed him."

Lexi smiled, brushing a wet clump of hair from Meg's face. "I know you took a lot upon yourself. You've got to let me in, OK? Don't have everything on your shoulders. You don't need to protect me."

Meg watched her sister, the vulnerability of her confession still present. "I'm worried something would happen … if you got hurt again. That's why. I'm your big sister, I'd feel responsible if anything happened to you."

"Na." Lexi shrugged. "Not anymore. I won't do anything stupid, not ever again."

Meg probed further. "How can you be so sure?"

"I just feel different now …" Her voice trailed off, as if searching for the right words. "But, Meg, you can't manipulate reactions. You can't control every aspect of life. OK? Promise me you'll let it go? I want us to be a team, equals, supporting each other. To grow old and watch old movies together." Lexi's smile held a secret.

"If you promise me, Lexi, that you'll never put yourself in a situation like that again … and you'll always reach out, even in your darkest moments?"

Lexi nodded. "I will if you will." The challenge in her tone was both playful and serious.

The mist enveloped them, a gentle cocoon wrapping around their shared vulnerability. Through the soft light on the hillside, they embraced, finally free from the weight of secrets.

31

ANGUS

Angus walked a dusty path resembling a desert, the sand shifting beneath his feet in the wind. Despite the scorching sun glaring down, uncertainty about his journey lingered. Figures from his life emerged on either side as the path widened, including his parents, friends Jake and Iona, Claudia, and Meg. He paused at Meg, her arms outstretched but unmoving. She uttered no cry for him, only gazing at him with pleading eyes. The sky began to blacken above them, hailstones hammered down, but she did not move, as if an invisible rope tied her feet down. He looked down at his own feet and suddenly he was plunged into a fast-flowing river.

"Angus!" A pair of big brown eyes stared at him. "Time to get up! The day is almost over!" Lexi giggled, her mood significantly brighter than the previous day.

Having spent hours searching the darkness for Lexi, Angus had returned the evening before to find the two girls happily indulging in noodles from his rations. In a foul mood, he shook off his drenched coat and boots and attempted to remain civil. The entire trip had unfolded as a whirlwind of drama, and he had no desire to engage in casual conversation with Meg, especially considering the unresolved tension between them. He had made polite excuses and curled up in his sleeping bag for the night.

The return journey to the kayaks had been a quiet one, particularly on Angus's part. He had focused on completing the task at hand; after all, he was their tour guide. He made them a quick breakfast of bacon and eggs and homemade bread he had snatched from home. He had little interest in being in that cold, miserable bothy any longer, and as soon as there was a break in the clouds, he hurried them out into the barren landscape.

His plan was simple: drop them off at the airport, be as civil as possible, and ensure they left glowing reviews. He had done everything he could, and despite the foolishness of exposing his heart, there was no reason for his friend's business to suffer due to this mess.

As they passed by the cairns once more, the stone markers made him briefly glance in Meg's direction, only to find her watchful eyes on him. He turned his gaze ahead, dismissing any lingering moments between them. Soon he would be alone, welcoming the distraction of his croft.

* * *

The van chugged along the road, sounding like an old man coughing in the early morning. Angus drove cautiously, his mind filled with contemplation about his next steps. He knew the girls would be eager to return home, but a nagging feeling tugged at him. As their tour guide, he had a responsibility to ensure they left with positive memories, but a more personal motivation whispered that he could, in some small way, make amends for his own misplaced feelings.

Making a slight detour, he turned down a road that the girls hadn't visited before. Lexi, unusually quiet in the back, tucked her phone away as they passed a manor house nestled amidst clusters of trees and hills.

"It's a nice spot," Angus began, his tone laden with an almost imperceptible urgency. "I thought perhaps I should show you something before you go. Now hear me out before I finish." His eyes met Meg's, her mouth tightening as if anticipating something unforeseen.

Before he could unveil his mysterious destination, the atmosphere inside the van shifted abruptly. "Bloody hell!" he shouted, slamming on the brakes. The screeching halt reverberated through the air, jolting the vehicle to a slanted angle on the deserted road.

In the middle of the road stood an enormous bird, clutching a piece of roadkill in its beak. It looked at them, its dark wings flapping vigorously, struggling for a moment before it took to the air and disappeared.

Angus could sense Meg tensing beside him, her hands pushing down on her seat.

"What was that?" Lexi cried out, her eyes wide with awe. "That was incredible! It was huge!"

"I know." Angus gripped the wheel tightly, his heart pounding in his chest. "I can't believe he dived down in front of the van! Bloody hell, I could've run him over!"

"Or her," Meg added quietly.

Angus turned to her, frustration palpable. Meg's response carried an unusual tone.

"It's a sea eagle, right? It could be a she," Meg said, her gaze still locked on the sky.

"Oh, a sea eagle!" Lexi marvelled. "That was the most amazing thing I've ever seen!" She laughed and clapped her hands together. "I wish I'd had my camera!"

"Meg seems to attract them. That's the second sea eagle we've seen," Angus informed Lexi irritably. Memories of the gala and their impromptu kiss on the beach flashed in his mind, along with Meg's peculiar expression as they watched the bird circling down to its catch. He had been unprofessional that day in so many ways, but to kiss a client had been a regret. Yet, she had a wild way of looking at him, like she wanted to kiss him. He had given in to his urges that day, but she had kissed him back.

A little shaken from what could have been an accident with the bird of prey, Angus cautiously continued their drive. He adjusted his breathing, letting himself cool down a bit, but Meg's presence beside him rattled him. He could feel her thinking, her mind racing with thoughts that remained hidden.

Hanging baskets brimming with heather and autumn crocuses swayed gently beneath a red sign for a quaint post office. Nearby, a cosy inn with two weathered benches out front hosted a pair of biker men, leisurely sipping pints of lager. Just behind the inn, a small church stood proudly on a hill, its ancient stones bathed in the soft glow of the afternoon sun.

Angus turned to them, his expression slightly sheepish. "This is where Father MacDonald is," he informed them, his words met with blank expressions from the sisters. "You don't need to do anything; I'm just letting you know. If you head up that hill, you should find him. Otherwise, I'm just going to run some errands, and I'll see you back here." His gaze lingered on Meg for a moment. Her cheeks flushed pink, and a hostile expression crossed her face. Without further explanation, he quietly closed the van door behind him and made his way into the post office. Once inside, he pretended to admire some postcards and a Highland cow calendar, but his attention was fixated on the window. Meg and Lexi were still by the van. He wasn't the type of man to pry into others' affairs, but he couldn't help himself. The revelation that Meg had shared, about their father being the local priest, Father MacDonald, had suddenly clicked into place. He had never considered the priest as a possible candidate before, given his occupation. Priests with families were exceedingly rare, and the few cases that did exist were often scandalous news.

He wiped the condensation from the window, squinting at his van. Then, they came into view. Meg leaned against the van's front bumper with a distant, almost glazed expression, while Lexi's hand gently gripped her elbow. He wished he knew what they were discussing. A growing concern enveloped him. Should he have left well enough alone instead of pushing them into something that might tarnish their mother's memory and cause even more heartache?

Before he could decide on a course of action, they moved away from the vehicle, disappearing into the sea of red and amber foliage that shrouded the end of the lane. He gritted his teeth, Should he follow them? What if this priest was cruel? If they exposed his secret, it could threaten his livelihood, and such threats often led people to react in unexpected ways.

Lost in a whirlwind of doubts, he turned from the window, only to find the postmistress and a balding man with a grey complexion huddled together, watching him with curious expressions. Feeling like an intruder, he inched away and returned to the van. He hoped that whatever unfolded, he wouldn't inadvertently become the cause of more misery.

32

MEG

Meg pulled her hair back into a bun, its neglected strands feeling greasy after a night of camping. Her morning routine had been reduced to the bare essentials – a hasty attempt to address the aftermath of a night spent outdoors. Brushing her teeth with her finger and some toothpaste seemed a sufficient compromise, given her initial expectation to return to Angus's, unwind, pack her belongings, and prepare for their impending flight – not to meet their father.

As the reality of the situation sank in, a rising panic gripped her throat. Unprepared and without any mental roadmap for interacting with the man who had left, she grappled with the daunting question of what to say to him. She didn't want this to happen, not yet. She had hoped that, after more time, Lexi would agree that opening the door to their past might be the worst scenario. Her sister had claimed to understand her interference, but what would happen now? It was all happening too suddenly to keep up.

The surroundings, however, offered no reprieve. Cars moved around them, people engaged in amicable conversations, stopping by the shop for newspapers, milk, or a loaf of bread tucked under their arms. The church, the smallest Meg had ever seen, perched on top of the hill, seamlessly blended into its centuries-old surroundings. The sky above was alive with the melody of birds. She gazed up, unable to see anything beyond the trees. On any other day, she might have explored, but now all she wanted was to leave. She didn't want to enter those walls, not if it meant confronting her past.

As she paused, catching her breath, Lexi gave her hand a reassuring squeeze, a silent acknowledgement of the inevitable. Lexi's composed posture conveyed everything without the need for words – the time had come. With a nod, Meg followed her little sister, the last few steps bringing them to the stone entrance.

"Do I knock or just walk in?" Lexi rested her hand on the doorknob, shrugged, and pushed the door open.

A stale, musty coldness, tinged with the faint scent of lemon cleaning polish, greeted Meg's nostrils as they entered the small porch area. Coat hooks lined one wall, and a stone font, waist-high, held water for churchgoers.

She huddled close to Lexi. They hadn't set foot in a church since childhood, and even then it was reserved for special occasions like Christmas or Easter. Everything about this unfamiliar place felt alien to them. They were impostors.

Lexi hesitated at the font, dipping a tentative finger into the basin.

"Lexi!" Meg hissed in the dim light, shivering from the cold.

"It's what you do, right?" Lexi replied, flicking a few drops of water across herself with little conviction.

Together, they ventured through the next door, leading them further into the open space. The church contained only ten pews on each side, and a humble altar consisting of a plain wooden stand with a Bible placed on top. In the centre of the altar, there was a table covered with a white cloth.

Contrary to Meg's expectations, the church's interior lacked the elaborate and beautiful gold ceremonial items typically associated with such spaces. Rain tapped gently against the arched stained-glass windows, the only real extravagance in this otherwise simple space. She squinted at a depiction of a woman wrapped in blue, holding a baby, surrounded by jewel-coloured cherubs playing trumpets and various animals. As her gaze lingered on the stained glass, something within the intricate details caught her attention. At first, it was just a subtle shape amidst the clutter of animals, but as her eyes focused, the form became clearer – a large bird of prey, its keen eyes seeming to lock on to the pair depicted below. A shiver crawled down her spine as the significance of this unexpected detail dawned on her – the sea eagle she had encountered on their journey.

"Good morning," came a voice from behind them, making her jump. A tall, slender man with greying hair at the temples walked through a side door. "I saw you come up the hill and wanted to see if there was anything I could help with. Or perhaps you'd just like some time alone for a wee pray?" The man clasped his hands together, his eyes crinkling in a warm smile.

Before them stood a completely different person, with a far happier countenance now than he had all those years ago. Meg had seen him before at the gala, but she had been too overwhelmed that day; most of his features had vanished from her recollection. The image she had of her father – shaggy dark hair and a slight frame – from a worn photo she kept in her sock drawer, was a stark contrast to the man before them.

"Um, yeah," she stuttered, trying to find her words. "Sure, why not?" She had forgotten the question, unsure of what she truly wanted, especially with her father and Lexi both staring at her.

His expression changed, with an understanding nod. “Oh, you’re not from these parts?” He patted his black jacket, producing a small pair of glasses, putting them on, only for them to immediately slide down the bridge of his nose. He propped them back up with a sigh.

“No, we’re from Australia, visiting the area,” Lexi replied in a clear voice. Her back was straight, her confidence striking to Meg. “This is my sister Meg, and I’m Lexi,” she introduced, her gaze locked onto the priest.

The small, cold church seemed to hold its breath, the silence broken only by the loud raspy caw of a crow from outside, startling them all.

The priest rested his hand on the pew beside him, muttering something to himself. Then he raised his eyes upwards, engaged in some silent communication. Meg followed his gaze but saw only wooden rafters, covered with a splattering of bat poo.

“I see.” His voice was low, barely a whisper.

Silence enveloped them again. She looked back at the stained glass, focusing on the bird of prey once again.

The old priest now followed Meg’s gaze. “I didn't think this day would come.”

“You know us?” Lexi inquired, drawing Meg closer as they faced the priest together.

He watched Meg curiously. “You look like her.” He sighed sadly. “She loved that window.”

Meg could feel Lexi tremble beside her; she tightened her grip.

“This was where we met,” he mused, and after a moment’s hesitation, took two steps forward, pushing his glasses back up. “You've come to see me?”

Lexi exchanged a meaningful glance with Meg and turned her attention back to the priest, her tone firm. “I think it’s time you gave us an explanation.”

33

MEG

Meg and Lexi perched on worn floral armchairs beside a large window, the stone church in view. The room felt stiflingly warm, thanks to a blazing gas fire beneath a mantelpiece overloaded with tacky ornaments. A gold clock ticked loudly next to dated cherubs and milkmaids carrying buckets. The priest limped slightly towards them with two cups of weak tea and settled himself slowly into a creaky wooden chair by the fire, wincing a little.

An oppressive silence hung in the room.

Meg shifted in the lumpy chair, which squeaked as she did so. "It's nice and homey," she said, clutching at any form of small talk.

He raised his eyebrows and nodded. "Ah yes, it is. My house helper, Morag, does her best to make the place look … cosy," he remarked, following Meg's gaze and leaning back into the creaky chair, which seemed unreliable to take his weight.

More silence. Apart from the ticking clock on the mantelpiece, which after closer scrutiny, Meg noticed read entirely the wrong time.

"Why did you leave us?" Lexi broke the silence, her voice

too loud for the small, carpeted room. She clutched her cup so tightly that her knuckles turned white.

The priest set down his tea on an equally cluttered table beside him and leaned forward, clasping his hands together as if in prayer. He tilted his head, looking at both of them. "You must be angry," he stated.

"Is that it?" Lexi laughed bitterly. "Is that what you have to say? Of course we're bloody angry!" Her voice rose even louder, and the priest recoiled.

Meg put her hand on Lexi's arm, about to speak, but she could see her sister wasn't finished.

"You left us and headed to the other side of the world – no phone calls, no letters, and now you're spouting the word of God?"

"I'm sorry for doing that to you, Lexi, and to you, Megan," he replied, shaking his head, a frown mark appearing between his eyebrows.

"You do not have the right to call me that," Lexi retorted. "It's Alexandria to you."

He nodded and smiled briefly. "Of course." He looked at the ticking clock on the mantel, patiently letting more time pass between them after the many years he had been away. "Alexandria," he mused. "A beautiful name. It was my mother's name. Did you know that?"

Lexi kept her mouth tightly shut, her fierce gaze meeting his serene and slightly detached one.

"I wish you'd known your grandmother, but sadly she passed away before I moved to Australia …" He stopped to give a brief cough, his eyes red. "I don't pretend that I was a good father; I know this. I was a confused young man, and I didn't want to drag you both down with me. That's why I left, and seeing you both now and what you have grown up to be … I believe I did the right thing in leaving."

"You didn't leave – Mum told you to go," Meg cut in, her

patience already wearing thin. "You would have dragged us all down with you, alright? It was Mum that made that decision."

He turned to face her, taking in her words slowly. "I'm sorry, child, but I did leave. Your mother could never leave me; I did not treat her right, and I owe her an apology – she deserved so much better. But I need to see her in person to even start to repair the—"

"Well, you're lucky then," Lexi interrupted with venom in her voice. "Mum died last year, so you don't need to go through the uncomfortable process of apologising face to face."

The room fell silent as Lexi's words echoed, each one landing like a heavy blow.

Meg's stomach twisted, a deep sinking feeling taking hold. Nausea threatened, and she clutched the arms of the lumpy chair, relieved at the support as the ground beneath her feet felt unsteady.

Their father's stunned expression looked as if Lexi had slapped him. He got up from his chair and slowly made his way to the window.

Lexi's face flushed with rage, and she looked down at the busy patterns in the carpet.

"I am so sorry," he said quietly. "I did not want things to go this way. Your mum was a gentle soul; I will pray for her – as I have prayed for her every day since I left."

"Why do you keep saying that 'you left'?" Meg snapped, her rage meeting her sister's. "Mum demanded you leave. You did not go of your own accord; you had no choice. Don't make it out otherwise."

"But I did leave, Megan," he said again in a low voice. The grey light from outside surrounded his silhouette, casting a resemblance to the woman in blue from the stained-glass window. "I could see I was spiralling, just as I feared. My own history crept up on me, and I knew if I stayed, I would cause even greater harm. Just like my own father did …"

"I heard her with my own ears. She screamed at you to leave and to never come back."

A grim smile appeared on his face, and he gently massaged his temples. "She asked me to leave, yes, you're right. Many times she asked me to go – but every time she would plead with me to come home. She'd search for me, wherever stupid place I was dwelling in; the bookies, the pub, she would always find me. The last time I left, I found my own lodgings, got some help. I thought I was maybe going to get my life back in order." He hesitated, turning to Meg. "But when I saw you that day guarding the house, and not letting me in for Lexi's birthday … I … I saw in your eyes just what I was. I needed to do more work on myself before I was worthy of you two to be in my life again." He swallowed. "I'm sorry, Megan, your mum would have done anything for you girls, but she would never leave me."

Tears sprang from Meg's eyes. "You came back? Are you saying I broke up our family?" Her hand covered her mouth. Her stomach twisted painfully, and she felt a rush of dizziness. The patterned room was closing in on her.

The priest took her hand. "No, you saved our family." Standing over her, he lingered awkwardly as she continued to sob, her grief finally coming out … from all the years of loss for one parent, to have the other gone for good. Her father, still close, patted her on the shoulder. He turned to retreat to the window again. Meg produced the letter she had been carrying all this time. The ripped-open envelope with smudged writing exchanged hands. No words were uttered; the priest scanned it, patting his black jacket for his glasses. Fumbling with the spectacles, he placed them on his nose and read the letter.

Meg, with a gentle touch, explained, “We had a bit of an accident during the trip. The rain caught us off guard.”

The priest, with anticipation in his eyes, asked. “What does it say?”

Meg hesitated, then softly responded, “Whatever you can gather from these words, they're hers. A love letter, directly to you.”

Behind him, rain grew heavier outside, hammering at the window pane. She watched the drops stream down. The house shook a little with a gust of wind. She looked down at her hands numbly and noticed Lexi’s intertwined with them. Her blonde messy locks tucked behind her ears, she looked away, neither of them watching the priest.

He looked back at the girls, then shook his head, his face pale.

Lexi mumbled, “It seems even at the end she wanted you to come back.”

Meg bit her lip, and her heart ached; her mother loved him until the end. All the fairy stories she had told them had been for him, to be closer in hopes of reuniting once again; that they would live happily ever after.

The priest re-read the letter, emotion engulfing him, and in that moment, Meg felt sorry for him. Sorry that his life had been full of regret.

“My dear Rebecca.” He clutched the letter. “I have made a mess of everything, my poor Rebecca, I’m so sorry,” he whispered to himself, closing his eyes. Lexi went to him and allowed him to lean on her. Meg wrapped her arm across his back, and the three of them stood there in a strange embrace. A strange embrace that none of them broke from.

34

MEG

"I think we did the right thing," Lexi said, kicking off her shoes and propping her feet on the mattress. "I mean, with Dad – Father MacDonald. Jeez, this whole business is so bizarre!" She shifted closer to Meg. "How do you feel?"

Meg lay on the guest bed, which wobbled with Lexi's movement. They had spent the rest of the day in a state of shock after meeting their father. Angus had left them to have sisterly time and discuss their next plan of action. Meg took it to mean he wanted to escape their complicated lives for good. Despite this, she couldn't help but smile as Lexi watched her with curiosity. She could feel their closeness, which she thought they had all but lost.

"I feel like I'm walking in a new land." She sighed, closing her eyes contently into the soft pillow.

"That's because you are!" Lexi scoffed. "We're in Scotland."

Meg lay blissfully aware of the hens roaming around the house, their clucks sounding outside Lexi's window. With Angus possibly gone for the night, she would need to usher them back into their shed before dark, which she didn't mind.

She had started to enjoy their unique personalities, which, for such small animals, conveyed a surprising amount of character.

She remained still, her body vibrating with exhaustion, from a sleepless night in the bothy to crying with everything she had in her. She was in a strange mood, one where everything felt at peace. She wanted to sleep forever, knowing Lexi was close to her, unharmed, and knowing that their father was there. Their father, once a distant figure, could now be part of the picture if they wanted him to be. Although his path lay in the church, there was a glimmer of hope. What would become of them all now? Would they keep in touch now? Or remain strangers?

There was no denying his pain; it lay etched on his face. Meg and Lexi may have moved on in their own ways, but their father seemed a shell, haunted by his actions. She once would have felt relief to know his suffering but now she just wanted no more sadness. A life with regret would consume you. It was true for her mother and for her father.

What was left for her now? With things becoming settled, she could now visualise Australia. Her dreams of becoming a singer had long been abandoned. Those days of exploring America on the back of a motorbike were long gone, but she wouldn't regret missing out on them. She was a different person then.

But was she truly happy now?

Angus had asked her that, but she couldn't answer him then, or even say it to herself.

"I've been thinking, Lexi," she began, wanting to stay in the shared cocoon with her sister. "You were right about Mum's ashes. We should scatter them at the castle that looked like every fairy tale she ever told us about. You were right; I felt her presence there too."

Lexi sat up. "Really? What about the other castles?

Weren't we going to scatter some of her ashes at each of them? Wouldn't she have wanted that?"

She shrugged. "I think we've done something Mum would have wanted all along." She smiled to herself, closing her eyes, seeing her mother on the blanket overlooking the sea, the swirls of Northern Lights around them. The knowing look in her eyes. "Do you feel it too? I feel she's happy … wherever she is now, I'm sure she's soaring through the skies."

Lexi's perplexed expression met Meg's, and she hesitated. "Well then, I also wanted to present another idea to you. Please don't be mad; it's just a thought. Should we invite Dad … I mean Father MacDonald to scatter her ashes? It might be good for him to say goodbye."

Meg's heart swelled with both pain and incredible love for her little sister. They had gone through so much to get here, and now that they could look ahead, she felt a freedom she had never known. "I think that's a wonderful idea."

* * *

Father MacDonald huddled under a small rowan tree, his flat cap and waterproof jacket shielding him from the elements. In one hand, he held a walking stick, and his white collar peeked out from beneath his chin. He took a deep breath, nodding to the girls to start their ascent. Megan and Lexi made their way up the hill overlooking the beach, this time without the sight of seals in the water. As they approached, they passed other tourists, who gave puzzled looks at the sight of a priest and two young women making their way up the hill toward a ruined castle, holding a velvet bag.

Upon reaching the summit, they quietly surveyed the surroundings for any lingering tourists. Meg was surprised to interrupt a teenage couple kissing under a stone archway, wrapped in a wool blanket on the cold stone slabs, lost in their own world of young love.

Lexi shrugged at her. "Being surrounded by love seems rather fitting."

Meg handed her the velvety bag and nodded with encouragement. "OK, set her free, Lexi."

Lexi, her eyes wide, opened the bag and gazed at what remained of their mother. She raised the bag, holding one corner out to Meg. "We do it together."

Together, they tipped its contents, letting the wind carry the ashes over the ruined castle and out to sea.

Their father stood in silence, watching with eyes that momentarily closed as he whispered some words to himself. Words that were carried away on the breeze, mingling with their mother's ashes.

A quiet sense of peace settled among them, and in that hushed moment, memories gently resurfaced. Despite the chaos and heartache, Meg came to a simple realisation – her childhood had been special, all thanks to her mother. Someday, if she had children of her own, she wanted to be just like her – baking, hosting tea parties, and infusing the household with warmth and liveliness. Though nursing the pain left by her father, Meg acknowledged that it was their mother who had breathed life into their house, ensuring that loneliness never lingered.

Meg nudged Lexi on the arm affectionately. "You OK?"

"I am. I miss her all the time, sometimes I can't get through the day. But … I know … everything's going to be OK. It has to, right?"

"I think some days will be painful. But that just means there was love, right? We loved her, and she loved us … that's why there's pain."

Accepting this, Lexi walked towards their father, his head

bowed respectfully. She placed her hand through his arm and for a moment he was taken aback, but just as Meg could see, he was understanding Lexi's ways. For as he said Meg had looked like their mother, Lexi was the embodiment of her completely.

She gazed out across the water, maintaining a safe distance from the cliff edge. Thoughts of Angus lingered in her mind. He had shared this special spot with them, guiding them to a fitting final resting place for their mother.

It was because of him.

She stooped under the stone archway, watching as the kissing couple walked off hand in hand. She carefully placed a loose, small rock on top of a few others, creating a somewhat wobbly tower. She recalled the cairns they had passed on the way to the bothy – Angus had mentioned they marked the path of the living carrying their dead to their grave. Wasn't that exactly what they had just done?

She tried to think of her mother. Yet despite her attempts to focus on her, Angus persisted, creeping into her thoughts. Instead of envisioning the soaring sea eagle catching the salmon, a darker image came in view with Angus on the same scratchy tartan blanket beneath a blackened sky. Something felt awry; she struggled to place her mother back in the dream that took them to Scotland in the first place.

Her goodbye to Angus had been curt. She had found the only car rental in the area and even though she told him she would leave a good review, he fell back to his grumpy ways. He barely looked at her. She had let him go. She couldn't talk to him, especially in amongst the confusion of her father and scattering her mother's ashes. The time had come, they needed to go home. They couldn't stay in a tour guide's house any longer; it was preposterous to even be there this long. She would talk to him on the phone, apologise for the chaos they brought into his life. Perhaps an email instead, when she was safely back home, sitting in her kitchen with the birds twittering outside. The only real sounds she would hear in her house. Only then could she try to explain that she hadn't actively deceived him.

Yet a nagging feeling persisted. She should have told Angus about her father. Perhaps he would have kept her secret, helping even more if he understood the importance of finding Father Graeme MacDonald.

She couldn't shake the sense that she had treated Angus unfairly, and the overwhelming feeling of having missed out on something weighed heavily on her.

* * *

They waved goodbye to their father, his hand creating a fleeting silhouette as his car disappeared into the distance, leaving behind a trail of smoke. Basking in the afternoon sun's warm embrace, Meg and Lexi found themselves in a nearby hotel, relishing the delightful combination of tea and scones. Amid the comforting aroma of freshly brewed tea, Meg seized the opportunity to dive into Lexi's potential love life – a welcome diversion from her own fading one.

"Have you been in touch with Mark?" Meg asked casually, spooning a rather large dollop of cream onto her jammy scone.

Lexi crooked an eyebrow, her voice low. "Erm … not for a few days. Why?"

"Oh, I just wondered if you were going to stay here a little longer, or maybe he might want to visit you back in Melbourne?"

"Whatever for?" Lexi sat upright, her hands flat on the table.

"Because you're seeing each other, or whatever you kids call it these days?" Meg said, aghast. Despite their growing closeness, it was evident Meg still needed to pry every bit of news from Lexi.

Lexi erupted into laughter, catching Meg off guard mid-bite, causing her to smudge cream on her cheek. "You think …" She struggled to stifle her laughter with giggles. "You have it all wrong. It's not Mark; it's Mrs Archer I have a relationship with—"

Meg, genuinely confused, interjected, "But she's a woman … and a pensioner!"

"Not that either, silly!" Lexi gasped. "Seriously, Meg, I don't romantically entangle myself with everyone I meet!" Leaning back in her chair, she folded her arms across her chest. "The truth is," Lexi began slowly, her voice carrying a hint of vulnerability, "I think I've found what I want to do with my life." She bit her lower lip, her gaze still locked on the table, almost as if she were revealing a secret to herself. "These last couple of weeks have opened my eyes. I see what makes me happy, and in a way …" She hesitated, her cheeks flushing with an uncharacteristic blush. "I see my own skills. I'm good at giving people energy, bringing happiness and fun, but also caring."

Meg grinned. "You are, Lex. You're great with people. I've always thought so." Setting down her scone, she watched her sister coyly. "So that's why you were there? You want to work in a nursing home?"

"Yes, maybe. All I know is I felt so elated after leaving there each day. I want to help people like Mrs Archer. So I've decided I want to go back to school. Mark says he'll put in a good word for me, and I might find some odd jobs when I go back to Melbourne." Lexi beamed at her sister, clearly already organising the next phase of her life independently.

She reached across the table, clasping Lexi's hand. "I'm so proud of you. You can do this. If this is something that will make you happy, then whatever you need, I will help you."

Lexi smiled, shaking her head. “Thanks, sis. I want to do this alone. I mean, if I can – I want to prove to myself that I can do this alone … Does that make sense?” She tilted her head, squinting at Meg thoughtfully.

“It sure does.” Meg could see a new future just within her excited sister's grasp.

35

ANGUS

The aroma of cheesy lasagna filled the room as Iona set the dish on the table. The kids were tucked in upstairs after Angus had played an exhausting game of Twister with them, leaving him to flop into a chair with a contented sigh. Iona chuckled at his dramatic display. "It's like you've been down the mines, not mucking around with the wee ones!"

"Playing is hard work!" Angus retorted, rubbing his aching arm after an intense balancing act during the game.

"When you're a dad, you won't know what hit you. There's a lot more than playing games … there are sleepless nights, constant crying, and that's just the parents … wait till you get near the nappies …"

He waved off the impending horrors of parenthood and dived into the lasagna. "Oh, I'm sure it's a breeze, and please, let's end the talk there at nappies." He blew on a forkful of pasta and savoured the dish. "You really are the best cook, Iona. I'd eat your food every day," he praised, earning waves of pleasure from Iona.

"Shame it's me who gets her cooking every day!" Jake interrupted their banter, jacket on, fresh-faced and leaning against the back door. Iona squealed with joy as he swept her off her feet for a twirl.

"I thought you were to be in London until next week?!" She giggled as he kissed her, and she playfully tapped his shoulder when he lowered her.

Angus stood momentarily to clap Jake on the back, then resumed his dinner. Having spoken to Jake almost every day, he had suspected his friend and employer might return as a surprise.

"What? No garlic bread?" Jake teased, prompting another playful slap from Iona.

"Good Expo?" Iona poured wine into their glasses, giving herself an extra measure and ignoring Jake's amused expression. "It's been a hard day, I've not been gallivanting like some!"

"Hardly gallivanting. I'm out getting more business for us!" Jake slyly clinked glasses with her. "Which looks like the winter might be busy too!"

"Oh, really?" Iona placed her glass down, locking eyes with him. "Do you think we'll need more staff?" The couple's expectant gaze shifted to Angus.

Angus tried to continue eating, but as the room fell silent, he sighed and put his cutlery down. "It's been good helping out, Jake, but I think it might be in your best interest to get someone to work for you. Someone interested and eager to please. I'm not that person."

"You are!" Jake bellowed, yet his jolly smile faded slightly. "You are interested in the area; you are a fountain of knowledge about this place. That kind of thing is difficult to train someone."

"Even so." Angus would not be swayed on this, or sweet-talked. He had made up his mind. "I'm sorry, Jake, but I just can't … I'm not tour guide material."

Jake sighed. "There's nothing I can say to tempt you?"

"Certainly not!" Angus chuckled. "Please do yourself a favour and get an eager tour guide … I'll help you find one – but not me!"

"OK, OK." Jake rolled his eyes to Iona, who had reassuringly put her hand over his.

"Maybe I could do it?" She shrugged, her blue eyes meeting Jake's.

"But the kids! You don't have any time left, not with the café too. I couldn't do that to you."

"No, I'd like to – we could work something out."

"You would do that? For me?" Jake's stunned reaction made Iona's smile grow bigger.

"Silly goat, I'd do anything for you." She stroked his hair, the gesture somewhat intimate. Angus looked away, a pang of envy enveloping him. After all the years his friends had been together, he still found it strange that once – long ago – Iona and him were in a relationship. Although it had been a lifetime, and her attentions on Jake had made more sense in the end. He was glad it was such a brief relationship; he had watched their strong marriage flourish, becoming more indestructible as the years passed. They were a unit, a partnership, and it only made sense that they would make the perfect business partners.

Jake held Iona's hand on the table between their dinner plates and refocused his attention on Angus. "What will you do?" he asked.

Angus shrugged. He had made plans since moving back to the Highlands, but now everything seemed up in the air. He had thought to focus on his farm. A secret part of him had hoped Meg might stick around, but the looming winter held only lonely nights for him. Since the sisters' reunion with their father, he had given them space and booked any further itinerary they had. Their goodbye was short, their minds preoccupied with new family ties. Angus did not want to get in the way and complicate things further. So he had sent them on their way with a stiff hug and a fake smile. He had been unable to look at Meg, and the thoughts of their farewell now made him regret his actions a little. Had he been a petulant child? She had lied to him all this time just to get her way. Not only how secretive she was, but the way she controlled her sister – not telling her about their father until she was caught. The things he had said to her, and what she gave back in return, well, it made him feel there was a link – a similarity, an attraction, whatever you want to call it. But perhaps he'd had a lucky escape.

He ignored the heaviness in the pit of his stomach, but pushed his dinner plate away, unable to taste another morsel now that Meg's green eyes invaded his thoughts.

"Did you know anything about my last tour group?" Angus asked.

"What, the Australian girls?" Jake ate quickly with one hand, the other still locked with Iona's. "Only that they had money to spend and were eager to find someone … that reminds me – did you find the elusive stranger?"

"Yeah, in a way. I think she only sought out our tour company for that reason. She had her own agenda, we were there to facilitate things." He grunted.

"Does that matter?" Jake took a sip of wine, his gaze on Angus. "Should we be questioning things?"

"Well, it meant that they had their own schedule. It made me feel like a lackey – a servant following at their beck and call, not being a tour guide at all!"

"Angus, you've got to calm down." Jake shook his head in wonder. "You are so serious sometimes; lighten up, man!"

"I just don't like being taken advantage of – or your company for that matter!" He took a sip of his own wine and placed the glass down so firmly that it splashed on the table.

"We're not here to question; we're here to provide a

service – to give people a taste of our country … at their convenience."

Angus tutted and gave a wry laugh.

"I thought you had cheered up lately – you seemed a bit … lighter on the phone. But you've gone back to your old crabby ways, then?"

"Don't do that, Jake." Angus winced. "I just don't like to be—"

"Yes, yes, taken advantage of!" Jake sighed. "I say this as a friend, OK?" He hesitated, tapping the table with his fingers gently, a brief glance at Iona. "You've got to relax. The whole reason you came here was to change your pace of life, and your outlook on life too for that matter."

He lacked the energy to retort to his old friend. He craved some space to think. Following the whole Claudia debacle, he had come to terms with his new life, the promise of a good life. But since meeting Meg, his desires had shifted. He had behaved like an infatuated schoolboy, placing undue importance on her when she wasn't even aware of him. In Australia, she would undoubtedly have suitors aplenty; how could any man resist her?

She was undeniably beautiful. He couldn't allow himself to dwell on her any longer; it would drive him to madness at this rate.

But underneath it all, as much as he didn't want to agree, Jake had a point. It was the reason he came back home; to embrace the good life. Now he just needed to rediscover what that truly meant.

36

MEG

Scrutinising the overhead screen, she felt a wave of relief as she discovered their flight was delayed. The journey to the airport had unfolded as a slapstick comedy, turning her into a jittery mess. They first found themselves in a standoff with a nonchalant tractor driver, blissfully indifferent to their frantic beeping. A herd of Highland cattle then staged a roadblock in a glen, resembling a colossal, furry hairball in motion. To add a cherry on top, Meg expertly guided the rental car into a pothole the size of a crater. Her unwavering refusal to let Angus take them nearly led to them missing their flight. If she were one for superstitions, she might have suspected a cosmic conspiracy behind their accidental detour. However, being the pragmatic soul she was, she attributed it all to her own charming idiosyncrasies.

Biding her time outside the restroom, she finally had the luxury to reflect on their trip while perched on her suitcase. Father MacDonald had surprised her with a question about visiting in the new year. Startled, she had boldly suggested he stay with her, realising later the audacity, given her limited knowledge of her father. What were his hobbies or even his dietary preferences? She wished for more time with him before catching her flight, but the pull of her own life beckoned, steering her away from her mother's empty footsteps.

Pulling out her phone, she glanced at the time in Australia, confirming it was still the middle of the workday. She dialled the office, only to be met with the secretary's perpetual lack of recognition despite her attempts to explain her identity.

“I’m sorry, Mr Simons is not in today, dear,” Patricia, the company's most trusted employee, informed Meg. “He's out playing golf.” With polite efficiency, she hung up, leaving Meg leaning her head against the wall. Her workplace seemed oblivious to her existence; despite over a decade of service, her boss's indifference manifested in unreturned emails and missed calls. Even the secretary, a daily exchange partner, couldn't place her. Could she believe that after all this time, she had been an inconspicuous figure, blending into the office backdrop? Frustration surged as she jammed her phone back into her handbag.

Just when she felt as worthless as she could, an affectionate couple's joyful reunion unfolded in front of her. Their laughter filled the air, a beautiful display of love that made her want to shut herself off from everything. She folded her arms and kicked the suitcase with her heel. Surrounded by people getting on with their lives, pursuing their dreams and desires, she felt lost in indecision. Work didn’t want her. Angus didn’t either.

But it was more than that – for the first time, Meg felt lost. She couldn't pinpoint what she truly wanted. Even Lexi, with all her past struggles, seemed brimming with enthusiasm, listing all the things she looked forward to upon returning to Melbourne. But Meg couldn't share in her sister's excitement. How could she, when Angus remained in the

Highlands? The thought of him thinking poorly of her weighed on her like an anchor.

She must block it from her mind entirely.

She turned her gaze away from the affectionate couple, who believed the bustling airport corridor was the perfect place for a passionate embrace. Manoeuvring around a corner with her dragging suitcase, she found solace in a seat by the windows. There, amidst the buses arriving and departing and a constant stream of people through the automatic sliding doors, a lingering question echoed in her mind: Would she find happiness by returning to Melbourne?

Are you happy?

Angus had asked her that same question. She hadn't answered, because she hadn't truly considered it. Day by day, she had taken steps in various directions, tending to her work, her home, finalising her mother's affairs, and embarking on this journey. Now, seated by the airport window, an uncertain future loomed before her. She had always found solace in control and predictability, finding comfort in knowing what each day held for her. But now, after all these years, the idea of returning to that controlled, mundane existence felt stifling. Did she really want to go back to a life where everything was planned and predictable?

Suddenly, an old man stood before her, a friendly smile creasing his face as he bobbed his head. He removed his tweed cap in a polite gesture. “Penny for your thoughts?”

Startled, Meg rose to her feet. She knew him. “Ronnie? You're at the airport?”

“I am that. I dropped off a friend visiting family in Denmark. Figured I had a bit of time to spare, so I offered him a lift.”

Meg marvelled at his kindness. “You're a good friend; that's a four-hour drive.”

Ronnie waved it off. “Gave us a chance to catch up, and

I'm always happy to help a neighbour. I was about to leave when I spotted a lady sitting on her suitcase, looking like she had the weight of the world on her shoulders."

"Oh … me?" Meg chuckled. "No, I'm fine. I'm just waiting for my sister."

Lexi arrived by her side. "That's me!"

Ronnie extended a hand to her. "Delighted to meet you."

Meg began to explain Ronnie's connection but faltered. She couldn't bring herself to say Angus's name. "He's a friend of …" To her horror, a wave of emotion overcame her, and tears welled up in her eyes. "He's Angus's friend," she finally managed.

Lexi and Ronnie exchanged concerned looks. Lexi tugged at her arm, whispering, "Are you alright, sis?"

"I don't know," she confessed, her gaze inadvertently drifting back to where the affectionate couple had been. "I don't know what's come over me."

"Love," Lexi stated matter-of-factly.

She frantically shook her head, laughing nervously. "Don't be absurd."

Ronnie glanced sideways from sister to sister.

Lexi then made a straightforward declaration, her voice loud over the flurry of people passing them. "Meg is in love with Angus, and I don't think she should come back to Australia. Not right now."

"I'm not staying. I have work," she protested, a flicker of uncertainty in her mind.

Arching an eyebrow, hands firmly on her hips, Lexi confronted her sister. "Meg, they don't value you there. You said so yourself."

"Absolutely not," Meg snapped. "I'm not doing anything so stupid!" She stopped, hesitating at Lexi's hurt expression. "What I mean to say is, it wouldn't feel right. Leaving you behind – it just wouldn't be the right thing."

Lexi persisted, "Meg, you've been putting everyone else first. But has it made you happy?"

She glanced from Lexi to Ronnie. Angus's words resonated in her mind:

Are you happy?

"I couldn't leave you, to do what? I can't throw everything away on a feeling?" She shook her head. "I'm not you, Lexi. I don't have that …"

"What, stupidity?" Lexi chuckled.

"No, courage."

"My dears." Ronnie sidestepped to allow more people to pass. "Is there something I can help with? I don't know too much on matters of love, but from past experiences, they usually involve just two people."

"Ronnie? It is Ronnie?" Lexi laid the flat of her palm on his forearm. He nodded, his cheeks flushing in response. "I know you were just hoping to drive back home, but you know Angus … please take this sister of mine back to him?" Lexi pleaded.

"Please don't listen to her!" Crossing her arms, Meg leaned against the wall. The couple from before had moved back into her peripheral vision, now groping one another and snogging. "I can't stay; I have to go home."

"You can stay!" Lexi insisted. "What's the worst that could happen? If he turns around and says 'nah, thanks', stay in an inn and come back to Melbourne the following day!"

Meg turned to Ronnie, seeking a voice of reason. He pursed his lips and raised his hands, offering, "That's not a bad idea, love. That way … you'll know."

"Thank you, Ronnie!" Lexi triumphantly raised a finger. "He's right; you've got to try it. If you don't, you'll always wonder." She smiled warmly. "I'll keep your house in order, your work will be fine. But honestly, Meg, consider working for yourself. With your skills, you could work anywhere!"

She gave her shoulder a reassuring squeeze, waiting for a response.

Meg was on the verge of speaking, but she stopped herself. Could this be what she needed to stop that uncertainty from flooding her whole being? She had seen what regret did to someone – her mother and father. If only they could have spoken to each other properly, they might have been able to address the issues that kept them apart.

If she let Angus go, would she regret it?

Her tummy somersaulted, her fingers tingled, yet the sensations didn't deter her. In fact, they felt warm and fuzzy within her, a stark contrast to the numbness of routine. She had always found comfort in control, but maybe, just maybe, it was time to embrace the unknown. This was it. They were right; she just needed to take a leap of faith before allowing doubt to seep in.

Taking a deep breath, she steadied her racing heart and willed herself to stop overthinking. Instead, she watched the faces of strangers melt past her, their lives moving forward in a blur of determination and purpose.

"You once said, Ronnie, you believed in signs?" She bit her lip, her voice a mix of nervousness and excitement. "Would you have room in your car for one more?"

37

LEXI

Lexi checked in her luggage and felt lighter, not just because of the lack of baggage but also the emotional weight she had cast off. She stretched her neck, relishing the newfound freedom coursing through her veins. Soon to be back in Melbourne, her to-do list beckoned, and she eagerly anticipated diving into it.

As she stood in line at the newsagents, clutching essentials – a chocolate bar and a magazine for her flight – she relished the feeling of being on time for once. The hum of distant conversations blended with the rhythmic clattering of suitcase wheels against the tiled floor. Overhead, the intercom crackled to life, announcing departure gates and last-minute boarding calls, its mechanical voice echoing through the vast terminal. Airports usually sent her into a frenzy, her tendency to run late a perpetual stressor.

She squinted at the person ahead. A man patted his back pocket, searching for change. It was only when she noticed familiar Thai script tattooed on his forearm that she recognised him – Leon.

He swiftly gathered his belongings and nodded to the lady behind the counter.

A shiver ran down her spine, awakening memories she had tried to bury. Panic gripped her, but beneath the fear, a fierce determination simmered. What should she say to him? Maybe the whole business with Angus's wallet was a misunderstanding that she had the opportunity to clear up. Frozen in place, she watched Leon slip away. Then, as if a switch had flipped, the newly assertive Lexi banished her former self.

Closure, she thought, her mind racing. *That's what I need. Answers. An end to the questions that have haunted me.*

She clenched her fists, feeling the weight of the past lifting, replaced by a burning desire to confront the man who had once manipulated her.

She abandoned her chocolate and magazine and manoeuvred ahead of the bustling crowd, following the shaggy-haired man in the loose blue shirt. Even now, there was a magnetism about him, an easy-going aura that drew attention without effort. As he patted his back pocket, searching for change or his mobile, Lexi couldn't deny the physical appeal that accompanied his mysterious demeanour. He scratched his hair casually, dipping the back of his shirt collar, which exposed a beaded necklace against sun-kissed skin. In that moment, Leon embodied a blend of athleticism and free-spirited charm, a man whose physicality hinted at a lifestyle shaped by both discipline and adventure.

Lexi's heart raced, not only from the unexpected encounter but also from the pull of his alluring presence in the busy airport corridor.

She clenched her teeth at her stupid emotions, even now. They had got her into this mess in the first place. She picked up her pace until she was right behind him. This wasn't just about catching a thief; it was about reclaiming control. She couldn't let this encounter slip away. *No more running,* she vowed to herself. *I've carried the weight of uncertainty for too long. It's time to face the truth, whatever it may be.* With a sharp tap on his shoulder, she demanded his attention.

"Oh hey!" Leon spun around, his face lighting up with a surprised but friendly smile, as if he had stumbled upon an old friend.

Her heart pounded, the anticipation escalating with each passing second. "Hey." She tilted her head slightly upward, her expression serious. "So, Leon, care to explain your disappearing act?" The words hung in the air, pregnant with the weight of unresolved questions.

"It's crazy to run into you here," he replied, glancing around as if the setting were merely coincidental. "How have you been?" His words felt like a deliberate sidestep, a careful evasion of the issue at hand.

She squared her shoulders. "Never mind. I asked you first. Where did you vanish to? Why did you leave without a word? You made me feel like a fool!" The confrontation had begun, and time seemed to stretch, each uttered word resonating with the gravity of her emotions. She tried not to show it, but her body trembled.

He chuckled and ran his hand through his hair, a calculated pause in his response. "Well," he began, his attention momentarily drawn to the departure screen above them, "I ran into someone I knew from high school. They were heading back to my island that night, and I didn't have much time, you see. So I left with them and made it home to see my mum. She was thrilled." His words hung in the air, and doubt crept into Lexi's mind like a persistent shadow. As he began weaving a tale of more chance encounters and hurried departures, she felt a tug at her convictions. *Could it be true?* Her eyes searched Leon's face for any sign of sincerity.

The pain of past betrayals echoed in her thoughts, and she hesitated. *What if he's telling the truth? What if I've let my past experiences cloud my judgement?*

As Leon continued his explanation, Lexi's emotions churned. *Don't be naive,* a voice warned her, reminding her of the scars left by trusting men too easily before. Yet, a small ember of doubt smouldered within her. *What if he's innocent?*

The seconds stretched, each heartbeat echoing the conflict within her. Then, a surge of strength cut through the uncertainty. She straightened her back, dismissing the doubt. *No,* she decided, *I won't let the past dictate my present. I deserve the truth.*

With renewed determination, her gaze narrowed as she regarded him sceptically. "Do you honestly think I'm buying that story?" She stepped in front of him, blocking his path. "I can't believe it. I genuinely believed you were a decent person. I defended you, but now I see what's been right in front of me all along," she said, determined to suppress any lingering feelings. "You did it, didn't you? You stole from Angus? You stole from me? Is that your M.O.? Befriend people and then pilfer their belongings? Honestly, I seem to have quite the knack for picking them!" She nearly spat out her words, disgusted.

Meg's words echoed in her ears: "You're more in love with the idea of romance than actual love."

Leon scoffed, shook his head as if she were a silly girl bothering him, and began to walk away once more.

"Hey! I'm talking to you!" Lexi shouted, drawing the attention of a few passers-by. She hustled to keep up with him, her feet almost running to match his brisk pace. He strode ahead, his backpack flung across his back, avoiding her gaze entirely.

"You're a liar and a thief!" she roared, frustration and anger coursing through her. "I bet you never lived on that island. I bet you've been doing this for so long that you don't even know what's true!"

All of her accusations seemed to roll off him like light, fluffy balls of wool. A sense of despair crept over her. Was this the closure she would get? Men taking advantage of her and then callously brushing her aside without a second thought? Her fury intensified. "If you take another step, I'm calling the police … or security … whatever!" she bellowed.

He rolled his eyes in exasperation. "Lexi, do yourself a favour and walk away. You can't prove anything."

"I could … I could tell them the whole story …" she stuttered, her confidence waning as she wondered if he was calling her bluff.

"Exactly … a story! That's all you have," he retorted. "Who's going to believe a silly girl who has a mental breakdown at the drop of a hat?"

She froze, her heart sinking. She had never even admitted to herself what had happened before Meg found her at her apartment that day. She had attributed it all to excessive drinking without considering the consequences. Leon had listened to her talk about her 'episode', and she had felt a connection growing between them. He had comforted her, wrapping his arm around her and admitting he had experienced heartache as well. "Love can make us do crazy things. It happens to the best of us; don't be hard on yourself," he had reassured her.

But the man standing before her now was the complete opposite of the friendly, gentle soul she thought she knew. This man was cruel.

"I told you that in confidence. Why are you being like this?" Her whole posture recoiled, and she took a step back. She hadn't expected her breakdown to be thrown back at her, forcing her to question if it had truly been a breakdown at all, or something far more deliberate and irreversible.

Meeting her gaze, he started to laugh, a chilling and heartless sound that echoed in the corridor. “Oh dear, did I hit a nerve? I wonder if Meg knew you were suicidal? Please don’t consider drastic measures on my account. Did you honestly believe there was love between us? My, my, you are a desperate little girl,” he taunted, his words cutting deeper than she could have expected. His entire demeanour shifted before her eyes, including his accent, which eluded her recognition. “I could sense your desperation from miles away. What is it with women? With a little coaxing … you're all so ravenous. You couldn’t wait, so you had me on the beach … twice as well!” He scoffed, “It was a little surprising for me!” then, noticing the anguish in her eyes, he continued to belittle her. “I would never be remotely interested in someone like you. Yes I rather enjoyed your slutty tendencies but you're lost, Lexi. Like a terrified deer, always waiting for others to make your decisions.”

“I do not!” she retorted, her voice quivering with newfound determination. She wanted to share the truth about finally taking control of her life, but why should she even want to continue this conversation? Did she still yearn for his approval?

Even now, she wanted approval?

No more.

“Disappear, little Lexi, just get out of my way. You're pitiful. I’m not surprised your ex cheated on you. How could anyone love a pebble in their shoe?” His words were meant to be hurtful, and they were.

Something inside her snapped, and without a moment's hesitation, she stepped up to him, gripped his arms, and kneed him in the crotch before another word could escape his lips. He cried out in agony and collapsed to the floor, clutching his injured privates.

She swiftly moved out of his way as he attempted to inch toward her, but he was immobilised by pain. “Goodbye,

Leon," she declared, turning on her heel and striding in the direction of her flight.

Adrenaline coursed through her veins, and her only regret was that Meg wasn't there to witness her triumph over this vile man.

38

ANGUS

After ensuring the hens were safely tucked away in their shed, Angus battled the biting winds, his thoughts lingering on the recent pine marten threats. A shiver ran down his spine as he fortified the shed with an extra layer, determined to shield his livestock from any potential harm. He rigged an automatic flashlight, hoping its sporadic beams would deter furry intruders in the night.

Escaping the relentless gale, he finally sought refuge inside the cottage. The moment he stepped over the threshold, a welcome warmth enveloped him. The crackling fire painted dancing shadows on the walls, casting a soothing glow that battled against the howling winds outside.

He moved to the kitchen, brewing a strong coffee to combat the weariness that clung to him. The rich aroma mingled with the scent of burning wood, a comforting backdrop to his plans for the evening. It was important he stay alert for the hours ahead. He planned to reach out to some old contacts in London, at least to test the waters before making any major decisions. Being here for the entire winter with only his livestock for company filled him with a profound sense of misery. Yes, he had his parents, and Iona was here with Jake, but he needed to rid himself of the persistent ghost of Meg from his thoughts. Staying here would mean her memory haunting every familiar corner. Jake would surely help look after his animals, or he could ask his neighbours. Surely someone would help, even for a couple of months in the bleak midwinter. A move made sense, even if it entailed risking his health once more.

There was nothing worse than dwelling alone with his heartbreak and regrets.

He opened his laptop and stared absently at the bright screen. He took a deep sip of his coffee and delved into the backlog of emails from old contacts. Surprisingly, since his move from London, he had continued to receive job offers from various competitors of his old firm. He took the time to respond, hoping to rekindle relationships he had let go of over the past year.

The wind continued to howl around the cottage, sapping the warmth from its walls. He tossed another log onto the fire and donned a jumper to ward off the cold. Lost in his thoughts and emails, he was startled by a knock at the door. It was unusual for someone to arrive at this time of night, he thought, but sensing it might be Ronnie, he was shocked to find Iona's face in the darkness.

"Is everything OK, Iona?" Angus asked.

Wrapped in her grey winter coat, Iona's cheeks were tinted with a rosy hue from the biting wind. She seemed to contemplate something for a moment, then nervously nibbled at the inside of her mouth. "I've come to pick you up," she said.

Angus, still holding the door handle, invited his friend inside, but she shook her head, gesturing toward car headlights at the end of the road.

"What's happening? Is Jake OK?" he asked, bewildered

by the late-night visit. "Oh, very well." He sighed and grabbed his waterproof coat from the hook by the door.

But before they could leave, Iona quickly turned around, her sharp eyes scrutinising his appearance. "You're not wearing that, are you?"

"I guess not, then!" Angus sighed once more, already growing tired of the cryptic game his friend seemed to be playing. He just wanted to focus on his new job prospects and get on with getting his life on track, making plans, and finding his happiness.

"Wear the black wool coat," she instructed, her voice firm. "Oh, and your nice leather shoes," she added.

He groaned, stomping on his shoes and throwing on his coat, then followed her out and joined her by the parked car.

"I knew that if I came up, you'd shut the door in my face." Jake leaned across the driver's seat, chuckling. "Get in, mate!"

"Guys! Could you please tell me what's going on?" he asked calmly, trying his best to hide his annoyance. This entire situation seemed quite fishy, and he was in no mood for it.

"There's a ceilidh on!" Jake exclaimed. "I knew if I phoned you, you'd make up some excuse not to come."

"My animals! There's a pine marten, I need to be here!"

"Oh, that – the pine marten has gone further west," Jake informed him. "Old Davey Doh told my dad they had attacks last night."

"Plenty of pine martens around, Jake!" Angus scoffed. "I don't think there's just one scouring the land, cherry-picking the best hens. They're ruthless beasts!" His response came out harsher than intended. He knew his friends meant well, but they knew nothing about crofting or farming.

Jake suggested a compromise. "How about this: we'll

come back in an hour or so to check it out. I can drop you back if you want then?"

Angus couldn't argue with that. If any pine marten attacks occurred, they'd likely be in the small hours of the morning. He had some time, but he wasn't keen on attending the ceilidh. Nevertheless, he felt there was no way out of this situation now.

Jake took his silence as a victory. "Good on ya! It's not every night we get a babysitter. Tonight is going to be a belter!"

Angus accepted his fate and settled into the seat. It was then that he realised he had spent so little time socialising or attempting to find happiness. He had been trapped in a bubble, a bubble of his own making. And for what? For someone who didn't return his feelings, someone he never really knew in the end.

Meg was soaring in the sky about now, returning to the life she wanted. He felt a quiet sense of peace for her; she had found her father and built a bond with her sister. Could he begrudge her that? She had what she needed, but that left him here, alone.

No more wallowing, he decided. Meg had embarked on her journey to find happiness, and now he would find his.

39

MEG

Meg swallowed, but the lump in her throat remained, threatening to choke her. She surveyed the small crowd in the dimly lit pub before her, recognising familiar faces from the short time she had spent in the area, yet one crucial person was absent – Angus. Her anxiety surged, her body trembling with nervous anticipation. She hadn't sung in years, at least not in front of any human beings, save for her steamy morning shower concerts. But during that long car ride with Ronnie, a sense of possibility had crept in, making even the most outlandish idea seem feasible.

"Are you ready, Meg?" Ronnie, her partner in this audacious venture, approached the stage, handing her a stiff drink. "The band wants to start soon," he reminded her, nodding toward the musicians gathered behind her, their pints in hand.

The crowd was growing restless. They expected live music, and even amid the chatter at the bar, the impatient huffs from the band behind her were unmistakable. Ronnie's patience, she realised, might not last much longer.

"We need to start, Meg. I'm sorry," he said, strumming his guitar, determination in his eyes.

Her legs felt like jelly, but she managed to step into the spotlight. The crowd applauded, bewildered by the delay in the live performance. Her heart raced, but she couldn't see Angus. He was supposed to be here. That was the plan.

"Meg, it's time – come on, lass."

"He's not here," Meg whispered to Ronnie, her voice trembling. "Iona was supposed to bring him, but—"

Ronnie strummed the guitar, cutting her off. "We need to start, Meg. I'm sorry," he repeated.

With wobbly legs, Meg made her way to the microphone. She could feel the eyes of the crowd on her. They expected music, but instead, they got an anxious, unsteady woman.

"Hello," she stammered into the microphone, her voice quivering. "Hi, um, I'm Meg. I'm from Australia, and I dedicate this song to someone special here tonight. Um," she stammered and gave a nervous laugh, trying to break the tension, "I hope you'll forgive the accent."

She took a deep breath, surrendering to the moment. She closed her eyes, pushing her vulnerability to the forefront. "Actually … this song is for Angus. I'm sorry," she said, opening her eyes and scanning the room. To her astonishment, Angus was standing at the entrance, eyes locked on her.

Ronnie began strumming, and, in that moment, she found her voice. She knew exactly what song to sing – it was the same song she had sung years ago at the talent show for her father. But this time, it wasn't about seeking her father's approval. This time, it was a declaration of love to the man who held her heart. She calmed her mind, and her heart took over, following the music's flow.

An older couple came to the front of the crowd, waltzing with the grace of years of shared moments. They sang along with the music, and to Meg's amazement, the entire pub joined in for the chorus:

O ye'll tak' the high road, and I'll tak' the low road,

And I'll be in Scotland afore ye,
But me and my true love will never meet again,
On the bonnie, bonnie banks o' Loch Lomond.

Applause erupted as she finished her serenade. Ronnie took a bow beside her, leading her off the stage. The band wasted no time and soon burst into a lively number.

"Well done." Ronnie patted her on the back, a proud smile on his face.

"Thank you." She laughed, feeling a rush of exhilaration. She walked toward the bar, her mind racing to catch up with her body's newfound courage. She soon found Iona but there was no sign of Angus.

"Where did he go?" she asked, desperation creeping into her voice.

Iona's frown conveyed the message before her words did. "I'm sorry," she said. "He left, Meg. Right now. He just walked out."

She shook her head, disbelief and disappointment heavy on her shoulders. She fought her way through the crowded pub, struggling to find the exit. When she finally emerged into the crisp night air, an icy wind swept over her.

The darkness swallowed her up, and she went towards the sounds of bleating sheep. Standing by a stone wall, overlooking what she presumed was a field, she only saw shades of darkness, accompanied by the occasional call from the sheep. Her breath formed clouds in the frigid air as the temperature plummeted within seconds. She had to make another plan, but what plan?

Angus had left. Perhaps that spoke more volumes than anything. She would have to book a room for the night, and leave behind this silly idea of hers to stay and start something.

"I couldn't believe it was you!" Angus called out, his

words hanging in the cold night air. His silhouette emerged, framed against the warm, inviting glow of the pub behind.

"It's something I should've done a long time ago. I knew I'd always regret it if I didn't," she said, staying by the cold stone wall.

"Well, you certainly captured everyone's attention. You have a beautiful voice, Meg. Truly, I'm delighted I was there to witness your stage debut," he said, remaining in the same spot, the light shining around him like a yellow aura, obscuring his features.

"Thank you," she replied stiffly, looking upward. The clear night sky twinkled with bright stars, and the Milky Way trailed above her. "But I didn't mean that would be my regret … What I meant to say is if I left you, I'd always regret it. I just couldn't, Angus." She paused, watching his still silhouette. "Well actually, I almost did – but on the way to the airport, it's crazy, it was like everything was stopping me from boarding that flight. Then I saw Ronnie …" She shook her head. "It was as if something, or someone, was trying to stop me from leaving before it was too late.."

"Well now, anyone would think the little time you had here has made a hardened lass like Meg MacDonald turn superstitious?"

She licked her lips, eager to say every word in her head. "Angus, why did you leave just now? Am I wasting my breath … did I imagine things? I'm sorry for everything. I'm sorry I didn't tell you about my father and for being so guarded."

He walked towards her slowly, his hands in his jacket pockets, his collar up against the cold. He leaned on the stone wall, towering over her. She hadn't realised how tall he was. "Meg, you don't need to apologise." He sighed. "I'm sorry for how I behaved. It was juvenile. I don't know why I took things so personally."

"Because you've been hurt before and you thought I was being open with you …"

"You were, though. I see that now. I just used the whole business with your family as an excuse," he admitted, scratching his jaw.

Someone opened the door, a burst of laughter and a crowd appeared, hovering at the entrance.

Angus pulled Meg closer. "You asked why I left?" He held up a small bundle in his hands. "Knew Jake had this in the car, from our camping days." He breathed, close to her. "If we hurry, I think there's something I can show you, just past the clearing."

In a state of confusion, she allowed him to lead her down a path with the stone wall on one side, trees on the other, which she recognised as the way to the sea. His hand supported her on the uneven ground, and they finally stopped at the edge where she could just about make out the water. The tide was out. Everything was still.

"Angus …" she whispered.

He reached for her hand and kissed it. "Will you have me?"

"I'm already yours," she confessed. "I couldn't leave. I just needed a little nudge to see it."

He folded his arms around her, pulling her close in the darkness. Instinctively their lips met in a passionate, long-awaited kiss. Warmth enfolded her like a summer breeze on this cold winter night. Their lips moved together with a gentle urgency, each moment deepening the connection between them. Faintly, in the recesses of her mind, or perhaps carried over the distant hills, she could hear the echoes of a familiar cawing sound.

The eagle's call.

She allowed the sound to wash over her, choosing not to

question or doubt its presence, but rather embracing and letting herself be swept away by the currents of love.

Angus held her face. Though his features were hard to discern in dark, she could feel him smiling in the way his fingers traced her skin. With a subtle tilt of his head, he whispered into her ear, "Meg, look behind you."

She turned, and what met her gaze in the darkness took her breath away. Green hues, soft and ethereal at first, began to paint the night sky, and then they were joined by delicate shades of purple that danced and intertwined in a celestial waltz.

"Is that …?" she breathed, her voice a hushed murmur.

"The Northern Lights," he murmured in response, his arms encircling her in a protective and loving embrace. He leaned in close, his lips brushing her ear. "I wanted you to see this, to share it with you." For a moment, he let go of her hand, to throw the blanket on the ground. She sat down beside him, her heart swelling with wonder at the sky above as it transformed into a magnificent tapestry, an otherworldly display of shimmering colours that made her feel like she had stepped into a dream.

"I've never seen anything so beautiful."

"I have," he whispered, close to her ear. "Ever since you came to me. You're all I can think about." His hand reached for hers, her head leaning against his broad chest, his heart pounding under his wool jacket. "I want to share everything with you. We can see so much together. Will you stay?"

Meg gazed at the display of colours, their reflection on the water ahead. "I think I waited my whole life for this. I feel it. Like I was guided here, to you." She smiled to herself. Maybe it was her mother, maybe it was even her father. Something lived in her that she thought wasn't there, a desire, a knowing that whatever would come, she would grasp it with her two hands and not let go.

Angus kissed her again. "So you will have me?"

Meg laughed aloud, but with her face close to his, she murmured, "With all my heart."

EPILOGUE

MEG

Meg had dedicated a substantial part of her day to cleaning the cottage, her heart aflutter with anticipation. Significant progress had been made, but there was still much work to be done. Her cosy office in the spare room had become a cluttered warren of papers and folders, the inevitable result of several months of managing her own business. It had been more demanding than she'd initially realised. At this rate, she contemplated, she might have to consider hiring an additional staff member. With the last folder safely tucked under her arm, she ascended the rickety step ladder and stashed it away in the dark attic. That folder could wait there until their guest departed.

As she was preoccupied with her task, the front door swung open and Angus entered, ushering in a gust of chilly wind.

"Meg, what are you doing?" he asked, his voice laced with concern.

She descended the small ladder, her expression one of determination. "Just cleaning."

He raised an eyebrow, his tone carrying a touch of amusement. “You've been cleaning for days. It's not as if we have royalty visiting. Lexi won't be expecting a spotless palace. She'll just be happy to see you, no matter the state of the house.” He took her hand and looked into her eyes with an affectionate smile. “And I'm worried about you. You’ve been at it tirelessly, and considering your condition, it's just not worth the risk. Promise me that you'll call me to handle any heavy lifting or climbing. It's my job to keep both you and our little one safe.” He brushed his fingers gently over the small bump under her sweater. “Please, my love. I understand that you're excited to see your little sister after a year, but don't do too much.”

Meg inhaled deeply and sighed with a mix of gratitude and exasperation. “I know,” she admitted. “I'm just … anxious, I suppose.”

“I get it,” Angus reassured her, planting a loving kiss on her forehead. “We're going to have an amazing time together. You'll see.”

Just as he spoke, a soft tap echoed at the front door. Their attention shifted simultaneously, and there stood Lexi, framed in the open doorway, elegantly brushing rain droplets from her coat.

“Lexi, you're early!” Meg shrieked, her eyes lighting up as she marched towards the doorway, pulling her sister into a warm embrace. The hug was interrupted by her protruding bump. “We were expecting you tomorrow!”

“Surprise!” Lexi grinned, allowing her sister to usher her inside, out of the chilly weather.

“Where's your bag?”

“Ah, well, that's the thing. It's not here,” Lexi confessed.

Meg's brows knitted in puzzlement. “What? Did they lose your luggage or something?”

Lexi shook her head, her expression mischievous. “Not exactly. I actually checked into the inn for the night.”

“What?” Meg stood upright, hands on her hips, her voice tinged with incredulity. “You did what now?”

Lexi chuckled at her sister's reaction, her posture relaxed. It had been quite some time since Meg had seen Lexi in person, and the transformation was remarkable. The once-frizzy bleached hair had been replaced by dark, sleek locks hidden under a stylish trilby hat. Lexi's face bore a new tranquillity, her eyes sparkling with newfound maturity. Her scruffy denim jacket had been swapped for a long, elegant winter wool coat.

Lexi proceeded to greet Angus with a warm hug and a generous kiss on each cheek. “Don't be mad, Megs,” she implored. “I wanted to spend some time with Annabel and the staff at the home. They've been so wonderful, helping me out with my coursework. I needed to show my appreciation.”

She gracefully removed her coat, hung it up on the new coat hangers by the door, and looked around.

Meg had spent her time focusing on the cottage's decor for the past few months, and while it was still a far cry from her modern house in Melbourne, she had made it into a comforting home, allowing her home back in Australia to be a base for Lexi during her studies.

“I promised I'd have dinner with Annabel soon,” Lexi continued, explaining her decision. “But I wanted to say hi to you tonight. I'm dying to hear everything, Meg. I want to know what it's like to move to the other side of the world for the love of a man.”

Meg sighed, her expression softening with affectionate exasperation. “I didn't exactly do that.”

“Well, it sure seems like it!” Lexi scoffed.

“She’s still playing hard to get,” Angus said playfully, a hand resting affectionately on Meg's shoulder. “We don’t talk about it too much.”

"That's because you said you'd move to Australia." Meg eyed him suspiciously.

"And I will, if you want to go back," Angus said, earnestly.

Her eyes twinkled with delight as she pressed her lips together to hide her smile. "Well, I'm feeling quite comfortable right now." She cast a sly look between Lexi and Angus. "Plus, this little one seems pretty content so far. We mustn't make any hasty decisions."

Lexi asked, "Do you know what you're having?"

Angus beamed with pride and, fluffing up some pillows on the couch, he helped Meg sit down. "A little lass."

"A girl?" Lexi squealed. "Oh, that's so wonderful! Have you thought of names?"

Meg and Angus exchanged a warm look and spoke in unison. "We like Rebecca."

Lexi's eyes misted over with emotion. "After Mum?"

Meg nodded, her voice soft. "She'll always be a part of our lives in some way."

Lexi reached out to grasp her hand tightly. "I'm so proud of you."

She blinked, a little taken aback by the heartfelt comment. "Proud of me? For what?"

"For stepping outside your comfort zone, for taking a leap of faith," Lexi explained. "You really did, Meg. You're a lot more like Mum than you know."

Meg brushed away a stray tear, her thoughts often lingering on her mother, especially with her own baby bump growing by the day. She had always assumed her mother would be there to guide her through motherhood.

Angus chimed in, "I'm glad she is, Lexi. If Meg hadn't come back, I'd still be wallowing in misery, too stubborn to change."

Meg chuckled and wiped away her own tears of joy.

"Well, it's not entirely untrue," she admitted. "But I'm glad I did come back. I wouldn't change a thing."

Lexi suddenly leaped from her seat, her eyes glued to her phone. "Oh, I'm so sorry, Meg, I've got to go. I have that dinner at the nursing home. Would you like to come?"

She followed Lexi to the door, standing beside her as she readied to leave. "I'll pass this time, Lex. I want you to have a nice dinner and catch up with everyone. But you promise you'll be back?"

"Of course!" Lexi responded eagerly. "I can't wait to stay here, eat Angus's cooking, and catch up with you properly."

Meg added, "Father will be here tomorrow."

Their relationship with their father had undergone adjustments, and it had taken time for Meg to call him Father. Now, it felt natural.

"I can't wait to see his new puppy." Lexi bubbled with enthusiasm. "It looked so cute in the photos."

Angus teased, "I've been trying to persuade Meg to get one too. But she says we should have the baby first."

"One step at a time." Meg laughed, placing her hand on her growing belly.

Lexi waved her goodbyes, hopped into a hire car, and started down the road toward the village.

Meg stood in the doorway and inhaled the fresh, cool air. The rain had subsided and the world outside was calm. The sounds of the animals filled the air – the contented grazing of sheep, the gentle clucking of hens in their shed, and the distant, low rumblings of the pigs in their pen at the end of the field.

Life, she thought, was all around her, inside her, and there was something incredibly beautiful about it. Angus wrapped his strong arms around her, one hand softly resting on the top of her bump, where he usually patted every night. But this time, a quick jolt made her gasp.

"She kicked. Did you feel that?" she asked, her voice full of wonder.

Angus chuckled, his eyes filled with love and excitement. "We'll be meeting you soon, little Rebecca. Just keep warm in there for now. Your mother wants to freeze us all out here!" He slowly led her back into the cosy warmth of their cottage, and Meg followed.

LOVED THIS SCOTTISH ESCAPE?

Enjoyed **The Love Letter**?
Your Scottish escape doesn't have to end here.

Meet **Callum** again — the quiet Highlander from the kayaks — in his own love story.
From Scotland With Love 🩶
Book One — just 99p

Small town • Second chances • First loves reunited • Feel-good romance

THANK YOU

Thank You 🩶

If you enjoyed this story, it would mean the world if you left a **quick star rating** on Amazon or Goodreads.

And if you feel like writing a review, that's wonderful too — but never expected.

Thank you for being here with me.

Claire x

ALSO BY CLAIRE GILLIES

A Season of Small Spells

On the Edge

The Love Letter

Arlochy series:

From Scotland with Love

Threads of a Highland Heart

Secrets in the Glen

WANT A LITTLE EXTRA?

Head over to www.clairegillies.com to receive a FREE download of short story prequel to From Scotland with Love.

AFTERWORD

Growing up as the youngest in a bustling household, I've always been fascinated by the complexities of family dynamics. Like most writers, I observe people and how they navigate their relationships, often using these observations to shape my characters. Having lived in many places and met people from all walks of life, I've gathered countless experiences that feed into my stories—one in particular that sparked the idea behind this novel.

I spent a period of my life in Australia, living in an unconventional house-share arrangement. My husband and I were given the basement of a sprawling old house—a former game room, with curtains draped over a large wardrobe to give us a bit of privacy. Despite its quirks, the house began to feel like another character in our lives, with its towering ceilings, echoing hallways, and two grand balconies. On summer nights, we'd gather on the balcony and watch the fruit bats swoop around a magnificent fig tree in the backyard. It was a strange but beautiful place, and in those years, time seemed to rush by in a contented blur.

Though I'd shared living spaces before, this particular setup was different—two of my housemates were sisters.

Living so closely with them, I became fascinated by how siblings can be so different yet so deeply connected, despite coming from the same upbringing. It reminded me of my own relationship with my sisters, which is complex and layered, much like the bond between the characters in my story. It was this experience that sparked the inspiration for the novel, an exploration of the enduring mystery of sisterhood.

As I wrote, I hoped to capture the essence of what it means to be a sister, the unbreakable ties that persist through the highs and lows.

I hope you enjoy this story, as much as I enjoyed creating it.

ABOUT THE AUTHOR

Claire Gillies writes heart-warming, uplifting women's fiction set in Scotland. Having grown up in the Scottish Highlands, Claire later lived in Australia for several years, working in retail and creating her own fashion label.

Now back in Scotland, Claire resides in beautiful Inverness-shire with her family. She finds inspiration in her love of folklore, costume, and history, which infuse and shape her writing.

When she's not writing, she indulges in her love for costume dramas like Poldark and Jane Austen adaptations, by curling up on the couch with a cup of tea.

Claire enjoys connecting with her readers on a personal level. Sign up to her mailing list and grab some goodies at www.clairegillies.com

Join the conversation!

Printed in Dunstable, United Kingdom

79226039R10170